# CONTROLLING
## *Chloe*

### SYNDICATE KINGS

**KATE OLIVER**

This book is a work of fiction. Names, characters, organizations, places, events, and incidents are either a product of the author's imagination or are used fictitiously. Any resemblance to actual persons, living or dead, businesses, companies, events, or locales is entirely coincidental.

Written by: Kate Oliver
Cover Designer: Scott Carpenter

Copyright © 2024 Kate Oliver

"ALL RIGHTS RESERVED. This book contains material protected under International and Federal Copyright Laws and Treaties. Any unauthorized reprint or use of this material is prohibited. No part of this book may be reproduced or transmitted in any form or by any means, electronic or mechanical, including photocopying, recording, or by any information storage and retrieval system without express written permission from the author/publisher."

# CONTENT WARNINGS

This book is a DD/lg romance. The MMC in this book is a Daddy Dom and the MFC identifies as a Little. This is an act of role-playing and/or a lifestyle dynamic between the characters and falls under the BDSM umbrella. This is a consensual power exchange relationship between adults. In this story there are spankings and discussions of other forms of discipline.

**Additional content warning**

This is Kate's darkest book to date. Some triggers to be aware of in this story:
   Thoughts of self-harm
   Discussion on page of past self-harm
   Emotional abuse and manipulation by a parent

Attempted sexual assault

Attempted drugging

Discussion of human trafficking

Light torture of bad guys (They deserve it, though. They always do.)

Abduction/kidnapping

Drugging

Please do not read this story if you find any of this to be disturbing or a trigger for you.

# 1
## CHLOE

Will I go deaf if I stab a cocktail pick in my ear?

Staring down at the bamboo stick spearing the green olives in my glass, I ponder doing it. Would it cause immediate deafness? Would I have to pull it out and then gouge it into the other ear so I can't hear on either side?

"What I'm trying to say is, it's actually a really big deal. One more step closer to the White House, if you know what I mean, babe."

I twist the pick in my fingers, seriously considering my options. The pain would surely be worth it. Would he notice the blood gushing from my ears? Or would he continue to drone on about himself like he's been doing since the moment he picked me up?

His eyes trail over the backside of a woman in a tight red dress. I arch an eyebrow and tilt my head to the side.

"I think I know her," he says with a cocky smile that makes me want to gouge my eyes out too.

How could he possibly recognize her when the only part of her body he saw was her ass? I gag internally.

What the hell was I thinking about agreeing to this date? Why do I continue to let myself be put in these positions? And why in God's name did I go along with letting this asshole pick me up from my house instead of meeting him here at the restaurant? Now I'm stranded with him unless I slip out and order a car service.

*Awesome, Chloe. Really brilliant. You're the star of intelligent choices once again.*

"Babe, you're not drinking your martini."

I roll my lips in, biting down to keep myself from responding in a less-than-ladylike way. However, I swear, if he calls me babe one more time, I'm going to snap. I'll make those true crime shows look like child's play.

My entire body was prickling with annoyance by the time we got here. Almost like bugs were crawling over me. All I wanted to do was go back home and scrub myself clean. When he picked me up, instead of coming to the door, he texted me from his car to tell me he was there. Then, the entire ride here, he talked non-stop about himself. And not a little bit. No. He went on and on and on. My neck still aches from how stiffly I kept nodding to make it seem like I was interested in even a single word he had to say. Surprise! I didn't give a shit about any of it.

Then we get to this place, and it's nice. Very nice. Dim lighting, candles on every table, and the staff are all dressed in crisp, black button-down shirts and black pants with clean white aprons. There's a shiny grand piano on one side of the bar, and the man sitting on the bench is playing a beautiful melody that he's completely lost in. We haven't ordered any food, but the smell of sizzling steak and garlic would have my mouth watering like a hungry puppy if I had any sort of appetite. Another shocker, the second he started talking, I lost it. I'd love to visit this place again. Without this douche canoe, of course.

After we found a table, he said he would go order our drinks from the bar. He asked me what I wanted. I'd already had a glass of white wine at home while getting ready, so I asked for a glass of Chardonnay. Mixing alcohol has never worked in my favor. And now, here I am, staring at the martini he was *sure* I'd enjoy more than wine. His words, not mine. *Idiot*. If I wanted a martini, I would have asked for one. He was probably too busy talking to himself about himself to hear my order.

"So anyway, there was this guy at the fundraiser, and we talked all night."

Meaning, he talked all night while the guy at the fundraiser probably wanted to put a bullet in his own head. I look around the place, enjoying watching the other couples who are obviously having a much better time than I am. Glasses clink, laughter fills the space, and people converse with one another. Women are dressed to the nines, and the men are in suits or slacks with dress shirts. I feel a twinge of envy as I watch a group of women laugh about something one of them said. Can I insert myself into their group and forget I ever met Bradley Du Pont? God, even his name is annoying.

Unable to take it for another moment, I push my chair back and stand. He looks at me in surprise as he pauses mid-sentence.

I smile and clear my throat. "I need to use the ladies' room. I'll be right back."

"Oh, right. No problem, babe. I'll get you a wine since you don't seem to like the top-shelf martini I got you."

Pompous asshole.

Several deep breaths later, I nod. I want to tell him I'll be leaving shortly after I get back from the restroom, so there's no need to get me another drink.

But the few minutes I'll have to wait between the time I get back and the time I can run out of this establishment will be torture, so downing a glass of wine during that time sounds perfect.

Without another word, I make my way through the bar. As soon as I'm locked in a bathroom stall, I dig out my phone to call my best friend and roommate, Paisley.

"Hey, girl! Are you having fun?"

"I'm two seconds away from committing a murder, so I need you to get me out of here. Call me with an emergency."

Without missing a beat, she says, "Okay. Do you need me to cry? Or scream? How urgent does your escape need to be?"

"Fucking urgent."

"Got it. I'll be super dramatic. Tears and screaming. How long until you need me to call?"

"Ten minutes. Not a minute more or I'll kill you."

"Sure thing. It'll give me time to get hysterical. Talk to you soon."

After we hang up, I step out to the sink and touch up my lipstick. Not because I want to look good for Bradley, but to buy a bit of time before I have to go back out there.

A woman walks in with a look of disgust on her face. She goes directly to the sink next to me and starts vigorously washing her hands. We catch each other's eyes in the mirror.

"Be careful when you go back out there. Some creep just hit on me and grabbed my hand," she warns.

I grimace and shake my head. "I'm sorry. That's gross. What does he look like?"

"Like what you would picture a pretty boy entitled asshole to look like. He thinks he's some hotshot who's going to be president one day. I'm pretty sure he has a date with him too, which is even worse. There's a wine glass and a martini glass at the table across from him. What a prick."

Honestly, I wish I could say I'm surprised, but I'm not. Not even a little bit.

I smile warily. "That would be me. I'm the date."

The woman's eyes widen. She looks worried I might freak out on her.

"My bestie is calling with a fake emergency so I can escape." I look at my phone. "In eight minutes. Eight long, torturous minutes."

"Oh, girl. I'm so sorry. That guy is slimy. How did you end up on a date with him in the first place?"

With a sigh, I shake my head. "Because I'm an idiot who's always trying to win the love of her father. And it always bites me in the ass."

She gives me a pitying look. "Do you want me to

go out there with you? Or maybe I could create a distraction so you can get out sooner?"

Even though this woman is a stranger, I already love her. Women who protect other women are my favorite human beings.

I smile. "Thanks. I'm good. I don't want to create a scene. I'd never hear the end of it from my father. A fake emergency will get me out quietly."

She nods then steps toward me to give me a brief hug. "Good luck, girl. I hope that guy gets what he deserves."

Yeah. Me too. If he ever becomes the leader of our country, we are completely and royally fucked as a nation.

"By the way, your makeup is stunning. How do you get your eyeliner like that?"

Warmth spreads through me. I've never felt more appreciative of a woman in my life. She's a stranger, yet in the few minutes we've been chatting, she's made me feel so much better. The world needs more of her.

"It takes a lot of practice. I have a YouTube channel where I give tutorials. I put this look on my channel the other day." I pull out a pen from my purse and rip a piece of paper towel to write down the name of my channel.

When I hand it to her, she smiles and holds the paper towel to her chest. "Thank you. I've always struggled with doing makeup. I'll definitely look you up."

We give each other one more brief hug before I sigh. "Guess I better go."

She looks as unsure as I feel. After taking several deep, calming breaths, I head back out to my date.

## 2
## BASH

"We'll provide the weapons at a third of what we charge everyone else." I run the tip of my index finger over the rim of my glass and glance around the restaurant. It's busy tonight. As it is most nights. You wouldn't think owning upscale restaurants and clubs would be such a money maker, but we've learned the two things the locals of Seattle love are a good steak and a heavily poured drink.

The two men I'm with stare back at me, smirking.

Knox speaks first. "Are you giving us a good deal because you want us to be in your debt?"

I smile at them and lift a shoulder. "I'm pretty sure, at this point in our relationship, we scratch each other's backs when needed."

"No offense, but I'd prefer not to think about scratching your back," Angel says with a grin.

We laugh. I give him the finger before I take a sip of my whiskey. "Why do you need guns from us anyway? I thought you had a supplier you've been using for years."

We've worked with Angel, Knox, and the rest of the Javier men for a long time. Though, not normally dealing weapons. They're not part of our organization, but they've done some jobs for us. In exchange, we've provided our resources when they've needed them. It's a win-win relationship, and it's gotten to the point where we consider them trusted friends.

Knox's eyes darken, and he takes a swig of his drink, his face contorted into a look of disgust. "The last two shipments have been sub-par. Half of them don't fire properly. In our line of work, we need reliable weapons that fire the first time we pull the trigger."

Angel nods. "When we had a meeting with them to discuss the problem, we got the feeling that they're getting into dirty business with some new people. The type of guys we've committed our lives to ending. We're looking into it, but we've cut off business with them in the meantime. We'd rather work with you guys. Where the fuck is Declan, by the way?"

I chuckle, shaking my head. "He finally took Cali on a honeymoon. They'll be back tomorrow."

"So, we're stuck making a deal with your ass in the meantime," Angel says, his tone light and friendly.

"It's not like I want to be sitting here with you assholes tonight either," I quip.

It's all love between us. When doing business deals like this, I wouldn't normally come alone, but because we know these men so well and trust them, there's nothing to worry about.

As a couple walks past our table, the hair on the back of my neck prickles. I study them as they're led to a table across the bar from us. The woman's honey-brown hair sways with her movements, and a few seconds after they pass, I get a whiff of something soft and floral that sharpens my senses. It's unique. A scent I've never smelled before. Whatever it is, I want another hit of it.

The man, who looks like he belongs to at least a dozen country clubs, is dressed in an obnoxious plaid suit. Who the fuck wears plaid anymore? Especially when you're standing next to someone as stunning as the woman he's with. I haven't seen her face, but I know she's beautiful. The dress she's wearing is both sexy and classy, and maybe I'm making shit up in my head, but it seems a bit innocent. It's yellow, which is kind of a surprising color for a place like this, and lands mid-thigh. The skirt flares out, creating a baby doll look. It's adorable. My cock thinks so too.

The woman moves stiffly, and every time her date

puts his hand on her lower back, she quickens her pace to get away from him. He doesn't seem to realize it or care because he continues to try to touch her. It pisses me off.

Angel and Knox notice it too. The three of us are bad men. The type you never want to cross because it won't end well. I can't count the number of lives I've ended. Boundaries rarely exist for us. We're some of the worst men in Seattle. The one thing we don't tolerate, though, is hurting women. We might turn their asses red and play roughly with them—consensually—but we never abuse or sell them. And we don't put up with others doing it either.

When the couple sits down, my heart pounds faster. Heat crawls up my neck as I stare across the bar. I have no idea who the slimy-looking guy is, but I know exactly who she is. My muscles are so tense, it's painful.

Who the fuck is this jackass?

"She looks like she'd rather be anywhere but here," Angel says.

I nod without glancing his way and continue to watch them, trying to decide what to do. She's my best friend Kieran's little sister. Chloe. Should I call Kieran and tell him to get his ass down here?

The guy flaps his lips, not giving her a chance to get a word in edgewise. Before long, he rises and goes to the bar. A few minutes later, he carries two drinks back with him. When he sets the martini glass down in front of Chloe, her face falls into a look of disgust.

Luckily, Angel and Knox no longer seem interested in keeping up the conversation. They're too busy watching this fiasco. Part of me thinks I should interrupt and scare that weasel off, but for all I know, he could be her boyfriend. She deserves way better than that fucker. There's no doubt in my mind. If he is her boyfriend, there's no way Kieran knows about him because I'm pretty sure he'd have a coronary over it. Not that I blame him. My brothers and I are just as protective of our little sister.

Right as I'm about to get up and make a casual, yet memorable, appearance at their table, Chloe stands and heads toward the bathroom.

"Where are your Little girls tonight?" I ask while keeping my gaze on the weasel.

Knox chuckles. "Probably giving Wolf more gray hairs. Lucy's having a slumber party with all the girls tonight."

I smile at the thought of all those women under one roof. I'm sure it's chaos. Angel and Knox have six other brothers, plus their dad in the family. Which means there are nine women driving Wolf to a heart attack. And he's probably loving every second of it.

The waiter drops off a glass of wine at Chloe's table and leaves just before the slimy-ass fucker grabs hold of a woman who walks by. She yanks her arm away and then scowls at him before flipping her hair over her shoulder and storming off. I don't know the situation with Chloe and this guy, but it's obvious he's scum. I want to deal with him the way the mafia likes to handle people who displease us. With a bullet to the head. Or use my sister-in-law's idea of handling things and feed him to the fishies.

Chloe still hasn't returned, and I wonder if she made a run for it out the back. I hope she did. Hopefully, she gets as far away from him as possible and blocks his number. I hope to God this asshole doesn't know where she lives.

The scumbag holds his hand over her glass for a moment and then picks it up by the stem. My blood runs cold as he swirls the drink around before setting it back down.

"Did you see that?" Knox asks.

I nod. "The woman is Kieran's sister. Can you stay here for a few? I'm going to need your assistance."

"Oh, shit," Knox murmurs.

Yeah. Messing with a mafioso's family member isn't a good idea. Ever.

"Of course," Angel says. They sit back down, ready to enjoy the show, I'm sure.

As I make my way across the bar, Chloe emerges from the hallway where the bathrooms are. I need to get to her before she takes a sip of that wine.

The bar manager sees me beelining and walks over, keeping stride. He can tell something's wrong.

"Start clearing the place out. Let them take their drinks to go for all I care. Don't create chaos. Tell them we have to shut down for the night."

I don't wait for a response because, while he might manage the place, we own it. He'll follow my orders without question.

Chloe sits as I arrive at her table. She glances up and does a double take, her eyes widening in recognition. It's been a while since I saw her last. In person anyway.

"Bash, hi," she says softly.

I stare down at her and nod. I'm so full of rage right now that I can't muster a smile for her.

The asshole clears his throat. Slowly, I turn my head to look at him. My expression is dangerous, and fear flickers in his eyes.

"Sebastian Gilroy. And you are?"

A blur of emotions runs through him. Irritation. Anger. Fear. Mostly fear. It gives me a sick sense of satisfaction. He knows who I am. He doesn't back down, though, proving he really is as dumb as he looks.

To my surprise, he reaches out a hand. "Bradley Du Pont. How do you know Chloe?"

My eyes slowly scan from his face to the hand he's

offering me. When he finally realizes I'm not going to shake it, he clears his throat nervously and lowers it.

He looks me up and down and then swallows, his Adam's apple bobbing in his throat. A fine sheen of sweat coats his forehead, and I feel a little better already. Intimidation is fun. Especially with dipshits like him. *Bradley Du Pont*. What the hell kind of name is that? And why does it sound familiar?

Moving my attention away from him, I finally smile down at Chloe, who looks like she wants to bolt. I'm sure she's wondering how long it will be before Kieran shows up.

I reach behind me to grab a chair from the empty table next to theirs, then pull it up right next to Chloe. She looks over at me, mouth slack like she doesn't know what the hell is going on. Which is accurate. She has no clue. But she's about to find out.

She lifts her trembling hand to the wine glass in front of her, but before she can pick it up, I wrap my fingers around her wrist to stop her.

"Bash, what are you doing?" she whispers.

Instead of answering her, I look across the table to Bradley and smile. "I think Bradley should try your wine."

His entire body tenses, but he relaxes quickly and gives me a slimy-ass politician smile. That's where I know him from. He's running for something. I don't have the first clue what, but I've seen his name and picture on signs.

Her phone starts ringing, but the tension around us is so thick that I don't think she hears it. Even though I'm not looking at her, I feel how stiff she is. I want to comfort her, but that will have to wait until I've dealt with him.

"I'm not much of a wine guy," he says.

Most of the restaurant has already cleared out. The music has stopped, and the hum of conversation and glasses clinking has disappeared. Out of the corner of my eye, I watch everyone leave, some carrying their drinks with them as they go. The manager did a good job—and fast. I'll compensate him generously for that.

I reach for the stem and scoot the glass across the table. "I didn't ask if you were a wine guy. I said you should try it. Go ahead."

Chloe tugs on my suit jacket. "Bash, what are you doing?"

Slowly, I put my hand on her knee and squeeze gently. She sucks in a breath but doesn't say anything more. Wanting to ease her anxiety as much as possible, I start to stroke my thumb along her outer thigh.

I keep my gaze on Bradley and nod toward the glass. "Drink up, pretty boy."

He sputters and looks around the bar, probably

just now realizing the place is empty other than the five of us.

"I wouldn't try to run if I were you. My two friends over there love a good chase. I also have six more men outside who like to play rough."

There are no other men outside, but it's fun to see the fear in his eyes.

"Drink the wine, Bradley," I say when he looks back at me.

This time, to emphasize my command, I lean back and let my suit jacket fall open, revealing the gun holstered under my arm.

His eyes widen as he starts shaking his head. "There's been a misunderstanding," he shouts, his voice cracking.

I let go of Chloe's knee and reach into my jacket. "You have one second to down that glass of wine unless you want a bullet in your head."

Chloe shifts beside me. I ignore her and watch with sick pleasure as Bradley picks up the glass with a shaking hand and starts to down it. When he's about halfway done, he starts to lower it.

I lean across the table and use my fingertips to lift the base, making him drink the whole thing. "All of it."

His eyes bulge, and his entire body trembles as he sets the empty glass down.

"How long before it's going to hit you, Bradley?" I ask.

He rolls his lips and looks away.

"What are you talking about?" Chloe tugs on my jacket again.

Her voice is shaky and unsure but sweet as sugar. She's scared, and I hate it. I have the urge to pull her onto my lap so I can comfort her, but as quickly as the thought comes, I shove it away. She's Kieran's sister, which means she's off-limits.

I turn to her and take hold of her hand. She's trembling, so I give her a gentle squeeze. "Your date here drugged your wine when you were in the bathroom."

She gasps and covers her mouth as my words sink in. Tears fill her eyes, and that urge to hold her returns. I ignore it for the moment. There's other business to attend to right now.

"So how long, Bradley? What was it? GHB? Ketamine?"

He swallows thickly, his eyes darting around the bar as if there's anyone here to save him. Too bad for him.

"Chloe, I didn't mean to," he says shakily.

She stares across the table at him, her eyes damp. Her trembling fingers are cold against mine. I want to hold her and promise that everything will be okay. That no one will ever harm her again. I want to protect her in a way I haven't felt in a very long time. Fuck. What is wrong with me?

"Is this guy your boyfriend?"

"No. I had never met him before tonight," she answers quietly, her gaze lowered to the table.

I clear my throat and force my focus to the asshole in front of me. "Being a slimy politician doesn't get you enough pussy, so you have to drug women? Or do you have a tiny dick, and you know you can't please anyone, so you have to incapacitate them? That way they don't go running for the hills when they see you naked?"

I'm pretty sure he used GHB since he's already starting to lean in his chair. It won't be long before he's out. I lift my chin to Knox and Angel who come over and stand behind Bradley with their arms crossed over their chests. He's already too high to notice them.

"Can you guys drop him off at our north warehouse for me? I'll owe you one."

Angel's nearly black eyes twinkle, and he smiles. "Nah. This one's on the house. We're happy to take out the trash. Mind if we work him over a little? I'm feeling a bit of rage coming to the surface right now."

I grin. "Have fun. Just keep him alive."

Bradley is limp in the chair now, his head rolling to the side. Knox and Angel yank him up as if he weighs nothing and cart him out of the place.

As soon as they disappear, I turn to Chloe. Tears track down her cheeks. She's shaking so hard, I'm afraid to touch her. I don't want to make it worse.

"I can't…I can't…" She's breathing too fast, and if she doesn't slow down, she's going to start hyperventilating.

Unable to stop myself, I reach over and lift her into my lap. "Easy, baby. Come on, I need you to take slow breaths. Chloe, listen to my voice and focus on me."

Her eyes are blank, but she obeys and looks up at me. She's still panicking. I cup her face in both my hands.

"Touch my face, Chloe. Tell me how it feels."

She's sobbing now, but she does what I say and runs her fingers over my chin. Her phone keeps ringing every couple of minutes, but I ignore it, keeping my focus on her.

"That's a good girl. How does it feel?"

Her fingers curl, and she lets out a deep breath. "Scratchy," she whimpers.

I stroke her cheek. "That's right. Tell me, what can you smell?"

She keeps her hand on my chin, flexing her fingers over the roughness of my short beard. "You. Citrus, I think. And…and whiskey."

That makes me smile. She's spot on.

"Yes. Good girl. Take a short breath in and exhale slowly for as long as you can."

As she does it, I praise her softly. I continue to repeat instructions to her for several minutes until her eyes begin to focus again.

"Did he...did he really put drugs in my wine?"

"Yes. I saw you two when you walked in. I could tell you were uncomfortable. When you went to the bathroom, I was watching him when he poured something into the glass."

She whimpers as more tears fall. "If you hadn't..."

I cup her face again, forcing her to look at me. "Shh. Don't think about the what-ifs."

Even though I don't want her thinking about it, I already know my mind will be reeling with all the what-ifs tonight when I try to sleep. My anger starts to boil to the surface again. He could have raped her. Or killed her. Or done a dozen other sick and disgusting things to her.

I'm not sure if she realizes that she's on my lap, but she snuggles into my chest, keeping one hand on my beard and the other tucked inside my suit jacket. I hold her for a long time in silence as I try to calm my rage. I need to take care of her. She needs me to be calm and steady right now. My emotions can be dealt with later.

"Let me take you home," I murmur.

She nods but doesn't say anything.

"Where's your car parked?"

When she doesn't answer, I pull her away from my chest so I can see her face. "Chloe, where's your car?"

Her bottom lip trembles. "He picked me up."

A fresh sob breaks free, and I let out a string of curse words. If she were mine, I'd spank her ass until she couldn't sit for a week for getting into a car with a stranger.

*But she's not your girl, so don't even think about it.*

I may not be able to spank her, but I can sure as fuck lecture her. And I will. But not tonight. She needs me to take care of her right now, not chastise her.

"Okay. My car is out front."

Without giving her a choice, I rise and carry her out to the dark night.

## 3
## CHLOE

Bash carries me to his black Escalade as if I weigh nothing and gently deposits me into the passenger seat. When I make no attempt to buckle my seatbelt, he reaches in and does it for me. Before he closes the door, he runs his index finger over my cheek. I close my eyes and lean into the warmth of his touch. It's a small thing, but it gives me the comfort I need right now. As soon as he pulls away, my entire body turns cold and shaky again.

I could have been raped tonight. The man my father set me up with, the one he said was a standup guy, tried to drug me and do God knows what to me.

He rounds to the driver's side quickly and starts the SUV, then leans over and turns on the heated seat on my side.

"What's your address?"

I sniffle and turn my head to look at him in the dim light. His features are set into hard lines. He's speaking gently, but fury burns in his eyes.

He watches me, waiting for an answer. I mumble my address, suddenly wrung out and exhausted.

"That's on the other side of town from your parents' house," he says.

"I moved out."

My phone starts ringing again, and I dig through my purse to fish it out. Paisley is probably freaking out that I haven't answered her calls.

"Hey," I answer quietly.

"Chloe, holy fuck, I almost called the cops. Why didn't you answer?"

She's shouting, and when I look over at Bash, he raises an eyebrow.

"I'll explain when I get home. I'm on my way."

Before she can start firing questions at me, I end the call and stuff my phone back in my purse.

"Who was that?"

I turn to look at him, trying my hardest not to gawk. It's hard, though. Sebastian Gilroy is the hottest man I've ever laid eyes on. I think an artist chiseled him directly from stone and then added a million tattoos to make him that much more appealing. Add in his brilliant green eyes that you could get lost in for days, his deep, velvety voice that makes me want to obey his every command, and the way he carries himself with so much confidence and a touch of arrogance; the man is a straight up walking, talking climax waiting to happen.

Not that I'd ever admit that. He's my brother's best friend. I've met Bash a handful of times, but I've never spent a lot of time with him. I don't think it's too far off to guess he's swimming in seas of beautiful women who want his attention. He wouldn't give a girl like me the time of day. Not that I'd ask him to, of course. No. Nope. Definitely not.

"My roommate."

He arches one of his dark eyebrows. "You have a roommate? When did you move? Does Kieran know you moved? He hasn't mentioned anything."

*Shit.*

I bite the inside of my cheek, unsure of what to say. Something tells me Bash will be able to sniff out a lie from a mile away. He's in the mafia. Which means he's a professional at reading people. Just like my brother.

"Chloe," he says, his low voice full of warning.

"I moved six months ago. And no, he doesn't know. I'm twenty-five. I don't need to tell my brother if I live somewhere else."

He glances at me, keeping one hand on the wheel as he drives toward my townhouse. "Why are you so defensive about it?"

My shoulders fall, and I slump back. "Because if

he found out I was no longer living with my dad, he would have insisted on coming to see where I live, then he would have made a big deal about the area not being safe—"

"It's *not* safe," he interjects.

I throw my hands up and shake my head. "See, that's why I didn't tell him. He and the rest of you would have had a hissy fit about it, and then he would have demanded to make the place more secure or worse, demand I move somewhere he can keep an eye on me."

The corner of his mouth ticks up. "We don't have hissy fits. Besides, what's wrong with that? We're men. It's our job to keep the women in our lives safe and protected."

I swallow and try to ignore the rush coursing through my veins at his words. Somehow, it's different when he gets all protective than when my brother does it.

"You know I'm not going to keep this from him, right?" Bash asks.

My head snaps toward him, and I scrunch my eyebrows. "What? Why? He doesn't need to know."

He pulls into my driveway and stares at the older townhouse like it personally offended him somehow. Then he turns to me, pinning me with his gaze.

"If something happened to my little sister, and he knew about it *and* kept it from me, I'd kill him. That's betrayal, and we don't do that shit. Loyalty is the most important thing to us. Plus, he's my best friend. So, either you'll go to him tomorrow and tell him, or I will. All of it. Are we clear?"

If he were to touch my neck right now, he'd be able to feel my pulse racing faster than the speed of light. His stern, threatening tone does something to me. Part of me wants to argue or disobey to see what he does. The other part wants to crawl into his lap and agree to do whatever he says so I can hear him call me a good girl again.

I already know there's no getting out of this. He means what he's saying. And as much as I want to be mad at him for it, I also understand his point of view. Even though I don't know many of the details of what my brother does in the mafia, I do know that loyalty and trust are two of the most important things in their world.

"Fine. I'll go to his place tomorrow and talk to him."

Bash raises an eyebrow. "What time?"

Damn him. He's probably going to show up just to make sure I do it. These men. They're so overbearing.

"Around ten."

He stares at me for a few seconds, probably trying to figure out if I'm telling the truth. It would be stupid of me to lie. Bash knows where I live now. I have no doubt that if I don't show up, both men will be on my doorstep at ten-o-five to give me the scolding of a lifetime.

Bash gets out of the car. Before I can ask what he's doing, he comes around to my side. When he opens my door, he doesn't hesitate before reaching in to unbuckle me. The warmth of his body and the comforting scent of his cologne wash over me. He saved me tonight, and if he hadn't been at that restaurant, I could be dead right now.

Emotion swirls inside me and fresh tears fill my eyes. I throw my arms around him. He pulls me out of the car, holding me tightly. I wrap my legs around his waist and cling to him like a baby koala.

"Hey. You're okay, baby. I got you."

"Thank you so much, Bash," I mumble into his neck.

He might be overbearing and bossy, but right now I'm so damn grateful for those things. He grabs my purse and closes the passenger door before he makes his way up to the front porch. The entire time, he keeps me in his arms, carrying me like he would a small child.

As soon as he steps up to the door, it swings open, and Paisley rushes out.

"Chloe! What the hell? Who is this asshole? Who the hell are you?" Her tone goes from worried to demanding in an instant.

Bash doesn't tense or try to put me down. Instead, he pushes past her and walks into our house like he owns the place.

"This is Bash," I explain in a wobbly voice. "He's my brother's friend."

I lift my head and look back at Paisley who follows us through the house. As soon as she sees my face, her expression turns horrified.

"What the fuck happened?" she shouts. "Why have you been crying? Did this guy make you cry? Did you make her cry, asshole?"

"Where's your room, baby?" Bash asks, ignoring Paisley completely.

"Upstairs."

He heads toward the stairs, and Paisley continues to trail us, asking a million questions.

"Why did he bring you home? Why have you been crying? What happened with Bradley? Why didn't you answer my calls?"

"Which room?" he asks.

"The second one."

When he gets to the second door, he throws it open and walks in. Then, slowly and gently, he lowers me to the bed before he turns to Paisley.

"That bastard drugged her wine. I happened to be there and witnessed it. She didn't drink any of it, but she's shaken up, so I'm going to get her ready for bed and stay here until she's feeling safe and calm again. Can you go get her a glass of water, please?"

I roll my lips in, trying to keep from laughing, as Paisley processes everything he said. Part of me expects her to push past him so she can get answers from me directly, but his firm tone and the way he keeps clenching his jaw must convey that's not a good idea because she lets out a sigh.

"Right. Sure. I'll be right back," she murmurs as she backs out of the room.

When he turns around to face me, I expect him to be annoyed or angry, but he's smiling.

"I like her. She's protective of you. Fierce," he says thoughtfully.

I smile and nod. "Yes. She is."

Then a zing of something that feels like jealousy runs through me. He likes her. Does he like her in a sexual way? I shake my head and push the thought away. It doesn't matter if he does. He's nothing to me.

"Do you want to take a shower before bed?" he asks.

I don't understand what's happening. I mean, I love how gentle he's being, but he doesn't need to stay and babysit me. Besides, I need some time to cry by myself.

"Bash, I'm fine. You don't need to hang out and watch over me."

He frowns and takes a step closer, then leans

down so he's only a few inches from my face. "Too bad for you, I didn't ask if you needed me to. I asked if you wanted a shower before bed."

My core clenches as his sparkling green eyes burn into mine. I've always known he was intense, but right now, with his stern expression directed toward me, I wonder if I need to proceed with caution.

I glance down at my dress and sigh. "I do want to take a shower. I...I feel slimy. Like he's on me somehow."

Without a word, he takes off down the hall to the bathroom. A second later, the shower turns on. I let out a sigh and get up to find some clothes to put on when I'm done. Hopefully, by the time I get out of the shower, he'll be gone, and I'll be able to hide under the covers in my room.

My eye lands on Quackers, my stuffed duck that I sleep with every night. I hurry to hide him under my blanket. Shit. Did Bash see him? How embarrassing. He probably thinks I'm weird. Definitely not the kind of woman he normally dates. Then again, that would mean Paisley's not his type either. I don't know why that makes me feel better, but it does. She's my best friend, and I want her to be happy. Just not with Bash. And I'm not going to think too deeply about why I don't want that.

"Will you be okay to shower alone?"

I whirl around and bring my hand to my mouth. "Oh, shit. You scared me."

"Language," he scolds softly.

My eyebrows furrow. "What?"

"No swearing. Now, can you shower alone? I don't want you in there by yourself if you might have another panic attack. Do you want me to have Paisley sit in there with you?"

Okay, I need a minute to unpack all of that. No swearing? As if he hasn't said the F-word a million times tonight. And he mentioned having Paisley come in the bathroom with me like she would jump at his command. This man. He's certainly confident. As he should be. He's hot. Rich. And in the freaking mafia of all things. And based on what I saw tonight when he was dealing with Bradley, he's pretty damn terrifying when he wants to be.

Bradley. I turn toward Bash with wide eyes. "What's going to happen to Bradley? You asked those men to take him to a warehouse. What are you going to do to him?"

Bash lifts a shoulder before he moves to me and cups my chin. His warm grip soothes all the thoughts racing through my head.

"Don't worry about Bradley. He's no longer your concern, and he won't bother you again. Why the fuck were you out with him anyway? You looked like you were having a shitty time from the start."

My shoulders drop. Shit. I'm going to have to answer a million questions tomorrow when my dad calls me. He's going to be upset and blame me because whatever business deal he's trying to finalize with Bradley isn't going to work.

Paisley returns with a glass of water, and I'm glad for the interruption. The last thing I want to do is answer Bash's questions. He's as nosey as Kieran.

"Thanks," I say as I squeeze past Bash's large frame. "I'm going to go shower. Paisley, will you bring me some aspirin?"

She bobs her head. "Of course."

I glance at Bash and lock eyes with him for several seconds. "Thanks for everything tonight. I'll go see Kieran tomorrow."

Before he can say anything, I grab my pajamas and scurry down the hall, hoping he realizes he's been dismissed.

## 4
## BASH

I grin as she hurries from the room without a backward glance. Then, I sit my ass down on the edge of her bed that's covered in a bright yellow comforter and rest my elbows on my knees. Paisley looks at me like she's unsure what to say or do. Not that I blame her. I'm big and intimidating. It doesn't matter whether she knows about my mafia ties. Even people who don't know me tend to stay out of my way.

"I take it you're not leaving?" Paisley finally asks.

"Nope. Not until I get the answers to my questions."

She fidgets with the hem of her oversized black sweatshirt. "Right. Um, well…"

"Don't worry about me. I'll sit here until she's

done in the bathroom. She needs some aspirin, though."

"Right. Yep. Thank you for helping her tonight. I didn't want her to go out with that guy. He seems like such a slimeball."

I raise an eyebrow. "You know him?"

"Oh, God, no. But I've seen him in interviews. He's running for mayor."

Not anymore, he's not. At least not once I'm through with him. He won't be running for shit because he won't be breathing.

"She won't have to worry about him again. I'm glad you were trying to look out for her."

A smile spreads across her face, and she finally meets my gaze. "Yeah, well, Chloe is my best friend, but she doesn't listen worth crap."

I like this girl. She's good for Chloe.

When I don't say anything, she straightens her shoulders and uses her thumb to motion behind her. "I'm going to take her some aspirin and then go to bed. It was nice meeting you. Sorry for calling you an asshole, by the way."

I hold up my hands and smile. "I get it. No hard feelings. It was nice to meet you too, Paisley."

When she disappears, I rise and slowly walk around the room. I shouldn't be snooping, but there's a lot of shit in my life I shouldn't do. It's never stopped me before, though.

I trail my fingers over an open dollhouse on top of her dresser. The tiny bed is even made with a frilly yellow comforter. Did she build this herself? One of the curtains is a little uneven, but it's otherwise perfect. My sister-in-law and her sister work on stuff like this. Hell, they have a whole goddamn zoo, complete with a piranha pond. They spend hours putting it together and rearranging it. I'm pretty sure Declan and Killian have spent a small fortune on the tiny toys.

Most of the walls in the dollhouse are the same yellow as her dress. I wonder if she painted them herself. The detail and time she put into this are impressive. I flip a tiny switch on one wall of the house and the interior lights up. She even hung a string of twinkle lights in one of the bedrooms. Fucking adorable.

I move on to her nightstand where she has a bunch of random stuff piled on top. Chapstick, a book, lotion, a remote, a few little candy wrappers, and multiple half-empty bottles of water. Her messiness makes my skin itch, but it's also cute. If she were mine, I'd get after her about it, though.

*But she's not yours, so get your mind out of the gutter, pervert. Jesus. Death wish, much?*

I almost regret opening the closet. The thing is stuffed to the brim with clothes, shoes, and purses, half of which are yellow. There's a trend going on here. I'm surprised the contents didn't burst out of there the second I pulled the door open. She needs more room to store all her stuff. A closet like mine, which is bigger than this entire bedroom.

A large, plastic tub at my feet is full of makeup. Palettes and lipsticks of all sorts. They all look old. When I open one, I'm baffled. The contents have been almost completely used up. Why is she holding on to all this stuff? Maybe it's a girl thing I don't know about. Makeup isn't exactly my specialty.

It takes me a minute to wrestle the closet door closed. The track is bent or something. Or maybe it's because this entire place is a rundown shithole, but I'll keep that to myself. I peer down into a laundry basket sitting in the corner. The way everything is tossed in there, I'm pretty sure these are her dirty clothes. And sitting right on top is a yellow pair of cotton panties. Fuck. My fingers tingle. One hit wouldn't be wrong, would it? At least I'd be able to stop wondering what her pussy smells like.

I stare at the panties for several moments and finally, unable to resist, reach down and gently pick them up. My cock stirs, and when I bring them to my nose and inhale, my entire body starts to buzz with adrenaline. She smells perfect. Sweet and feminine. She smells like mine.

Shit. What am I doing? I drop the underwear like they've burned me and shake my head. She's not mine. She's Kieran's sister. And I sniffed her fucking panties like a deranged stalker. I'll never forget her smell, though. I need to find out what perfume she wears. It lingers in the air. I might not be able to have her dirty panties, but I can sure as fuck buy a bottle of her fragrance. My cock is rock hard, and if I don't get it under control, she's going to walk in and be scared to death.

I move to the edge of the bed and sit near the big lump hidden under the comforter. She stuffed a bright yellow plush duck under there before she headed for the shower. Part of me wants to pull it out and have it on my lap when she returns, but she's already had a traumatic night, and the last thing I want to do is upset her more. She obviously stashed the toy under the blanket because she didn't want me to see it.

A few minutes later, she walks into the bedroom but halts the second she sees me. "I thought you were leaving."

I stay where I am, though what I really want to do is pick her up and carry her to bed. What the fuck is wrong with me? I can't think like that. It's wrong. She's Kieran's sister. I'd be pissed if he hooked up with my sister. Actually, that's a lie. I wouldn't be upset. I trust the men around me. I know they would never hurt her. And I know if she ended up with any of them, she'd be well taken care of. However, just because I feel that way doesn't mean Kieran would.

"I never said I was leaving. I asked you a question and you didn't answer. So, I waited."

She shifts nervously, her eyes darting around the room. When she looks at me again, I raise my eyebrows. "Why were you out with him, Chloe?"

Her shoulders drop, and fuck me, I wish I hadn't noticed because I can see her nipples through her thin tank top. It takes incredible strength, but I force my eyes back up to hers and wait for an answer.

"It doesn't matter why," she says quietly.

That's exactly why it matters. Because there's something off. She didn't go on that date willingly, so whatever the reason, I need to know so I can handle it.

"Chloe, answer the question. Now."

If I weren't so tense, I might laugh at the way her eyes widen at my firm tone. Normally I'm one of the more easygoing men in our organization. At least, I come across that way. What a lot of people don't know is that I'm a control freak, and I can be a pure monster when I need to be.

"Geez. You're as bad as Kieran."

I smile. "Baby, I'm worse than Kieran. And unless you want me to call him right now and have him come over here, I suggest you start talking."

To my surprise, she sits on the bed beside me. Not

close enough to be touching but close enough that I can smell the vanilla body wash she used. My cock twitches to life again, and I've never been more thankful to be sitting so I can keep it hidden.

She lets out a deep sigh and flops back onto the mattress. I wish she hadn't done that. Now I can see a sliver of her tummy, and I can't stop imagining myself hovering over her.

"My father set it up. He was trying to seal a business deal with Bradley, and he asked me to go out with him."

I twist my upper body to look at her, but she has an arm resting over her eyes.

"He asked? Or he demanded?"

She and Kieran have different dads. The only thing I know about her father is that Kieran hates him and thinks he's a piece of shit. And if my best friend thinks that, it's true.

"He…strongly encouraged."

Tired of question dodgeball, I grab her arm and pull it away from her face. "How exactly did he strongly encourage it, Chloe? And give me a straight answer. I'm growing impatient."

Her eyes narrow, and her jaw flexes. "Has anyone ever told you that you're extremely overbearing?"

I flash her a smile. "Yes. Scarlet and Cali tell me that all the time. Now, answer the question."

"Who are Scarlet and Cali?"

Jesus, this woman is exasperating. "Declan's and Killian's women. Why? Are you jealous?"

She scoffs. "No. God. Not even."

"I'm going to count to three, and if you don't answer my question by the time I get to three, I'm calling Kieran. One."

She slaps a hand on the bed and sits up. "He told me I had to go out with Bradley or he wouldn't pay my college tuition next term. I'm so close to being done with school, and I don't want nearly eight years of practically killing myself for a degree I have no desire for to go down the fucking drain. Happy? You got your answer, so you can leave now."

I'm on my feet so fast, she gasps. "What the fuck? He told you that? What the fuck is wrong with him? And what the fuck do you mean you don't want to do the job you went to school for? Why did you choose that major then?"

"You say fuck a lot," she murmurs.

The rage burning inside me is too hot to acknowledge what she said. Instead, I start pacing the room. That bastard. What kind of man would use his daughter to close a business deal and blackmail her by threatening to cut off funding for her education?

Chloe must realize how pissed I am because she doesn't say anything. My mind is racing. Bradley is going to die, and part of me wants to make her father disappear too. I need to talk to Kieran about it first, though.

"Get in bed, Chloe," I finally say.

When she doesn't move immediately, I pick her up to place her under the covers. She struggles in my arms as I yank the blankets back, exposing her duck, and then deposit her back onto the bed. Before she can try to hide the stuffed animal again, I grab it and push it into her arms.

"Where's your phone?"

She squeezes the toy and stares up at me like she's not sure what's happening. "It's in my purse."

I look around the room until I spot the small clutch.

"Hey!" she says when I open it. "Do you always do whatever you want?"

"Yes. Put the code in." I hand the phone to her and wait.

She stares at me for several seconds before she sighs and taps in the pin to unlock it.

"God, you're worse than my brother," she mutters.

I ignore her and call my number first then program my name into her phone. After that, I open the browser, find what I'm looking for, and hit install.

"Oh, yeah? How so?" I wait for her answer while watching the program download at the same time.

"You're bossy, overbearing, rude, bossy—"

"You already said bossy. Saying it a second time doesn't count."

She huffs and squeezes her stuffed duck tighter. As soon as the app installs, I set it up and close it before handing her phone back to her.

"I put my phone number in there, and I have yours. If you're not at your brother's at 10:00 a.m., you'll be in trouble."

Her mouth falls open. I'm damn pleased with myself. She can act as scandalized as she wants, but her eyes don't lie. Those blue beauties tell me the only truth I need.

I move toward her bedroom door and turn back to look at her. "Oh, and Chloe?"

"What?" she snaps.

"You looked incredibly beautiful tonight. It's a shame you wasted it on that piece of shit. I'm sorry your dad gave you that ultimatum. It won't happen again."

I walk out of her room, go downstairs, and head out of the front door, locking it behind me. As I stand on the front porch and look around the neighborhood, I shake my head. This fucking place is not an acceptable home for her.

I can't worry about that tonight, though. Kieran and I will handle it tomorrow. For now, I have a sorry excuse of a man to go see.

## 5

## CHLOE

As soon as the front door closes downstairs, Paisley rushes into my bedroom, her jet-black hair flopping around in a loose ponytail. "Dude, what the hell happened tonight? That was some intense shit. Tell me everything. Who is that Bash guy? You totally need to fuck him. He's hot. I had to go to my room and fan myself."

I'm still in shock. Mostly, though, Bash's parting words keep replaying in my mind.

*"You looked incredibly beautiful tonight. It's a shame you wasted it on that piece of shit. I'm sorry your dad gave you that ultimatum. It won't happen again."*

He thought I looked beautiful. Sebastian Gilroy said I looked beautiful. It's pathetic how excited that makes me. I wave my hand in front of my face, trying to cool my heated skin. I've never had this kind of reaction before. Not this intense. I've never felt the need to change my panties because of words a man said to me. Not until now. He's the most gorgeous specimen I've ever laid eyes on, and he thinks *I* looked beautiful. Damn.

"Earth to Chloe. Hello! I need deets."

Paisley crawls into my bed and makes herself comfortable. I fall back against the pillows and hug Quackers to my chest. I can't believe Bash saw my stuffed toy. God. How embarrassing.

Whatever. He's annoying and bossy. Just because he gave me a compliment doesn't mean I like him. I meant it when I said he's worse than my brother.

I don't see Kieran as often as I'd like. My father never wanted me to get mixed up with the mafia, but any time I do see Kieran, he's ridiculously over-the-top protective and bossy. He always asks me a million questions. Am I eating enough? Am I sleeping enough? Do I need any money? Is my car up to date on oil changes? It's annoying. It's also endearing.

Since we're only half-siblings, and my father thinks Kieran is a bad influence on me, he tries to keep me from seeing him as much as possible. Our mom died a few years ago, and my dad tried even harder to keep me away from him after that. I don't know why I let him control my life so much.

But I've been living with Paisley for nearly six months, and I haven't made an effort to spend time with Kieran, so that's on me. He's the one who texts me at least once a week to check on me. I have a feeling he's going to be hurt when he finds out I moved and never told him. That thought makes my tummy twist into knots. I respect Kieran, and the last thing I want to do is disappoint him. Fuck. Stupid Bash. Maybe I won't go over there tomorrow morning.

Who am I kidding? Bash said if I didn't show, I'd be in trouble. I ache between my thighs at that thought. What did he mean by trouble? A vision of being bent over Bash's powerful thighs while he turns my ass red runs through my mind. My heart pounds and my nipples ache. I like that idea way too much. There's something wrong with me.

"Oh my God, if you don't start talking, I'm going to smother you with a pillow," Paisley whines.

I blink several times and giggle. "Sorry. Tonight's been a bit wild. I'm still trying to sort through everything in my head."

She snorts. "No, you're trying to picture Bash naked in your head. What happened with Bradley the fuck boy?"

My chest aches as I tell her all about the night after I got into Bradley's pretentious sports car. By the time I tell her the last thing Bash said to me before he left, I'm exhausted. Part of me wants to cry and part of me wants to kick my roommate out of my room so I can grab my vibrator and pretend it's Bash.

"Holy fuck. Wait, I need to back up a second. You said he asked those guys to take Bradley to a warehouse. What does that mean?"

Shit. I've been friends with Paisley for years, and she's always known I have a half-brother. I've never told her what he does for a living, though. Kieran always warned me against telling people because there are enemies everywhere and they could try to hurt me if they know I'm related to him. Paisley isn't one of those people but when we first met, I hid this from her, and now all this time has passed. I trust her completely, though.

"What I'm going to tell you has to stay between us. Like, you can't tell another soul. Ever. Not even a dog on the street. It goes to your grave. I've never told anyone."

Her eyes bug out, and she licks her lips as she waits for the bone I'm dangling in front of her.

"Pinky swear. To our graves, I won't tell anyone. Not even the CIA would be able to get it out of me."

We hook pinkies and kiss our thumbs. It's our ritual whenever we need the other to keep a secret. There isn't a single other soul in the world I would trust with this information.

"My brother is in the mafia."

"The mafia?" she shouts.

"Shh! Oh my God, be quiet."

She slaps a hand over her mouth and bobs her head, her eyes as round as saucers. "Sorry. Sorry. The mafia?"

"Yes. He's one of the leaders of the Irish mafia here in the States. His father was in the mob too. It's usually a family occupation."

"So, he...like...he kills people? Pulls out their fingernails and shit?"

I laugh and roll my eyes. "I don't think he pulls out people's fingernails. But, yeah. He kills bad people. They don't murder people for fun. They always have a reason behind it."

Paisley stares at me for several seconds until I'm squirming under her gaze. Maybe I shouldn't have told her.

"It doesn't bother you that he does that stuff?" she finally asks.

I shrug. "I know my brother. He has a good heart. He only hurts bad people. They protect women and children and never hurt them. They don't have anything to do with prostitution or anything like that. There's been some sort of pact in place for a long time between all the syndicates, so they don't go to war with each other. It's like a big corporation that has both legal and illegal businesses."

She smiles but shakes her head. "I love how naïve you are, Chloe. The fucking mafia? Seriously? They do some bad shit. I've read books. We've watched mob movies together."

"Pais, sorry to tell you, books and movies are nothing like it is in real life. I mean, I'm sure there's some stuff that's the same, but I think most of it is pretty normal business stuff."

After a few seconds, her eyes widen. "Does that mean Bash is also in the mafia?"

I bite my lip and shrug. "Yes. He and Kieran are best friends. Bash's father was the head of the Irish syndicate here in the States, and now Bash's older brother Declan is the boss."

Her expression is almost comical. Her eyebrows are pinched like she sucked on a lemon, but her mouth is hanging open, and she's blinking so fast, I wonder if she's short-circuited.

"This is… How… I can't believe you never told me. This is like, holy shit. This is some heavy information, Chloe. I was kind of rude to Bash. He might come kill me now."

I laugh so hard that tears spring to my eyes. This is exactly why I didn't tell her. I love Paisley like a sister, but, man, her imagination is wild. It doesn't help that she loves dark romance books even more than I do.

"Bash isn't going to kill you. Kieran, Bash, and the rest of them are so protective of women, it's irritating. I never told my brother I moved here because

I knew he would flip his lid about the area and make me get some high-end security system or something. They're over the top. It's annoying."

If hearts could appear in someone's eyes, she'd have them. Black hearts, of course, because aesthetics are important. "It's actually pretty sweet. To have someone who cares about you so much. I wish I had a brother like yours. You're lucky."

My heart squeezes in my chest. I know I'm luckier than most. I grew up with a comfortable lifestyle and a brother who loved me a little too much sometimes. Unlike Paisley, who had a rough upbringing.

"I'll let you know how lucky I am when I get back from my brother's house tomorrow."

"What do you mean?"

I huff. "Bash is making me tell Kieran all about what happened tonight and that I moved out. He said either I told him or he'd tell him because he won't keep stuff from my brother."

She bites her bottom lip to try to keep from smiling, but it doesn't work. Then she starts giggling. "Sorry. That sucks, but it's actually kind of funny. I think I like Bash. And your brother, even though I've never met him. They seem like good men, despite being gangsters."

Letting out a sigh, I squeeze Quackers tighter. "Yeah. They are."

"I hope you didn't have a date with your vibrator because I'm sleeping with you tonight."

Well, there went my plans.

As soon as I pull into Kieran's driveway, Bash pulls up behind me in his black Escalade. So much for hoping he wouldn't show.

He's dressed in a crisp black suit with a black button-down shirt and no tie. He looks like the devil in a tailored Armani disguise. They always say the devil is attractive, and now I think I understand. Attractive yet terrifying. Perfect description for Sebastian Gilroy.

His hair is styled like he's about to be in a magazine shoot. Short on the sides, longer on top, and teased to give him that just-rolled-out-of-bed-but-did-this-on-purpose look. His beard is groomed to perfection. Everything about him screams sex appeal.

Unlike me, who barely slept. Between talking with Paisley until the early hours of the morning and thinking about Bash, I don't think I got more than a few hours of sleep. Thank goodness for quality concealer and dry shampoo. I might be feeling rough, but I was able to pull myself together before I came here. Just in case I happened to run into the devil in disguise.

"Morning, lass," he says with a smug smile when I step out of my car.

"You didn't have to come, you know. I said I would be here, and I know better than to lie to you."

He arches an eyebrow and pierces me with his gorgeous green eyes. "Do you? I'm not so sure, Little one. Guess we'll find out in time."

Whatever the hell he means by that? I let out a sigh, long and dramatic. He saunters up to me, and my eyes are drawn to his tattooed knuckles. They're swollen and red, several of them cut open. They weren't like that last night.

"Bash, what the hell happened?" I reach for his hand, but he pulls it away.

"Don't worry about it, Little one. Quit stalling and go knock on the door."

With a huff, I glare at him and spin on my heels. He follows closely. Part of me wants to tell him to get lost, but another part of me wants him here because I know Kieran is going to blow a gasket when I tell him everything. Hopefully, Bash will be my shield.

As soon as Kieran opens the door and sees me, his expression brightens until he sees Bash. Then his entire demeanor changes, and the side of my brother I rarely see is there. The deadly side.

"Tell me," he growls.

He doesn't move away from the door to let us in. Nope, he stands there like he's about to go to war. I'm pretty sure he and Bash know each other well enough to read each other's body language. Either that or Bash already told him, and now Kieran wants to hear it from me.

Annoyed with the big brute already, I press my hands to his chest and push him back. "Sure, I'd love to come in. A cup of coffee sounds lovely, big brother. Thanks for offering."

Both men stomp through the house, trailing close behind me. I roll my eyes even though they can't see them. I have a feeling the next hour is going to be grueling.

I lean against the kitchen counter and wait as my brother pours a cup of coffee. When he goes to the fridge and pulls out a bottle of vanilla creamer, I arch an eyebrow.

"I didn't take you for a creamer kind of guy."

He grunts. "I'm not. But I know you are, so I keep it stocked in case you stop by."

A lump the size of a tennis ball lodges in my throat. Guilt swirls around me like an angry thundercloud. I'm such an asshole. I can't remember the last time I came here, yet he keeps my favorite kind of creamer in the fridge. Is there an award for the world's shittiest sister? Because if so, I win.

When he hands me the steaming cup, I give him a

grateful smile and sigh as I breathe in the vanilla scent. I don't even get my first sip down before Kieran snaps.

"What the fuck is going on? You have your coffee. Now, what's wrong?"

I'm pretty sure most grown men would cower at my brother's feet if he spoke to them that way. Not only is he big, muscular, and tattooed on nearly every inch of his skin, but he has a deep voice that matches. He doesn't frighten me, though. I know the loving guy underneath. The one who would never harm a hair on my head. He can't walk into a room without inciting fear in most people. But I know I'm completely safe. And loved. Even so, he does intimidate me a little when he's like this.

I look to Bash for help, but he crosses his arms over his chest and smirks. "You said you'd tell him yourself. I'm here to make sure you tell the truth."

With a huff, I circle the kitchen island and climb up onto one of the stools. "It's not a big deal."

Bash snorts. "Don't start out by lying, Chloe. Jesus. Liars get a red ass. Is that how you want this to go?"

I gasp and narrow my eyes at Bash. "What the hell is wrong with you? Who talks like that? Kieran, tell him to leave."

When I look at my brother, he crosses his arms to mimic Bash's stance. "He's right. A red ass for lying.

Truth. *Now*, Chloe. I'm growing impatient. I'll only give you so much lenience."

God, these men are too much alike. I can't believe Bash threatened me with a spanking. That's absurd. I'm a grown woman. My clit has a pulse, though, and my cheeks, both lower and upper, feel warm and tingly. Why does the idea of Bash disciplining me turn me on? Didn't corporal punishment go out of style like fifty years ago?

I sigh and lower my gaze. They're both glaring at me. Kieran would never hurt me, but his patience is hanging by a thread, and I don't want to be the reason it snaps.

"A guy slipped a date rape drug into my wine last night. Bash happened to be there, and he intercepted it."

"What?" Kieran roars so loudly I startle, causing my coffee to slosh over the sides of the cup.

Bash is at my side in an instant, pulling the hot mug from my hands. He uses a towel to wipe up the mess before he sets the cup down in front of me. "Careful," he murmurs.

I tremble as I look up at my brother. He's about to lose control. The vein in his neck is popping out, and his face is beet red. He's vibrating with anger as he looks from me to Bash, clenching his fists at the same time.

"Did you kill him?" he demands.

Bash looks at me then back at Kieran and says something in Gaelic that I don't understand.

My fingertips go ice cold. *Did you kill him?* Shit. My brother and his friends kill bad people. Bash would see Bradley as a bad man. And he is. But to kill him? Oh, God. Did Bash kill for me? The thought sends a thrill through my entire body right down to my clit. What the hell is wrong with me? I need to go to therapy and stop reading all those dark romance books. Someone killing for me isn't romantic.

It's bad.

Really bad.

And hot.

So hot.

## 6

## BASH

"He's not dead yet. Close. He's a politician, so before I kill him, I need to make sure nothing will come back on your sister first," I say in Gaelic.

Kieran punches right through the drywall. Chloe jumps and looks at me worriedly. I shake my head and hold up my hand, so she doesn't try to go to her brother. He has a few more walls to punch before he'll be calm enough to talk to.

Sure enough, he throws another fist in a fresh spot. He has a punching bag in his gym, but it would be pointless to tell him that. Sometimes you actually have to break some shit to feel better. It's the only reason I'm not a walking time bomb this morning. I got to break lots of things last night. Bones. The most satisfying thing to break. Especially when they belong to predators like Bradley fucking Du Pont.

We watch Kieran stomp around throughout the open living space like a pissed-off bear for a few minutes before he comes back into the kitchen.

"Who the fuck is this guy? How do you know him?"

Chloe swallows, the bravado she had earlier now gone. "He…uh…he…um. My father told me to go out with him. He's some kind of business associate."

Kieran rears back and growls. "Your father set you up with a fucking predator? Did you want to go on this date?"

She flicks her eyes to me, but I stare at her and try to convey that I expect her to tell the truth. Either way, Kieran will know the truth. I'd like it to come from her. Although, the thought of spanking her ass for lying does something to my cock. Something I have no business feeling. She's my best friend's sister.

"He told me if I didn't go, he wouldn't pay my tuition. I'm so close to being done. I can't afford to pay tuition on my own. I can barely afford rent. So, I agreed to go."

Kieran's eyes darken, and he glares across the counter at his sister. "What. Do. You. Mean. *Rent*? He has you paying him rent?"

From the look on her face, she hadn't meant to let

that part slip. Better to get it all out now because I'd force her to tell him anyway.

She shakes her head and stares into her coffee. "I moved out six months ago. I couldn't stand living with my father anymore. I got a job at a coffee shop. It pays just enough to cover my part of the rent. He agreed to keep paying tuition as long as I show up to any events he wants me to attend."

Kieran looks at me, hurt in his eyes. He loves his sister so fucking much. Even though he doesn't see her as much as he'd like, he's always talking about her. I know it bothers him that they aren't close, but he also knows a lot of that has to do with her father.

"Why didn't you tell me you'd moved?" he asks quietly.

Chloe looks up at him, her blue eyes sparkling with unshed tears. "I'm sorry, Kieran. I've been under my father's thumb for so long, and it was my first time getting some freedom. I know how you are. You're so overbearing sometimes, and I was afraid if I told you, you'd come over and get all protective and bossy."

"The difference between me and your father is that my bossiness is to keep you fucking safe!" he shouts.

She straightens in her seat and blinks back her tears. I don't want to overstep, but I also don't want him taking his anger out on her when it's meant for her father and that fucker who tried to drug her.

I step forward and put a hand on Kieran's shoulder. "Take a breath, man. I know you're upset, but you know now. Directing your anger at her is misplaced."

He's breathing heavily, but he dips his chin in agreement. When I step back and look at Chloe, she gives me a small smile and mouths, "Thank you."

"I'm sorry, Kieran. I didn't mean to hurt you. I know you're different than my father. I guess I wasn't thinking about your feelings. I was so excited to get out on my own for the first time."

Kieran's gaze softens. "I'm happy you got out of your father's house. You should have told me, though. I want to keep you safe, Chloe. I don't want to control your life. Not like he does."

She pushes to her feet and slowly walks around the kitchen island. When she stops at Kieran's side, she looks up at him, uncertain for a beat. Finally, she wraps her arms around his waist, and my best friend drops his shoulders and lets out a long exhale. I shouldn't be jealous that she's hugging him. Should not and am not are two different things, though.

When they release each other, the tension in the room has mostly dissipated.

Kieran glances at me and switches to Gaelic. "We're going to pay her father a visit."

"Aye," I reply.

She moves her gaze between us. "I don't like it

when you speak Gaelic in front of me. What did you just say?"

I look down at her and wink. "Nothing, lass. I'm going to let you two catch up for a while." To Kieran, I say, "I'll be at Declan's whenever you're ready."

He nods.

Before I leave, I stop in front of Chloe. "The next time you think about telling a lie to one of us, remember what I told you happens to naughty girls who fib. Be good, Little one."

Her mouth drops open, and her eyebrows pull together as she narrows her eyes, but her pupils dilate. "You are such a caveman."

I throw my head back and laugh. "I've been called worse, lass."

When I glance at Kieran one last time, he's staring at us with a strange expression. As soon as he notices my gaze on his, he tips his chin up. "See you in a few."

"Aye."

---

"WHAT DOES this fucker do for a living?"

Kieran turns down a long driveway and parks. I've been here once before for a party. Years ago.

Before their mom died. That's the only time I've met Chloe's dad. I didn't like him from the second we shook hands. He had one of those wimpy handshakes that tells you he's not trustworthy. If I wanted to hold a dead fish, I'd go fishing.

"He's an attorney for a bunch of high society fucks. Politicians, judges, CEOs."

We get out and walk up to the front door of the massive home. The older craftsman-style mansion has a running fountain in the middle of a circle driveway. I don't remember it looking this run-down. The gardens are overgrown, there's paint chipping off the shutters, and moss growing on the roof. Everything was immaculate when I was here last. Then again, Chloe's mom was alive then, so maybe she was the one who managed the house.

Kieran rings the bell, and a moment later, a woman in a maid's uniform opens the door.

"Is Ronald here?" he asks.

She smiles politely. "May I tell him who's asking?"

He moves into the door frame, and I follow. The woman steps back fearfully, giving us enough space to enter the house.

"I'll let him know who I am. Thanks for your help, ma'am," Kieran says with a smile.

"Wait!" she calls out as we make our way through the house.

Kieran knows where he's going. I stride silently behind him, and when we come to a set of French doors, he kicks them open. A woman screams. Ronald looks up from his chair in surprise as he hurries to zip himself up.

"Jesus Christ!" the older man shouts.

The woman rises from her knees. All I see on her face is fear. I'm used to it. It's almost normal when we walk into a room. But she's not afraid of us. It's something else. She's young. Too fucking young. I'm all about age being just a number, but he's in his sixties, and I'm debating asking for her ID to make sure she's legal. I don't like it.

Kieran stomps toward Ronald and grabs him by the throat. "Do you know what you did? Huh?"

I nod my head toward the hall, signaling for the woman to leave. As soon as she does, I close the doors and lock them.

"She could have been raped. Or killed. You fucking piece of shit," Kieran growls.

When I approach, Ronald is struggling to get free of Kieran's hold, his beady eyes are glassy, and his pupils are blown wide. Is he high?

Kieran finally releases him and puts his hands on his hips, and glares at the older man.

"How dare you come into my home like this!" Ronald shouts.

Without giving any warning, I pull my arm back

and swing, hitting the older man in the jaw. He staggers, his hand going to his mouth. Blood is already dripping from his lips.

"Tell me why you set her up with Bradley Du Pont." My tone is even. Calm. Serene. That hit made me feel so much better.

"She—she wanted to go out with him!"

I swing again, hitting him in the same spot. "The fuck she did. She said you blackmailed her into going. You know who we are, Ronald. This can go badly if you lie to us. Very badly. So, I'm going to ask you again, why did you set her up with Bradley Du Pont?"

The older man grabs tissues and uses them to mop up the mess around his mouth. My knuckles are throbbing. I love the pain. It keeps me focused and gives me a sense of inner peace. It's sick and twisted that I enjoy bloodying my hands, but I've never claimed to be a saint.

Kieran picks up a glass bottle from the bar and hurls it against the wall behind Ronald. It shatters, and the scent of whiskey fills the room. Damn. Old Ron drinks the good stuff. "Talk, asshole. Why did you set *my* sister up with a predator?"

"What are you talking about?" Ronald demands.

I raise my eyebrows. "What are we talking about? We're talking about that asshole slipping GHB into your daughter's wine last night."

Ronald shakes his head. "Bradley's a good guy. He's running for mayor. He asked to go out with her."

Kieran crosses the room in only a few strides so he can corner Ronald again. "The question is, *why*? *Why* did you blackmail her to go out with him? *Why* did you threaten to cut off the money for her schooling if she didn't go out with him? *Why*, Ronald?"

Ronald shakes his head and dabs the tissue to his lips. "I've been trying to get him to hire me as his lead legal counsel. He's wealthy. His reputation is stellar. It's good for my business."

I let out a huff and flex my hands. "It's good for your business? Yeah? Is your business worth your daughter nearly being raped?"

"I didn't know he would do that! He's always been a respectable guy," Ronald says. "I never would have set her up with him if I'd known what he was going to do. She's my daughter, for fuck's sake."

"Your daughter who you blackmailed to get her to go on a date!" I roar.

Kieran shoves Ronald and shakes his head. "Your daughter's schooling is no longer your concern. I will be paying for it from here on out. And if I hear of you trying to set her up with any more men, I will come for you, Ronald. I don't give a fuck if you are her father. I will come for you, and I think you're smart enough to know what happens when the mafia comes for someone."

Ronald's face turns deep red and his chin wobbles as he trembles. "She's my daughter!"

I advance on the older man, and he shrinks back into the corner of the room again. "You put your daughter at risk for your own gain. She is no longer your responsibility. We'll take care of her from here. And if I find out you're trying to set her up with any more of your clients—or any man for that matter—I will come and slit your throat myself. Are we clear?"

He swallows as a bead of sweat rolls down his temple. "Yes."

"Who the fuck was that girl? How old was she?" Kieran demands.

Ronald sputters. "She's a hooker."

Kieran's face twists into a look of disgust. Then he spits on Ronald's shoe. "You're scum. Always have been. Always will be. I can't wait until your daughter finally realizes it."

I turn on my heels and stalk out of the office. Kieran follows, slamming the doors behind him. The maid is nowhere to be seen, nor is the woman who was with Ronald when we walked in.

As soon as we close the doors to Kieran's Range Rover, I shake my head. "He was high on something."

Kieran doesn't say anything as he turns onto the

main road and heads toward the estate we all live on. "You like my sister."

Fuuuuuck. I've never lied to Kieran. The mafia foundation is built on loyalty and trust. We take it as seriously as we would marriage vows. But damn, he might put a bullet in my head the moment I tell him the truth.

"Of course, I like her. She's family."

There. That's not a lie. She might not be Irish, but she is part of our family because she's related to Kieran.

He pulls the SUV over. "We've been best friends for nearly all of our lives. If you think I can't read every fucking emotion on your face by now, you're a bigger idiot than I thought. You like her more than just family."

I slowly turn to him. The vein in his forehead is popping out. Never a good sign. I exhale deeply and run my fingertips over my temple. I need an aspirin. Or a drink. Maybe both. Down the pills with some whiskey straight from the bottle.

"You have to know I would never act on it. I respect you too much. I'll only ever treat her as family."

He doesn't say anything, just puts the car in gear and starts driving again. I hate myself right now. I've probably pushed away my closest friend. Not that I blame him. Declan, Ronan, and I are just as protective over our sister.

"How long?"

I furrow my eyebrows. "How long, what?"

"How long have you wanted her?"

Shit.

"Since her eighteenth birthday party. I never acted on it, though, and I never will."

"That's seven fucking years, Bash. You've liked her for seven goddamn years? And you kept it from me?"

"I was never going to act on it. I knew it could never happen, so I tried to forget about her. Tried to keep my distance at family events when I could."

He shakes his head and scowls.

We fall silent for several minutes. I'll be devastated if this fucks up our friendship. I'm closer to Kieran than I am to anyone else.

"You need to make her yours," he finally says.

My head snaps up to look at him so fast that I might need a neck brace later. "What?"

"Out of every man in this world, I trust you the most. I know you would never harm her, and I know you can give her what she needs. I'm her brother. I can't give her the things her Daddy can. You have my full blessing."

I've never been so stunned in my life. "Kieran."

He shakes his head. "I mean it, Bash. You're a

good man. One of the best. And she's an amazing woman. I can see you two together. She's going to run circles around you and drive you up the wall, but you can handle it."

I don't know what to say. It's not very often that I'm speechless, but I need a minute to process all of this. Luckily, my phone vibrates, giving me the time I need. When I pull it out and unlock the screen, it opens the tracker app that sent the notification. Maybe I should feel guilty for downloading a GPS tracker on Chloe's phone last night. It was a stalkerish thing to do, especially considering I had no plans to make her mine. That's the thing about me, though. There are very few things I feel guilty about. And this isn't one of them.

The app shows she's at work. Safe and sound. The muscles in my neck finally release some tension. Kieran gave me his blessing, which means I'm responsible for her safety now. Good thing I'm already ten steps ahead. Without his blessing, I would never act on my feelings for her, but it doesn't mean I wouldn't have kept an eye on her to make sure she stays safe. Especially after last night.

If anything goes down inside that coffee shop, the men I have keeping an eye on the surveillance cameras will let me know. I need to send a thank you card to the owner for already having a system in place. Saved me the time of having to do it myself in the middle of the night. I close the app, slide my phone into my jacket pocket, and then look at my friend.

"I want to make her mine."

The corners of his lips twitch slightly like he's trying not to smile. "It goes without saying if you hurt her in any way, I'll slit your throat myself and give her your head."

"I'd put a bullet in my own head if I ever hurt her."

This time, he does smile. "I know you would. That's why you have my blessing."

# 7
# CHLOE

Work is the last place I want to be today. My emotions are all over the place. Now that I've had time to process what happened with Bradley, I'm going through waves of anger that then turn to tears.

I've always considered myself smart. I got good grades in school. I'm about to take the bar exam to become an attorney. I read for fun. They may be filthy smut books, but those still count.

Despite all of that—and the warnings flashing like bright red sirens in my head when my father told me to go out with Bradley—I didn't listen to my own gut. And if it hadn't been for Bash, it could have ended badly.

A few times, I've wondered if Bradley is dead right now. And then I try to figure out if the possibility upsets me. If I'm disgusted that Bash may have killed the guy. Then, I started googling therapists because the thought of him doing that for me turned me on more than anything. Seriously, what is wrong with me?

I shouldn't be attracted to Bash. He's a cocky asshole who threatened to spank me. Like I'm some disobedient child. Rude.

*Haven't you always dreamed about a man who takes total control?*

Ugh. I hate that inner voice. The one that always calls me out on my shit. Finding a man who takes control has always been my deepest fantasy. Not that I've had a lot of time to date over the years since law school is pretty intense, but the times I have, I've always felt disappointed.

Then I read dirty books about dominant men, and I want that. I want someone who will take care of me. Not financially. I'm going to become a lawyer—as much as I don't want to—so I'll be fine in that sense. What I want is more about not having to think so much. Not having to make decisions. I won't be a doormat. I'm not weak. Or stupid. But I'd like to be able to hand over the reins to someone and know that they will always do what's best for me. For us.

The way Bash stepped in and took over last night. Then this morning, when my brother was freaking out. I felt completely safe with him. And as much as I want to spew a bunch of bullshit to him about his thoughts on spanking me, that's all it would be. BS. I've never been spanked before, but I've fantasized about it more than once. About the pain. I've wondered how it would feel compared to the pain I've caused myself over the years. Would it satisfy the need? Would it give me the release I seek?

I keep myself busy, wiping down the coffee bar, organizing sugar packets, and refilling espresso beans. The fresh smell of a new bag of beans always gives me a boost of dopamine. Potent and rich. The scent alone is almost a caffeine rush. I'll never understand people who don't like coffee.

Since I'm working the afternoon shift, the shop isn't busy. My coworker sits at one of the tables doing homework. She'll pop up whenever a customer comes in to help, but the owner doesn't mind us doing schoolwork during the slow times. It's been a blessing because working and going to classes doesn't leave a lot of time for assignments. I'm looking forward to the break I have coming up next week. Then, just two more quarters of this to get a degree I never wanted.

*You'll be a lawyer. You can join my firm, and I'll make you rich. If you don't go to school to become a lawyer, I'm not paying your tuition. Rich men love an attractive attorney. They'll pay you anything you ask.*

My stomach clenches, and waves of nausea hit me as my father's words play in my mind. I might become an attorney, but I will never work for my father's firm. He belittled me enough growing up. I know his own father was tough on him and that's why he is the way he is, but it still hurts. So, while I'll be an attorney, I'll find my own path.

He hasn't called to check on me today. To ask how things went with his good friend, Bradley. I'm sure he's busy with work. Maybe he'll call me tonight. Maybe I'm hoping he'll suddenly care or show interest in my life other than things I can do for him.

I wish I hadn't let my father stop me from seeing Kieran more. When I was younger, I believed all the things he told me. *"He's a gangster. He's a criminal. He's ruthless."* I let his opinion of Kieran sway my own feelings for the longest time. My brother might be a mobster, but his heart is gold. He would do anything for me. I don't know why I kept the fact that I moved out from him. Yeah, he would freak out over the area and do a bunch of stuff to make my place more secure, but isn't that what I want? Someone to take care of me? He's my brother, so it's a totally different thing, but also kind of not.

I swipe the tears gathering in my eyes and pull my phone out of my back pocket. First, I find Bash's name in the contacts.

> Chloe: Thank you for being there today with my brother.

After that, I find Kieran's name.

> Chloe: I love you, Kier. Would you be up for a movie night tonight?

The doorbell jingles, and when I look up to greet the customer, the words get caught in my throat.

"You rang, baby girl?" Bash gives me that smug smile of his as he saunters toward me.

"What are you doing here?"

He winks at me, and the citrus scent of his cologne surrounds me like a soft blanket. I need to find out what he wears and buy a bottle.

*Because that's not weird, Chloe.*

I internally roll my eyes. I'm so annoying sometimes.

"I came to see you. And ask what you're doing after work."

My mouth goes dry, and suddenly I'm self-conscious about my appearance. Here he is in a full suit while I'm in a pair of ripped skinny jeans that are a size too small, a black Rolling Stones tee that I got from a thrift store, and a pair of yellow Converse. My hair is in a high ponytail, but I know without looking in the mirror that it's not neat and tidy like it was this morning.

"Little girl, I asked you a question," he murmurs.

I tilt my head back to look at him. His eyes are sparkling and his lips… damn, his lips are nice. How is it possible to be this hot? What did he call me? Little girl. My tummy does a fluttery thing, and all my muscles tighten in my core.

"I, um, why do you want to know?"

He raises his eyebrows and takes a step closer. "Because I do. What are you doing after work, Chloe?"

I'm not sure whether I should be nervous at his question or not. What is he doing here in the first place? I don't remember telling him where I work.

"I'm going home."

His gaze travels down my body, his tongue darting out to wet his lips as he does so. "Good girl. I'll see you there."

"I'm sorry, what?" My face pinches as I try to process his words. What the hell is happening?

Instead of answering my question, he leans closer. "Have a good rest of your shift, Little one."

Then he turns on his heel and stalks out of the shop, and I'm left dazed and completely confused.

MY PHONE STARTS RINGING as I make my way out to my car.

"Hey, Paisley. I'm about to head home."

"Thank God. Bash is here with three other big dudes, and they're setting up security cameras and changing out the locks on all the doors and windows. I tried to stop them, but the big hairy one they keep calling Wolf laughed at me and started taking the doorknob apart anyway."

"What?" I screech. "Let me talk to Bash!"

There's some rustling as Paisley tells him I want to talk to him.

"Hey, Little girl, are you on your way home?"

"Bash, what the fuck! What are you doing at my house?"

He lowers his voice as he speaks again, "Little girls who use dirty words get punished. Do you want to be punished, Chloe?"

My entire body flushes, and I'm about to lose my shit on this guy. Who does he think he is? I slam my car door shut and start the ignition. "What is it with you and punishing women? Do you get off on hurting them?"

"I never said anything about your punishment being painful. In fact, it could be quite enjoyable. For both of us."

My heart is pounding so hard, I can hear it. What in the hell is going on right now? And what does he mean by enjoyable? Was that a sexual innuendo? Is he flirting with me? Because my body is reacting completely differently than my brain. I'm going to need to change into a fresh pair of panties when I get home. After I murder Sebastian Gilroy.

"Is my brother there?" I demand.

"Nope. Just me and some of my associates. Wear your seatbelt on the drive home and no speeding."

"Sebastian, what the hell are you—"

I don't get to finish because the phone beeps in my ear signaling the end of the call.

"Gah!" I scream.

Instead of calling Paisley back, I find my brother's name in my phone.

"Hey, Chloe," he answers casually.

"Did you send Bash over to my house to install security cameras?" My voice is shrill as I shout, but I don't care. These overbearing men are going to feel my wrath.

Kieran chuckles. "Nope. Don't know anything about that. That's all Bash."

"Why, Kieran? Why would he do that if you didn't tell him to? Why? Tell me!"

"Jesus, Chloe, take a fucking breath before your head pops off."

I obey his command and take several breaths. He's right. I am about to detonate. But only because there's a hot as fuck mobster at my house right now installing a whole-ass security system. Who does that? I mean, I wouldn't put it past my brother, but Bash isn't my family. We hardly know each other, and now he thinks he can boss me around and call me names that make me weak in the knees? No. Nope. Not happening.

"Kieran, why is Bash at my house?" I grit out.

He sighs. "Maybe he likes you. Maybe he's trying to protect you and keep you safe in his own twisted, overbearing way. And before you get all pissy about it, maybe you need to admit you like him too. Because you do. I saw it this morning."

That fluttering returns to my tummy. Bash likes me? That's not possible. Maybe he wants to fuck me. That would be more likely. I don't do flings, though. I'm too emotional and needy. Plus, I have no doubt that if I had sex with Bash one time, I'd catch feelings, and it would be a disaster. Hell, I think I already have feelings that I have no business having.

"He doesn't like me," I insist.

"Yes, he does. I spoke with him about it. Look, you're my sister, and I love you, but you need someone like Bash. He'll take care of you. Even if you don't like the way he does it sometimes."

I stare at the dash of my car, trying to figure out what he means. I have a feeling there are a lot of layers to that statement.

"If he likes me, it's only because he wants to hop into bed with me."

That's all any guy has ever wanted to do. Once they see my scars and how fucked up I am, they want nothing more to do with me. That's why it's been two years since I've had sex with anything other than my vibrator.

"If that's all he wanted with you, I wouldn't have given him my blessing. I'm going to ask you something, and I want the honest truth. Promise?"

My shoulders drop. I'm not going to like his question, but I love him and I want us to be closer. "Promise."

"You've known Bash for years. Maybe not as a close friend, but you've been around him and seen the kind of man he is. So, despite his strong-armed approach, do you like him? Do you find him attractive? Do you want a man who will take care of you and always put you first?"

I let out a huff and shake my head. "I don't think I want to answer that question."

"Then you have your answer right there, Little one."

Stupid brothers. Stupid Bash.

## 8

## BASH

Paisley hasn't stopped pacing since I arrived with Wolf, Colt, and Angel. When we first got here, she went paler than she already was, and I thought she was going to pass out. I wonder if Chloe told her what I do for a living. Even though I would never hurt her, the fear worked in my favor because she let me into the house.

When I told her what I was there for, she tried to talk me out of it, but I was too busy telling Colt where I wanted the cameras to listen. Whether Paisley realizes it or not, all this security stuff is here to keep her safe too. If I had my way, I would have shown up with a moving company and had both women moved into one of my houses by morning. Since things are so new, I figured that might be taking it a step too far. Maybe next week. After Chloe has time to adjust to the changes she's about to experience in her life.

My phone rings shortly after I end the call with Chloe and, when I see Kieran's name on the caller ID, I grin.

"She must have called you."

"Aye. She's as mad as a hornet."

Wolf installs a third deadbolt into the front door, and I lean against the wall. "Am I going too far?"

"Probably. At least she knows there's a camera system going in. Cali didn't have a clue Declan was watching her before they got together. So, there *is* that."

We chuckle. We don't understand the concept of boundaries. Especially when it comes to the women we want. And I want Chloe. She's going to fight me, test me, and probably piss me off, but I'm going to love every minute of it.

"You have your bulletproof vest in your car? Might want to put it on," Kieran says.

"Does she have a fucking gun?"

"Aye. I gave her one on her twenty-first birthday. Didn't want her going out partying without protection."

Shit. I probably need to find it before she gets home. Although, I'm glad she has it, and I'm grateful to Kieran for making sure she was as safe as possible.

"Thanks for the heads up."

As I end the call, Chloe storms in, pushing the front door open so hard, it nearly hits Wolf in the face.

"Oh, sorry!" Her eyes widen as she takes him in.

My girl. Mad as hell but still apologizing for almost hurting someone. Cute little thing.

Wolf grins at her. "No problem, Little one. The one you want to hit is over there."

Her gaze follows the direction of his thumb. When her eyes land on me, she stomps over and puts her cute little hands on her hips. "What are you doing, Sebastian? Seriously? What the fuck?"

Without a word, I flip her over my shoulder and band my arm around her thighs.

"What the hell!" she squeals and hits me in the back several times.

Taking the stairs two at a time, I go into her bedroom and toss her onto the bed. "Remember what I said about saying naughty words? Do you know what happens to Little girls who curse? Their Daddies punish them."

Her pupils go wide and her mouth falls slack. When she presses her thighs together, I smirk and prowl toward her.

"You're not my Daddy, and you can't punish me." She lifts her chin defiantly, and I love it. My strong girl.

I press my knee between her legs, so she's forced to open her thighs. Then I lower myself to hover over her, my hands resting on either side of her head. The defiance disappears, replaced with heavy breathing as she bites down on her bottom lip.

"I might not be your Daddy yet. But I want to be. And you might argue about me punishing you, but we both know you want it. Hell, I think you crave it. Every time I talk about it, your body tells me so."

She shakes her head. "Does not."

Using my thumb, I stroke her cheek. She leans into my touch, and when I rub the tip over her plush lips, her eyes close. I don't like it. I want her to see exactly who's touching her.

"Look at me, baby." When she obeys, I smile at her. "Good girl."

As if she suddenly remembers that she's pissed at me, she shoves at my chest. I don't budge, and her face scrunches up in irritation.

"Get off me," she says breathlessly.

"Say please." I grin.

She huffs and shakes her head. "You're a big jerk."

"Baby, I'm more than a jerk. But I'm your jerk now. Fight it all you want, but I'm not going anywhere."

Something flashes in her eyes. Doubt maybe. Like

she doesn't believe me. Silly girl. She'll learn. As quickly as it comes, it disappears, and she's back to glaring at me.

"I don't understand what's happening, Bash. Why are you here? Why are there three terrifying mobsters downstairs installing stuff?"

"They aren't mobsters."

She shoots me an exasperated look. "Okay, whatever. Why are you here?"

"Because the first time I met you on your eighteenth birthday, I was entranced. I have never had a reaction to a woman the way I did to you. When your brother introduced us and we shook hands, I felt like I'd been hit by lightning." I stare at her for several beats. "Do you remember the night of your parents' anniversary party?"

"Yes. Of course, I do. It was right before my mom got sick."

"That night, I was going to find a bathroom, and I overheard you talking to one of your friends. It actually might have been Paisley. I wasn't paying attention to her. You were crying, and you told her you wanted one of the guys at the party to leave because he wasn't getting the hint that you weren't interested. You told her you were tired of being around men you didn't feel safe with. Do you remember that?"

Her gaze travels over my face. "When I went

back to the party, the guy was gone. I never heard from him again."

"So, tell me this, Chloe. Do you feel safe with me?"

We stare at each other for a long moment before she gives a slight nod and whispers, "Yes."

"Do you know why you never heard from that guy again?"

She shakes her head.

"Because I made it crystal clear to him that if he ever came near you, I'd break every single bone in his body. At the time, I knew nothing could happen between us because you were my best friend's sister. Loyalty is everything to me, and I would never betray him. Despite not being able to have you, I knew I'd still do anything it took to make you feel safe."

I let my gaze roam over her delicate features for a few seconds before I go on. Her lips part and her hands are still resting on my pecs. I'm hoping it's a good sign that she's still touching me.

"I kept my distance. I didn't ask Kieran about you because I didn't want to tip him off that I've thought about you every single day since that night. I tried not to. But every time I closed my eyes, there you were. I kept my obsession a secret, but all it took was your brother seeing us together for him to know I have feelings for you. He gave me his blessing today.

Not having that was the only thing that kept me from hunting you down and pursuing you years ago. So, tell me right here, right now you want nothing to do with me and I'll leave. If you don't tell me that, if you don't say those words, the chase is on, Little girl."

## 9
## CHLOE

I can't catch my breath. Is he insane? He's liked me for seven years? That…that can't be right. Sure, I've thought he was hot since the first time I met him. Droolworthy. I might have even thought of him a few hundred times while using my vibrator, but that's beside the point.

Now, after supposedly liking me all this time, he's gotten my brother's blessing, and he expects me to fall in line with his, well, whatever it is he's thinking. Bash is one of the top-ranking men in the Irish mafia. He's used to getting anything and everything he wants. And what's with all this Daddy stuff? I'm not hating it. But I'm confused. I've never had a man like this in my life. I mean, my brother is intense, but he's my brother. It's different with him. With Bash, it's like all his attention—all his focus—is solely on me, yet it hasn't even been twenty-four hours since he saved me.

"I'm getting impatient, Chloe. I'm going to count to three, and if you don't tell me you want nothing to do with me, that's it. This is the only time I'll give you an out. One."

My eyes widen. If I tell him I want nothing to do with him, it would be a lie. A big one. I wonder, though, if I don't say it, what does that mean for me? He's already shown me that he won't think twice about doing whatever he wants when it comes to me. He came here with his friends while I wasn't home to install a bunch of security stuff, for God's sake. He'll walk all over me if I let him.

"Two."

That's the thing about me, though. I won't let him. I'm not going to lie down and let him do whatever he wants. I'm not that kind of girl. At least, I don't want to be. I've done enough of that with my father, letting him mow me over to be the perfect daughter. And what did that get me? A bunch of scars, a degree I never wanted, and a date with someone who tried to drug me. I don't know Bash very well, but something tells me he would rather die than let anything happen to me. He's a protector. Even if the way he protects is a little...unhinged.

Lying to him would probably be the smart move. The safest move for my heart. Because I think Bash could be the guy who could actually shatter it to pieces if he wanted to. My brother wouldn't have given his blessing if he thought Bash would ever do that, though. Kieran would literally kill him if he did. They might be best friends, but Kieran and I are blood. He's more protective of me than anything.

I meet Bash's gaze and stare at him. He might get his way right now but I'm sure as hell not going to always let that happen.

As if he can see the decision settle in my mind, he smiles. "Three."

And then he crashes his mouth to mine.

His kiss is rough and claiming. Passionate but demanding. I grip the front of his shirt and wrap my legs around his waist. Our teeth clink together as he pushes his tongue into my mouth. My entire body is on fire. My core aches and my nipples send a zing right to my pussy as they press against my bra. His cock is rock hard against me. I'm nobody special. I'm certainly not the type of woman I would expect him to like. I'd expect him to be with a runway model instead of someone short and chubby like me, who has a stuffed duck in my bed that I have to sleep with every night. It thrills me that I can make him react like..*that*.

When he pulls away, his eyes are blazing. "You're mine, Chloe. Do you understand? *Mine*."

I roll my eyes. "You're delusional, you know that?

You can't come in here and declare that I'm yours. It doesn't work like that."

His lips curl into a smile. "Wanna bet? I gave you an out. You didn't take it. So now, you belong to me."

Part of me wants to smack the arrogant smile off his face, but the other part of me is a needy bitch who likes his caveman side. My drenched panties like it too.

"We need to deal with your punishment for swearing," he murmurs.

My mouth drops open. "You can't punish me for swearing."

He arches an eyebrow. "Yes. I can. I'm your Daddy now, and no swearing is one of my rules."

*I'm your Daddy now.*

Is there a hose around here somewhere? Because I need to cool down. I shouldn't get a thrill this intense over those words. Even if having a Daddy Dom has always been a fantasy of mine. I used to think I was a freak, but then I realized it's more common than I imagined. Paisley is into it too. It's why we're such good friends. We know each other's deepest secrets and desires. Despite my love of the color yellow and hers for black, we're two peas in a pod.

"Do you want to know what happens to Little girls who break the rules?"

My gaze snaps to his. Do I want to know? Fuck

yes, I do. But also, I shouldn't *want* to be punished. Definitely not. My heart pounds so hard against my ribcage that I'm afraid it might break a bone. Being spanked is intriguing. I've read so many books that have scenes where the man spanks his woman, and as embarrassing as it is to admit, I've read most of those scenes one-handed. I was using my other to touch myself until I got off on the vision of me being the one getting spanked.

His pupils dilate as he watches me squirm while dirty thoughts consume me. Then, he flexes his hips slightly, pressing his erection into my core. "Little girls who swear get their mouths fucked by their Daddy. But since it's probably a bit too soon for that to happen, maybe I should put you over my knee instead."

Holy hell. I chew on my bottom lip as I think about Bash fucking my mouth. That doesn't seem like a punishment to me. It seems like a treat. Then I picture him putting me over his knee, but the sound of a hammer interrupts my thoughts. We're not alone here.

"You can't spank me. They'll hear."

Jesus, what the hell is wrong with me? I basically told him if there weren't other people here, he could spank me. Now he's going to think he can do that anytime he wants when we're alone.

"You think I give a fuck if other people hear you

getting your bottom spanked?" He's not smiling. Nope, there isn't an ounce of sarcasm in his voice. He really doesn't care if other people hear. But I do.

"I don't want anyone to hear."

He stares at me for a long moment. Several emotions pass through those emerald eyes, and I want to ask what he's thinking, but then he sighs. "Fine. But you're still going to be punished."

"I don't want to be punished."

Good God. I sound like a whiny little girl. And the way one side of his mouth pulls up into a smirk, he thinks so too.

"Little girls never *want* to be punished, but they need to be, so they remember to be good girls in the future."

"I am a good girl."

What the hell is wrong with me? Why am I indulging him on this? Why am I playing the part instead of telling him to fuck right off to hell?

His mouth spreads into a genuine smile. "You are a very good girl, baby. But you were naughty. So, here's what's going to happen since I'm not going to fuck your mouth, and I can't spank you with other people here. You're going to go stand with your nose in the corner for five minutes and think about a better way to talk to Daddy in the future."

That sounds awful. I think I'd rather him fuck my mouth. That seems much more fun. Despite hating the idea of standing in the corner, there's an ache between my legs that says otherwise.

Before I can argue, he rises and leans down to grab my wrists, then pulls me up to stand. I stare up at him, waiting for him to tell me he's kidding. Instead, he places his hands on my shoulders and turns me toward the only empty corner of my bedroom. Then he swats my bottom. Hard.

"Owwie!" I spin around and glare at him while rubbing my butt.

"Get moving, otherwise I'll spank you with or without people hearing."

His tone leaves no room for argument, and if I know one thing about Bash, it's that he doesn't make empty threats. None of them do.

With a huff, I turn and stomp toward the corner. "This is ridiculous."

"Keep talking, and I'll add more time."

Well, that's rude.

It's like time stands still. In a way it's good because with me facing the wall, I don't have to see his beautiful face. It gives me a chance to sort my thoughts without being distracted by him. On the other hand, I miss his touch. The warmth his enormous body provides. The way he looks at me like I'm the most interesting thing he's ever laid eyes on. His smirk after he's said something dirty. That dang citrus scent that makes all of my senses come alive.

He declared that I'm his. What that all entails, I'm not sure. Does he mean I'm his girlfriend? That seems a little juvenile. Do mafia men have girlfriends? Maybe I should ask Kieran.

I shouldn't have cursed at Bash. I know this isn't the best part of town. The locks in this place aren't super secure. He's here doing this nice thing for me, even if he is going about it the wrong way, and I was yelling at him in front of his friends about it. Something tells me Bash is always going to do things his way, even if I don't appreciate that. He's not a man who does anything by anyone else's rules but his own.

"Time's up. Come here, baby."

He's sitting on my bed with his thighs spread wide, holding out his arms for me to come to him. Maybe I should be spitting mad that he punished me, but the only thing I want right now is to curl up with him and let him snuggle me.

As soon as I get to him, he tugs me down on his lap and holds me close to his chest while stroking a hand up and down my back. "That's my good girl. I'm proud of you for accepting your punishment."

Feeling relieved, I burrow my face against his neck. "I shouldn't have cursed at you."

His hand stills for a brief second. "You're not always going to like how I take care of you, Chloe. I'm a control freak. I'm possessive and overbearing."

"You fool people."

He leans back enough so he can see my face. "What do you mean?"

I reach up and tuck the tips of my fingers into his shirt so they're resting right on his pulse.

"I always thought you were the easygoing one. Like nothing in the world bothered you."

His heartbeat starts to race under my touch. "I wear a mask to the outside world. All of us do to some extent. We have to. We can't show weakness, fear, or anger because it could be used against us. But while I might have seemed easygoing, I was always watching. Always listening. Always ready to do what had to be done to protect my family and our legacy. Only a few people get to see the real me. The people I care most about and who mean everything to me. And when I need to be, I'm a monster, but because I wear the mask, the bad guys don't know that about me until it's too late. You, Little girl, are part of this family. You're a part of me now, and I will do whatever I need to do to protect you and take care of you. Even if you don't always like it."

Wow. Okay. That shouldn't be the most romantic thing I've ever heard, but it is. Maybe my brother's mafia blood rubbed off on me somehow because all this dark stuff he keeps saying turns me on instead of making me want to run for the hills.

I think about Bradley and the way Bash jumped

right in to protect me. He stayed calm the entire time he was scaring the daylights out of Bradley.

"Did you kill Bradley?"

Why did I ask that? Do I want to know the answer? If he tells me and then I'm questioned by police, will I be able to lie? Because I would lie my ass off so Bash wouldn't go to jail. I'm supposed to become a lawyer. Lawyers are supposed to follow the law, not aid in murder. Even if he deserved it.

"Not yet. Kieran and I paid him another visit this afternoon. He's still alive. For the time being."

I pull my bottom lip between my teeth and nibble on it for a few seconds. "Are you going to kill him?"

He stares at me for a long moment without saying anything. I know what the answer is, but I want to hear him say it. I need to hear him say it.

"Nobody hurts what's mine and lives to talk about it." His voice is low and deadly.

A shiver runs up my spine, goosebumps spreading over my flesh. Bash might be a monster, but I've never felt so safe in my life.

## 10

## BASH

I'm not going to keep the truth from her. If she were a different woman, I'd probably introduce her to my lifestyle a bit slower, but she's Chloe. She knows what we do. She may not have grown up in the mafia life, but her brother did, so she's not clueless. Besides, if this is going to work, we need to keep things honest. I won't allow her to lie to me, so I won't do it to her.

She snuggles deeper into my arms and sighs. I lower my face to her neck and give her a gentle kiss. Her fragrance surrounds me like a cloud of comfort mixed with arousal. My cock stirs. My dick has been hard non-stop for the past twenty-four hours.

"What perfume do you wear?"

"Hmm? Oh, it's called Juliette Has a Gun."

I pause with my lips hovering over the pulse point of her neck and smile. "Interesting name."

"It's my favorite," she murmurs as she leans into me.

I take another deep inhale. "It's one of mine too."

What I don't tell her is that my all-time favorite is the smell of her dirty panties. Her perfume is a close second.

"I'm taking you to dinner tonight."

She pulls away from me and raises her eyebrows. "First of all, the polite thing to do would be to ask. And second, no you're not. I have a movie date with my brother."

A low growl works its way from my chest. "I don't think I like the idea of you hanging out with another man."

Her mouth falls open as she glares at me. "He's my *brother*."

"Exactly. He's a man. I don't like it." I'm teasing her. Mostly. The jealousy I'm feeling is more because he gets to spend time with her tonight, and I don't.

"You are certifiable."

I laugh. "Probably. Can I come for movie night?"

Fuck it. I don't care if I seem clingy. I want my girl on my lap tonight, even if it's just snuggling while we watch something.

"No."

Another growl works its way up. "Why not? Kieran's my best friend, you're my girl. It makes sense for me to come."

She smacks my chest and shakes her head. "You're not coming. I haven't spent nearly enough time with my brother over the years, and I feel horrible about it. I need some one-on-one time with him. Maybe, if you *ask*, tomorrow night we can have dinner."

If I kill Kieran, she won't have to spend time with him. Then again, if I off him, she'll be sad, and I don't want that. Shit. I guess I'll have to deal with it. Maybe I'll go over to Declan's and see what Cali and Scarlet are up to tonight. They're always fun to hang with. I love watching them run circles around my brother and Killian.

"Fine. Tomorrow night, then."

"If you ask. You can't demand all the time, Bash."

"It's Daddy to you, Little girl."

She quirks a brow and pushes out her lips into a stubborn pout. "I'm not one of your men who's going to fall in line just because you say so."

I wink at her and grin. "Maybe you should. It would be so much easier for me."

She giggles and rolls her eyes. "I have a feeling too many people jump to do your bidding every time you issue a command. Too bad for you, I'm not going to be one of them."

My skin heats, and my heart pounds against my

ribcage. I press a kiss on her forehead. "That's good, baby. I like you sassy. Gives me more opportunities to spank your ass."

Someone starts hammering downstairs, reminding me why I came here in the first place. I wonder if Paisley is still down there wearing the carpet thin with her pacing.

"Let's go downstairs. I'll introduce you to the guys and teach you how to use the security system."

I help her to her feet. As we make our way out of her room, I notice a small shoebox of makeup and remember the box she has at the bottom of her closet. This stuff looks used up and old too.

"What's all that makeup for?"

She glances down at the box and smiles. "Oh, uh, I just love collecting makeup. I sometimes film tutorials and post them online. It's no big deal. I save all the unique containers. I don't know why. It's probably a weird thing to do."

"Hey," I say as I grab her elbow. "It's not weird, baby, and I don't want you thinking that. I think it's cool. I didn't know you did makeup tutorials."

Sadness flashes in her eyes. "Makeup is my one true passion in life. But it's not an acceptable career path according to my father. So, I do it for fun. When I finish school, I'll have more time for filming."

My gaze is fixed on the box of makeup. She heads out of the bedroom and turns the corner to go down the hall. I start to follow but stop again when I reach her laundry basket. She's mine now. Completely and utterly mine.

"Are you coming?" she calls out.

I quickly snatch up a pair of black cotton panties and shove them in my pocket. "Coming, baby girl."

"So let me get this straight. Kieran's half-sister is your girlfriend?" Cali asks.

I shrug. "She's going to be my wife. And my Little girl."

Scarlet stares at me like I'm an alien. "And Kieran is okay with this?"

Declan, Killian, Grady, and Ronan are all looking at me, fully amused by the girls grilling me. Fuckers.

"Yes. We talked. He's good with it."

Cali raises her eyebrows and smirks at Scarlet then looks at me again. "When can we meet her?"

I exhale deeply. "Don't even think about trying to get her to join your little troublemaker club."

Both women scoff.

"We don't have a club, silly. That's ridiculous. But maybe she could be our friend at least. We're family after all." Cali's eyes go round and wide. "Aren't we?"

Declan barks out a laugh while Ronan brings his fist up to his mouth to hide his grin. The little brat just had to hit home on the family part. She knows how important that is to me.

I sigh and drop my shoulders, pinning her with a stern look. "Yes, stop trying to guilt me. You know we're family. But you two are walking chaos."

Scarlet shrugs. "We're also the only reason you guys ever laugh, so there is that."

"Daddy, can I have more wine?" Cali holds up her glass as if she's waiting for her husband to serve her.

He quirks an eyebrow. "Where did your manners go, Little girl? Do I need to give you another reminder?"

She shakes her head so hard that I'm surprised it doesn't fly right off her shoulders. "Please can I have more wine, Daddy?"

Declan smiles and grabs the bottle from the wet bar. "Good girl. This is your last glass for the night, though."

When Cali lets out a dramatic huff, Declan snatches her glass away. "Little girl…"

"Okay! Okay, I'm sorry, Daddy. I was just being sassy." She holds out both her hands and makes a grabby motion with her fingers.

Watching the two of them makes me wish Chloe could be here tonight. I want to argue with her like this. To threaten her with spankings and pour her wine for her. To know she feels safe to be sassy and bratty. I want it all. When I told Cali that Chloe would be my wife one day, I wasn't lying. And if it's up to me, it will be sooner rather than later.

"Can we start the movie now? We haven't watched *Beauty and the Beast* since last week," Scarlet whines.

The men all groan, but we grab our glasses of whiskey from the bar and find spots to sit. I know this entire movie line by line by now. It only takes one look at the two women who have captured all our hearts, and my annoyance disappears. I'd do anything for them. Just like I'd do for Chloe. Which is the only reason I haven't shown up on Kieran's doorstep demanding to join them. She asked for one-on-one time, and since I know she's totally safe with him, I'll sit my ass here and watch this damn shifter dude lock Belle up in his lair. Actually, it's not a terrible idea. Maybe the Beast is onto something with that. Would Kieran approve, though? Or is that taking it too far?

Probably too far.

For now.

"What are we doing here? I thought you were taking us to lunch."

I smile in the rearview mirror at Scarlet and Cali. Grady chuckles beside me. "We are going to lunch, but I needed to stop here first."

Scarlet scrunches her nose. "At Blush? It's the best high-end makeup store in the city. A bottle of foundation is like eighty dollars."

"I know it's the most high-end. That's why we're here. Let's go."

We get out of the SUV and wait until two men exit SUVs parked on either side of us. Declan and Killian don't let the girls go anywhere without a small army of guards. Not that I blame them. I'm actually on board with it. Which is why I had Chloe followed home last night by a couple of men. Can never be too safe when it comes to the treasures in our life.

The store goes silent when the eight of us walk in. I suppose six big men in black suits walking into a makeup store isn't something that happens every day. I scan the place. Rows of displays on either side gleam with different bottles, tubes, jars, and pencils. Every row is a different brand, but all of them are high-end and packaged to match the expensive price tags.

The obnoxious lighting glares off the bright white floors. To one side, several women sit at vanities while employees in black aprons give them makeovers. The entire store smells like a mix of different fragrances, none of which appeal to me because they're not Chloe's.

A tall, slender woman approaches nervously and looks at Cali and Scarlet. "Welcome to Blush. Is there something I can help you find?"

"We're going to need a couple of sales associates to help my sisters pick stuff out. And baskets. Several baskets."

The woman looks at me and bats her eyelashes. "Of course."

Cali turns to look up at me. "What's going on, Bash?"

"Chloe loves makeup. She films makeup tutorials and likes to collect the pretty containers. So, you two are going to pick out anything and everything in this store that she might possibly like. No limit. And pick some shit out for yourselves if you want. Got it?"

Scarlet lets out a little squeal and throws her arms around me. "I take back what I said to you when Killian handcuffed me to the car. I do like you. She's a lucky woman."

I laugh and wrap my arm around her shoulders. "Love you too, brat. Now go. Have fun. Try to find some sparkly shit, she seems to like that stuff."

Two sales associates have appeared in front of us with baskets in their hands, looking more than ready to assist the women. Two of our men accompany each of them as they start wandering the store.

The first woman who greeted us comes over to me and touches my arm. "Is there something *I* can help you with?"

I lower my eyes to where her fingers are on me. My skin crawls even through the layers of clothing. The woman is attractive. There's no question about it. But she's not Chloe. The only hands I want on me in that manner are my girl's.

"No. I'm good," I say flatly as I stare straight ahead, keeping an eye on Cali and Scarlet.

When she doesn't move, I finally slide my eyes in her direction. She sticks her bottom lip out in a forced pout and uses her index finger to run a line up my sleeve. "I'm sure there's *something* I can help you with."

"Remove your hand from me, now. The only woman I'm interested in is my *wife*," I say quietly enough that only she can hear.

Her eyes widen in obvious surprise, but she does as I say and lets out a huff before stalking off in the other direction. It doesn't matter that Chloe and I aren't actually married yet. She will be my wife one day soon, and in my mind, I already consider her mine.

Grady lets out a low whistle. "Damn, man."

"Shut up." I walk off toward the perfume section.

Another associate is straightening all of the fancy glass bottles. She turns toward me when I get close. "Anything I can help you find?"

"Do you have Juliette Has a Gun?"

Her eyes light up. "Oh, yes. That's a popular one."

"I'll take every bottle you have."

The way her face pales, I'm worried she might pass out. "We have at least fifty bottles of that perfume in stock. We just had a shipment come in. Like I said, it's a popular one."

I nod. "Good. I'll take them all."

Cali is nearby looking at a makeup display. She must take pity on the woman because she comes over to me and smiles. "Don't worry. He can afford it. It's better if you start packing them up instead of asking questions. He's sort of a caveman and doesn't communicate very well."

When the woman finally scurries off, I give Cali an appreciative smile. "Good girl. Why isn't your basket full?"

She rolls her eyes. "I'm taking my time to choose carefully."

Shaking my head, I move to the display she was standing in front of a few seconds ago and start grabbing boxes by the handful. I think they're lipsticks, but some of them are brown and are called contour sticks. Whatever that means. I don't care. If she doesn't use them, she can donate them or keep them for the containers.

"Bash, this stuff is super expensive."

I grab another handful—this time, jars of some sparkly gel stuff—and drop them in the basket. "Do I look like I give a fuck about the price? The only thing I care about is making Chloe smile. So get to shopping."

She huffs but starts grabbing more makeup, murmuring something under her breath about unhinged mafia men being a pain in her ass. It's like she forgets we're billionaires who own our own planes and yachts. Money is no object to us. But the happiness of our girls? That's everything.

"I heard that. I'm telling your Daddy about your filthy language."

"Snitches get stitches, Bash. Just remember that." She sticks her tongue out at me and stomps off toward another display.

While they continue to shop, I pull out my phone to text my girl.

> Bash: Dinner tonight at 7.

> Chloe: Nope.

> Bash: What do you mean nope? That wasn't a question.

> Chloe: Exactly. It wasn't a question, Bash.

Her words from yesterday run through my mind. She wants me to ask. Like I'm courting her or something. We're not teenagers. I'm not dating her. She's mine.

> Bash: Sassy girls who don't address their Daddies correctly get spankings, you know.

> Chloe: And Daddies who don't ask don't get to have dinner with me.

I chuckle and shake my head.

> Bash: Chloe, my sassy Little girl who desperately needs a red bottom, will you please have dinner with me tonight at 7?

> Chloe: Sure! I thought you'd never ask. I'd love that.

Little brat.

> Bash: I'll pick you up at 6:30.

> Chloe: What should I wear?

Bash: Wear anything you'd like. You're beautiful in everything. But if you really want my opinion? The yellow cotton summer dress with the bow on the back that you wore to your brother's birthday dinner last year is my favorite.

Chloe: …

Chloe: You remember that?

Bash: I remember everything about you. Can't wait to see you tonight. Be good.

## 11

## CHLOE

"Hey, Dad." I perch the phone between my ear and shoulder while continuing to file my nails. I need to paint them badly. Maybe a soft pink. Or yellow. Yellow is always a good choice.

"Chloe. Your brother and one of his thug friends dropped by yesterday."

My stomach clenches, and the urge to vomit seeps up through my chest. I was afraid of that. Neither Kieran nor Bash told me anything about it. I'm sure it's because they're trying to protect me from the big, bad world.

"Yeah. Well, Bradley is a bad guy," I say quietly.

"He's not a bad guy. He made a bad choice. There's a difference, Chloe. Like going to see your brother. That was a bad choice."

"One of his friends saw what happened, and that's how he got involved. Either way, he's trying to protect me, Dad."

"I didn't raise you to need to be protected, Chloe. I raised you to stand on your own two feet. You're never going to make it as an attorney if you crawl to your brother whenever something bad happens."

Every muscle in my body tenses. My temples throb with the start of a migraine. His words always cut deep. Which is why I used to cut deeper. To neutralize the pain. Not anymore. The urge is still there, though.

No matter what I do, it's always the wrong thing in my father's eyes. Maybe if I had been the son he wanted, it would be different.

"I didn't crawl to him. I didn't tell him to go see you."

"My business deal is ruined now. I needed that contract. It's all fucked-up now. It's putting me in a bind, Chloe."

I close my eyes, trying to keep the tears at bay. "I'm sorry. I didn't ask him to drug my drink. If Bash hadn't seen it and intervened, I might be dead right now."

He snorts. "Don't be ridiculous. Jesus, you're always such a drama queen. He wouldn't have killed you. He wanted to have some fun with you."

Seriously? Is he for real right now? I drop the

nail file and pull the phone away from my ear to look at the screen, just to confirm it's my actual father who called me and not some prankster. Bile rises in my throat as I stare at his name on the screen. My heart cracks down the center. Has he always been this way, and I chose not to acknowledge it? Ignorance is bliss and all that?

"I'm not paying your tuition anymore. If you can't help your own father out, I'm not going to help you. Don't bother contacting me anymore. Since you seem to want to run to your brother so much, he can be your family. You're no longer my daughter or my concern."

The phone beeps and the line goes dead. I stare at the device for several minutes, processing what just happened. My entire body is numb, and I can't think clearly. How have I never seen this side of him? The realization that I probably have and decided to be blind to it hits me like a ton of bricks. Am I that naïve? That stupid?

His painful words are the only thing I can hear playing through my mind, and I want them to go away. I need them to go away before I lose it. Before I crumble like I've done so many times in the past when he's hurt me. I'm not the same girl I was ten years ago, though. I'm stronger now.

I don't feel strong, though. I feel weak and broken. Confused. Even though it's been years, I still have a collection of blades in my bathroom. Would it give me the same relief it did before? Would I feel better afterward? Or worse? I'm pretty sure I'll feel worse. Although I don't know how I could possibly feel worse than I already do. My own father, my flesh and blood, disowned me.

Instead of going into my bathroom, I crawl under the covers and pull Quackers to my chest. Maybe a nap will help. As I rub Quackers soft yellow fur, the tightness in my belly slowly starts to unclench and the only thing I can think about before I drift off to sleep is how much I wish Bash were here.

"Why am I so nervous?"

Paisley grins at me in the reflection of the mirror. She's on my bed with her feet in the air and her head perched on her hands. "Uh, gee, I don't know. Maybe because you're going on a date with a mobster who basically broke into your home with his mobster friends to install a security system."

I spin around to face her and roll my eyes. "He didn't break in. You were here. And those other guys aren't in the mafia."

She raises her eyebrows and looks at me like I've

grown an extra boob. "Defending him already. That's good. It will come in handy when you are questioned by the cops."

"I'm not going to get questioned by the cops. And I'm not defending him. I'm just…"

"You're just already falling for him and want a piece of that dick he's probably swinging around like a baseball bat."

God bless America. I love Paisley. I do. But she's so damn blunt sometimes and usually right, and I hate it.

"I'm not in love with him. I like him. And I feel safe with him, you know?"

"Hey, if you can get past all his red flags, I can too. Red flags, where? All I see is green," she says with a grin. "Besides, even though I've never met your brother, you've told me how protective he is, so I trust that he wouldn't let Bash date you if he felt it was dangerous. Which, if you ask me, is pretty damn hot. Hey, is your brother as hot as Bash?"

I giggle and roll my eyes. "I don't look at my brother that way, but women seem to ogle him whenever we're in public, so I'd guess the answer is yes."

Paisley hums and taps her finger on her chin. "Maybe I need to meet him. Is he a Daddy, though? I mean, if his best friend is, then he might be too, right?"

Just the word Daddy makes my skin heat. Bash

keeps referring to himself as Daddy, and the things it does to me are sinful. Last night, I wore the batteries out on my vibrator after I got home. I don't know what it is about calling a man Daddy—or him calling himself that—but it makes me squirmy and hot. Especially because with Bash, I don't think it's just a name for him. It's the way he is. He takes care of everything, and in his own fucked up way, he goes out of his way to make me happy. The fact that he remembered what dress I wore to dinner a year ago says a lot about him. He pays attention. I have a feeling if I become the center of that attention, he won't miss a thing.

I look at my reflection in the mirror and smooth my hands down my front. After our text conversation, I was relieved because I didn't have to fret over what to wear. He told me exactly what he wanted and despite me being sassy with him all the time, I want to please Bash. In more ways than one.

"You look so damn adorable. You should put your hair up in some space buns with bows. It would match your dress, and *Daddy* would probably love it."

"Don't call him Daddy," I bite out before I think better of it.

Paisley giggles. "Calm your tits. I'm kidding. Obviously, he's *your* Daddy. I just like saying Daddy. I haven't been able to call anyone that in forever."

With a sigh, I sit on the edge of the bed and lean

into her shoulder. "I know. I didn't mean to snap at you. I'm not normally so jealous."

"Maybe it's because you actually have real feelings for him, unlike the other idiots you've dated."

She isn't wrong. I don't think I've ever had feelings for a guy like I have for Bash. It's kind of terrifying. My brain tells me to proceed with caution while my body tells me to dive in headfirst. Then there's my heart. That one isn't telling me anything. Nope. Instead, it's hoping that Bash will keep me in the safety of his bubble, love me unconditionally, and take care of me in a way I never got from my father. Stupid hearts. Always hoping.

After I woke up from my nap, I stayed buried under the covers for a long time and let my thoughts run wild. Memories of my childhood. Of my mom. I miss her so much. She was always the peacekeeper in the house. She shielded me as much as she could from my father's harsh words. Then she would make excuses for him. Usually, those excuses consisted of him being stressed at work. And he wonders why I didn't *want* to become an attorney. Too late for that now, though. Like an idiot, I let him make that choice for me. Because stupid me, I wanted to get his approval just once. A simple, *I'm proud of you* or *you're doing a great job.* I don't think I ever heard those words out of his mouth.

I didn't get out of bed until Paisley bounded into

my room and told me to get my ass in the shower and *scrub your coochie, so you can be prepared to be ruined by Bash's cock*. Her words. Not mine. It made me laugh, though, which is what I needed.

Now, the situation with my father is mostly at the back of my mind, and all my nervous energy is focused on the fact that I have a date…in less than ten minutes. I shake my hands and take a few deep breaths, hoping my racing heart will stop pounding so damn hard. It's Bash. I know him. Sort of.

The doorbell rings, startling me. Paisley practically leaps off the bed in a blur of black and runs out of my room to answer it. Bash isn't the kind of man to text me from the car. He's nothing like any other man I've met. My core clenches. *Am I ready for this?*

"You're the most beautiful woman I've ever seen."

I gasp and spin around. Bash takes up the entire doorway, his gaze sparkling as he looks at me. He's gotten a fresh haircut and trimmed his beard, so the lines are sharp and clean.

"I've seen a lot of beautiful things in my life. Diamonds. Rubies. Sunrises and sunsets. Marriages. And not one of those things comes close to how breathtaking you are."

My knees wobble, and my shoulders relax, all the anxiety about the evening ahead floating away. I'm breathless as I stare up at him. I try to swallow, but my mouth is so dry I can't quite seem to accomplish that.

He pushes off the door frame and comes to me. As though he can't stop himself, he cups the back of my neck and pulls me toward him until our lips are locked together and he's exploring my mouth like a starved animal. I whimper and moan like a cat in heat, but the way I'm feeling right now, I might as well be. My panties are drenched, and my clit has a pulse.

When he pulls back, his fingers tighten on my neck as he stares down at me. Gold flecks dance in his irises. Using his free hand, he runs his thumb under my mouth.

"I didn't mean to fuck up your lipstick, but I needed to kiss you."

"It was worth it," I say breathlessly.

His lips pull back into a smile that could practically cause an orgasm. If he had kept kissing me, that might have happened anyway.

"I have something for you. They aren't nearly as beautiful as you are, but hopefully, you'll still like them."

Tilting my head, I stare at him with furrowed eyebrows. When he pulls a small velvet red box from his pocket, my eyes go round. He opens the box and perched perfectly inside are a pair of diamond earrings. Not just any kind, though. The diamonds are a gorgeous yellow color, cut into perfect pear shapes. My mouth drops open, and I bring my hand to my chest.

"Bash! These are beautiful and way, way too much. Flowers are acceptable on a first date. Diamonds are not."

He chuckles and lowers his face until his lips are nearly touching mine. "If I have to remind you to call me Daddy one more time, you're going over my knee for a long hard spanking until it's crystal clear to you."

I gulp and stare up into his blazing eyes. I'm quickly learning when Bash is being deadly serious and when I can push him. This is not a time to push. "Okay, Daddy."

"That's my good girl. My beautiful, good girl."

Warmth seeps through me. Such simple praise, but it pulls at every one of my heartstrings. I lift up onto my tiptoes and leave a soft kiss on his lips. When I try to pull back, he cups the back of my head and kisses me deeper before letting me go.

"Do you want to wear these to dinner or some other time?" he asks, holding up the box.

"Ba… I mean, Daddy, these are stunning, but they're too much. I don't need gifts."

He shrugs and starts to pull the earrings out of the box. "Nothing is too much for you. You may not need gifts, but I want to give you gifts so accept them and say thank you, Daddy."

I shake my head, but a smile is pulling at my lips. Stubborn butthead.

"Thank you, Daddy."

## 12

## BASH

My poor girl is nervous. I was afraid her cuticles were going to be bloody by the time we reached the restaurant. If I hadn't reached across the middle console and intertwined my fingers with hers, they probably would have been.

Now that she's had a few sips of her wine, her shoulders are no longer up to her ears, and her expression is more relaxed. Her skin glows, and her eyes sparkle. Those earrings I gave her have nothing on her beauty. It's not even close. Her makeup is flawless, and I can tell she spent time doing it. I can't wait to show her the surprise I'm putting together for her. It'll take a few days, and I can hardly stand the wait.

"I've never been here," she says as she looks

around the restaurant, stopping briefly to watch the three-piece band. "Italian is my favorite."

I pick up my glass and swirl the amber liquid around. "I know. That's why I chose it. Vino's is the best Italian restaurant in Seattle."

She pauses with her wine glass midair and snaps her gaze to mine. "How do you know?"

"I meant it when I said I remember everything. What kind of food did you have at your eighteenth birthday party?"

A dimple appears as she tries not to smile. "You're observant. So, you assumed it was my favorite from that?"

My lips curl into a smile. "That, and the three plates of Bolognese you ate that night. It was safe to assume."

Her hand trembles slightly as she brings her drink up to her lips. When her throat works to swallow, I adjust in my seat to give more room for my thickening cock. Is that what she'd look like on her knees before me while she sucks me off? Shit. I can't think about that right now. Otherwise, I'll end up dragging her out of here so I can fuck her in the car, and that's not how I want our first time to be.

"So, um, how does this work?"

Tilting my head to the side, I lift an eyebrow. "How does what work?"

She motions between us. "This, uh, us dating?

I've never dated anyone in, uh," she looks around the restaurant, "your line of work before."

Heat crawls up my neck. My baby girl doesn't understand yet. She'll learn. I'll make sure of that.

"We're not dating, Chloe. What we're doing is much more than that. You're mine. Forever. Until death do us part, baby. You're going to be my wife."

Her mouth falls open, and she starts blinking rapidly. After a few seconds, she shakes her head. "You can't say stuff like that, Bash."

"What did you call me?" I ask in a low voice.

It takes a second before she realizes what I mean. "I can't call you that in public."

"Oh, yes, you can. And you will. I won't punish you if you don't call me Daddy when we're in front of people who aren't part of our inner bubble, but when we're alone, like we are now, you'll call me Daddy."

She shifts in her seat and stares at me as if she isn't sure what to think or say. That's okay, though. Her heavy breathing and squirming tell me everything I need to know. She might not *want* to like what I said, but she does.

"Right, well, as I said before, you can't say stuff like that. We barely know each other."

"I don't say things I don't mean, baby girl. And I'm never going to keep my feelings from you. It might take you some time to accept it, but you're mine. Forever."

With a huff, she shakes her head, but she's smiling. "Okay, I can see I won't win this argument, so we'll put it on the back burner for now."

I grin, knowing she'll bring it up again at some point, but my answer will be the same. "Sure, baby. Whatever makes you happy."

"What I was originally asking when you went off the rails is, how does this work? I haven't been in a relationship with anyone like you before, so I feel like I'm a bit lost."

"Well, it works however we want. Let's start easy and get to know each other. Tell me about your love of makeup."

The way her face lights up warms my entire body. Her piercing blue eyes dance with excitement. If it makes her this happy that I asked about it, I'm going to do whatever it takes to make sure she has an endless supply of whatever cosmetics she wants.

"I loved playing with my mom's makeup when I was a kid, and she always let me. She said I was wearing her lipstick by the time I was two. When I got older, I started filming tutorial videos for different looks and put them on YouTube. It's so fun. I wanted to go to business school, so I could maybe start my own cosmetic line someday, but that didn't happen so it's a hobby now."

I'm pretty sure I already know, but I need to hear

it from her beautiful, heart-shaped lips. "Why didn't you go to business school?"

Her expression instantly sours. She holds her wine glass so tightly that I'm afraid it might shatter.

"My father told me it was a ridiculous idea to have a makeup line, and that he wasn't going to fund college for me unless I went to law school. Everyone in his family has been a lawyer, so that was the only acceptable occupation for me to choose."

Suddenly, I have no appetite for food. The only thing I'm hungry for is her father's blood on my hands. I had a feeling he forced her to take that path. I flex my hands a couple of times while trying to calm down. I'm pissed at him, not her.

"Do you want to be a lawyer? Even a little bit?"

She stares at her wine for several seconds before she meets my gaze. "No. I don't. It's never been something I've been interested in."

I nod and clear my throat as the server arrives with our dinner. As soon as he disappears, I lean back and watch Chloe twirl the pasta around on her fork. She closes her eyes and lets out a moan of appreciation, and I swear to God, I just came a little. Fuck. I want to hear that noise while I'm driving into her.

When she opens her eyes and notices me staring, her cheeks turn pink. "What?"

Shaking my head, I pick up my fork. "Nothing, baby girl. Just admiring the view."

We eat in silence for several minutes. I always forget how good the chicken piccata is here. But since she loves Italian so much, I'll be bringing her here often.

"So, tell me about the tutorials you do when you film. How do you do it? Where do you get your ideas for looks?"

The excitement returns to her eyes, and her hands move through the air as she explains the different types of products, the looks, and where she gets her inspiration. With each word, I fall for her a little more.

As we leave the restaurant, my skin heats, and my stomach tightens with dread. I don't want to take her home. I've spent the past seven years without her. I don't want to be apart from her for even a minute.

"Will you come stay the night with me?"

It's not a question I'm used to asking. Normally, women are begging me to take them home with me. Chloe isn't most women, though. She's mine. And I'm not above begging her. I wouldn't drop to my knees for anyone else, but for her, I'd do it in a heartbeat.

She looks up at me with uncertainty painted over her features. "I'm not sure that's a good idea."

We're standing at the passenger side of my Escalade with the door open. "Why not?"

When she pulls her bottom lip between her teeth, I reach up and tug it free with my thumb then run the pad over her plush, pillowy mouth. "Why not, baby girl?" I ask again.

"I'm scared. We barely know each other. You're sort of, a lot. Not in a bad way necessarily, but it's overwhelming. I can't think around you."

If only she knew I feel the same. Every rational thought I might have in my fucked-up head disappears the second I'm around her.

"Nothing has to happen. I'll sleep in my suit if you want me to. I want you wrapped up in my arms all night, though."

She giggles and lifts her chin to meet my gaze again. Her eyes sparkle in the moonlight. "You don't have to sleep in your suit. Promise nothing has to happen?"

I capture her chin between my fingers and lower my face so it's only inches from hers. "Nothing will ever happen that you don't want. I might control you and leap over all sorts of invisible lines, but the one thing I will never do is force myself on you in a way you truly don't want."

Her breath catches, and a whirlwind of emotions

runs through her eyes like a movie reel. "Okay. Nothing happens, though."

"Scout's honor."

An unladylike snort comes from her. "Somehow, I don't believe you were ever in the Boy Scouts."

My lips pull back into a face-splitting grin. "Maybe not in the traditional sense. More like the mafia scouts where our word is everything. Way better than the other kind of scouts."

She bursts out laughing. It's the most beautiful sound in the world. When I grab her by the hips and lift her into the car, she squeals and grabs my forearms but continues to giggle as I buckle her in. I start to pull away, but she grabs my hand.

"Will you kiss me?"

Slowly, I lean in and brush my fingers over the wispy hairs that have fallen free from the buns on top of her head. "You never have to ask, Little one. I'll kiss you anytime you want."

Then I seal my lips over hers and kiss her like my life depends on it. It feels like it does. She's the air I need to continue breathing. My girl.

## 13

## CHLOE

I'm a squirmy mess, sitting in a pair of soaked panties while he drives to his house. It's probably for the best that we don't mess around. I meant what I said when I told him he overwhelms me. Sometimes it's a good feeling, and sometimes, I don't know what to think about it.

Bash is the kind of man who will completely consume me. Hell, he already does, and it's only been two days. As hard as it is with him, I'll have to learn to stand my ground on some things. My father ran my whole life for so long, and I let him do it while lying down like a dog. I won't let the same thing happen with Bash. Although, comparing the two is absurd. Bash is nothing like the man who raised me.

"How come I've never met your sister?" I ask. "I've met you, Declan, and Ronan, but never her."

His expression softens. "Paige is attending college in Ireland. Her mom was there."

My eyebrows furrow. "Her mom?"

"Yes. Our mom died when I was young. Our father married Paige's mom ten years later. That's why she's so much younger. After our father died, her mom decided to return to Ireland where she'd grown up. Paige stayed in the States to finish schooling. Her mom fell ill when she was close to graduating high school. Declan offered to send her to Ireland for college so she could spend time with her mom before she died."

My heart squeezes in my chest. I know what it's like to lose a mom. I can't imagine doing it in a foreign country, away from everything I've ever known.

"She's all alone?"

He shakes his head. "Her best friend, Tessa, is with her. We have some extended family there too, so she has plenty of people surrounding her. As soon as they graduate, they both plan to return to Seattle."

"That's good. How old is she?"

"She's a little younger than you."

I nod. "What did she go to school for?"

A smile spreads on his face, and he lets out a quiet chuckle. "Interior decorating. She was always redecorating stuff. It drove my father up the wall, but he never said anything to her because it made her happy. He would glare at everything she'd done, but when she asked whether he liked it, he always praised her. It wasn't a big surprise to any of us when she told us what she wanted to go to school for. We're hoping she'll be too busy starting her business when she gets home to focus on our houses."

Tears burn in my eyes. "Your dad seems like he was sweet."

He shrugs. "He was a good man. Loyal and trustworthy. Wanted what was best for the family business. He was fair and loved his family more than anything. Before he died, he made us boys promise to take care of our sister but to let her choose the path she wanted. Of course, we would have let her either way. Just because she was born into the mafia doesn't mean she has to stay on that path. It's different for the men."

"How so?"

"To us, women are gifts to this world. They aren't pawns or things we use for negotiations like some other families. Men born into the mafia are expected to follow that path, but for the women, at least in our family, the only requirement is that they let us protect them."

I stare at him for a long moment, shocked. "What planet did you guys come from? I don't understand how a mafia family can be more reasonable about things than my own father."

His eyes darken, and his jaw clenches. "Your father is a piece of garbage. Sorry to say it, baby."

Normally, I would try to make excuses, but I have none. After our conversation today, I think my eyes are finally wide open to the person he is. I wish it had happened sooner. Maybe it would have saved some unnecessary pain over the years.

"He called me today," I whisper.

Bash glances over at me for a brief second before he looks back to the road. "What did he say?"

"He said you and Kieran went to see him." When he doesn't reply, I keep going. "He told me Bradley isn't a bad man. He just made a bad choice. Then he told me I was no longer his daughter, to never contact him again, and he hung up on me."

He lets out a string of words in Gaelic, and based on his tone, they weren't nice ones. When he reaches over and takes my hand in his, he gives it a gentle squeeze. "He doesn't deserve you, Chloe. He never did. You belong with us now. You always have, but we're going to take care of you from now on. Understand?"

The lump in my throat is too thick for me to say anything, so I nod. We stay silent for the remainder of the drive. When he pulls into his garage and the door slides down, closing us into his space, my tummy tightens with anticipation. I have a feeling that after tonight, there's no turning back.

I reach for the latch to get out of the car, but Bash lets out a low growl, stopping me in my tracks.

"Don't even think about opening your own door, Little girl."

My mouth falls open as he gets out and rounds the front to my side. When he opens the door and holds out his hand for me, I shake my head at him, but I can't stop my smile. He's so bossy and overbearing, and I love it. I probably won't always love it, but I've never been treated like this by a man. Like I'm precious.

He escorts me into the house, and I look around in awe. All six of the top men, including Bash and my brother, live on one gigantic estate but each has their own mansions. Declan's is the biggest because it holds all the offices and who knows what else. They're all spread out, so there's some level of privacy for the men. I have no idea how they were able to get their hands on such a huge piece of property this close to the city, but I suppose mafia influence can go a long way when it comes to getting what you want. My understanding is that the estate has been here for several generations, so maybe it was before Seattle became a huge metropolitan area.

The dim lights reflect off creamy walls. A cluster of black sculptures perch over the fireplace. As we pass through a living room that smells like Bash's citrus cologne, I run my hand along the back of the enormous couch and picture him sitting here, watching TV. I want to be part of that. To curl up on his lap.

When he leads me to the foyer and a grand staircase, I can't help but wonder whether he gets lonely here. Even though it's cozy and welcoming, it's so big. I'd think it would feel like living in a museum. Then again, I'm pretty sure the men spend most of their time at Declan's. They're a tight group.

"Do you want some dessert or wine before we go up?"

I shake my head. "No. I'm still so full from eating all of my dinner and some of yours."

He chuckles and places his hand on my lower back. "It pleases me to see you eat. If we hadn't been at a restaurant, I would have had you on my lap and fed you myself."

My nipples harden at the thought. I want to experience that. In fact, I think I'd like to eat every meal on Bash's lap.

"Come on, baby girl." He leads me up the stairs. "Hold the railing so you don't fall."

My eyebrows lift, but as soon as I meet his gaze, I

realize he's not joking. Not even a little bit. So, I reach out and grab onto it.

"Good girl."

My heart rate goes wild. How can two simple words catch me by such surprise? I want to do whatever it takes to keep hearing them.

We go down a long hallway to a set of double doors. He pushes them open, and I nearly gasp. His bedroom is larger than my entire townhouse. My feet sink into the plush carpet, and I can't wait to take off my shoes to feel it between my toes.

"The bathroom is in there. Closet is over there. We should have stopped at your place to get your pajamas and duck."

I grimace and swallow. He's seen Quackers, but I'd hoped he'd forgotten about my stuffed toy. My eyes lower to the floor, and in an instant, he's in front of me, gripping my chin to lift it.

"Look at me, Chloe." He waits until I meet his piercing gaze. "Don't be embarrassed, do you understand me? I love the innocent side of you. I love that you have a stuffie, that you make miniature dollhouses, and that you wear adorable dresses. I'm a Daddy Dom. I like that shit. So don't ever feel embarrassed. I'm going to buy you a lot more stuffed animals and little dollhouses and shit like that."

"You don't think it's weird?"

He lets go of my chin and picks me up by my hips. I wrap my legs around his waist, and my arms around his neck, not wanting to fall. Although, he would never let that happen. When he sinks into one of the chairs in the sitting area, he brings me down onto his lap so I'm straddling him. This is probably a bad position. My panties are soaked and pressing against him. His slacks are definitely going to be wet when I get up.

"Sweetheart, I don't think a single thing about you is weird. I love that you have a side of you that lets go. I will always encourage it. I'll take care of you and nurture you, and I'll enjoy every second of it. Don't hide from me. Don't keep any part of you from me. I want it all. I want your strong and stubborn side, and I want your innocent and soft side. Okay?"

I cross my arms over my chest and narrow my eyes. "I'm not stubborn."

Amusement dances in his irises as he tries to keep from smiling. "Okay, baby. Whatever you say."

When I don't say anything, he continues. "Tomorrow, I want to introduce you to Cali and Scarlet. They're just like you. They have stuffed toys, they make bracelets, create art, cause chaos, and give all of us gray hairs. Once you meet them, you'll understand that you are exactly what I want and need. I need your innocence when I come home. I need your light. Okay?"

My muscles twitch, and my tummy flutters. I'm not sure why I'm nervous about meeting Cali and Scarlet. What if they don't like me? What if I don't fit in? Will Bash want me then? Will he change his mind?

"What's going on in that beautiful mind of yours?"

His hands rest on my knees, massaging gently and soothing some of my anxiety. His touch always seems to comfort me. Inch by inch, my muscles relax, and I let out a long breath.

"What if they don't like me? I can tell they're important to you."

Continuing to stroke his thumbs over my knees, he stares at me, his gaze serious. "They *are* important to me. But you're the center of my universe, Little girl. Got it?"

God, this man is so intense sometimes. One second, he's carefree and smiling, and the next, he's ready to take on the world for me.

"You can't say stuff like that," I whisper.

His fingers tighten on me. "I can if I mean it, and I do mean it, Chloe. Every single word. This might all be new to you, but I've had seven years of wanting you and not having you. Now I have you, and I'm never letting you go."

Slowly, his hands move up my thighs, lifting the hem of my dress. I'm so distracted by the way he's looking at me that I don't notice as his fingers move over the first bump. As soon as they do, he looks down, and his entire face changes. Black storm clouds hover in his eyes as he pushes my dress higher before I can stop him. With each new line he sees, his rage becomes more and more visible until I'm so uneasy that I try to back off his lap.

It was inevitable that he'd see them eventually. I'd just hoped it wouldn't be this soon. His hands grip my outer thighs, stopping me from moving another inch. I'm afraid. Not of him. He won't hurt me. I know that. But I'm afraid of what he might think of me right now.

"Who the fuck caused all of these?" he grinds out between clenched teeth.

I close my eyes and try to keep the tears burning the back of my eyes from springing free. It's hard to breathe, so I force myself to take several deep inhales before I answer, "I did."

Keeping one hand on me to hold me in place, he moves his other and traces one of the lines with his index finger. His nostrils flare and his breaths come out in short, hard gusts. "I know you did them. What I'm asking is who the fuck made you feel like you had to slice yourself up to soothe the pain they caused?"

The lump in my throat has tripled in size. I shouldn't say a word. It will only make things worse. I can't lie to Bash, though. Even if I tried, he would know. He already knows the answer. He wants to hear it from me. I swallow and try to breathe through my panic as he continues to trace each line on the top of my thighs.

"Who, Chloe?" he whispers harshly.

"My father."

## 14

## BASH

"Are there more?"

She shakes her head. "No."

My heart is pounding so hard it's painful. My girl. My precious baby girl. How could this have happened? How could her own father treat her so badly that she had to take a razor blade to her skin to neutralize the pain?

My entire body vibrates with the need to slice his throat and watch with glee as he bleeds out in front of me. He deserves it. And he'll get what's coming to him. His death won't be quick. I don't give a fuck if he is her father. No one, and I mean no one, hurts my girl.

Seventeen lines.

All perfectly straight and evenly spaced. They aren't fresh, thank God. Each one a representation of the pain she experienced. Each one a time in her life I wasn't there to protect her. Never again. She will never feel this kind of pain again.

"Daddy," she whispers softly.

I take a breath and stare at the lines. A bead of sweat rolls down my neck. Can't she see how hard I'm working to catch my breath? I can't do it. Can't get myself under control. "Give me a minute, Chloe. I need a minute, baby."

She nods and doesn't move while I continue to trace my finger over each mark. Seventeen. He will pay for this. Seventeen times, he will pay. More. A lot more. Because that's the thing with me. If you hurt what's mine, the revenge is paid back tenfold.

When my heart rate finally starts to slow, I raise my gaze to hers. Her blue eyes are wet with tears, and it kills me. She looks so fucking scared.

"You're mine. Do you understand?" I growl.

She sniffles. "Yes, Daddy."

Framing her face with my hands, I pull her toward me and kiss her. It's not soft or sensual. It's claiming. Dominating. Primal. When I let her go, we're both gasping for air. I promised her nothing would happen tonight, and I meant it. Tonight, the only thing I need is to take care of my Little girl so she feels the kind of love she's never experienced before.

"Let's find a shirt for you to sleep in."

She smiles, and I help her climb off my lap. I stand and nausea bubbles in my stomach. I've seen a lot of shit in my life. More blood than any normal person. I've slit throats, dismembered bodies, and put more bullets in people than I can count, but none of that shit has ever kept me up at night. What I saw on my girl—knowing what she went through—will haunt me for the rest of my life.

I've got to pull myself together. My focus is her. Getting her ready for bed. Tucking her against my body and hoping I can somehow erase all the bad things that have ever happened to her.

I find the softest T-shirt I can and turn to her. She's retreated into herself, her eyes downcast, and her bottom lip trembling slightly. Her scent surrounds me like a blanket. Just being close to her soothes the monster inside me.

"Baby, look at Daddy."

She does, and when her blue irises meet mine, I fight back the tears burning in my own eyes. My chest is so tight, I wonder if I'm having a heart attack. Can you die from heartbreak? My pain doesn't matter, though. She's all that matters. "I don't know what you're thinking right now, Chloe, but I know I don't like it."

"Do you think I'm a freak?"

I yank her against my body and squeeze her tightly. "No. I think you're so fucking strong. You deserved so much more than that fucking asshole. It kills me that Kieran didn't know what was happening. He would have put a stop to it."

A small sob escapes as she buries her head against my chest. "My father did whatever he could to keep me away from him."

"I know. I know he did. No more, though. You belong to this family now."

We hold each other for a long time. When she lets out a deep sigh and her shoulders relax, I finally release her.

"Will you trust me to get you ready for bed? To get you changed into my shirt?"

She peers up at me from under her lashes and gives a slight nod. "Yes."

Taking her hand, I lead her to the bathroom. When I stop and turn, she's looking around, taking it all in.

"Why do you have a bottle of my perfume?"

I glance at the white bottle on the counter. I also have one in my closet, my office, my nightstand, my car, and my kitchen. But I'll keep that to myself for now.

"I wanted to smell you whenever you're not around."

The corner of her mouth twitches. I shrug. "Don't judge me. It's not creepy."

For the first time since we got home, she giggles.

Then she raises her hand and motions with her index finger and thumb a few inches apart. "It's a little creepy."

"Get used to it, baby. You think that's creepy, just fucking wait."

She laughs again and shakes her head. "I should probably be running for the hills, but instead of being frightened by all your unhinged behavior, I feel safe."

I kneel at her feet and reach for her shoe. "You are completely safe with me, Little one. In every way. Physically and emotionally. Hold my shoulders and lift your foot."

Her fingers warm me through my jacket as she obeys. When she's barefoot, I rise and gently turn her around.

"We need to talk about your rules," I say as I untie the bow of her dress and then unzip it.

"Rules?"

"Yes. Rules. You'll have rules you'll follow, or you'll find yourself in the corner or over my knee. Or both."

She stares at me in the reflection of the mirror. "Like what kind of rules?"

I turn her around to face me and pull her dress off her shoulders, letting it fall to the ground. The lace bra she's wearing is sheer enough that I can see the rosy color of her nipples. My heart lurches while my cock stirs to attention.

Not wanting to linger or stare since that's not what tonight is about, I reach behind her to unsnap her bra. "First, no swearing. We already talked about that one. Next is no lying or hiding yourself from me. I want to see you. All of you. And I don't just mean physically. Do you understand?"

When I pull the bra away from her chest, she shivers. I'd bet a good amount of money it's not because she's cold. If I were to dip my hand between her thighs, I wonder how wet I'd find her panties to be.

"Yes. What about you? Are you going to lie to me?"

I shake my head. "Never. Next rule, and it's important; I need to know where you are at all times. That way I can assess how safe it is and decide if you need to have guards with you.

Her eyebrows furrow. "I thought there was a pact in place, so you all got along?"

"There is. Among all of the syndicates. But there are groups out there who aren't part of it. We always have enemies. You might feel like it's controlling or an invasion of your privacy, but it's purely for your safety. It's my job to keep you safe now, and I take that very seriously. Okay?"

She nods but doesn't say anything, so I keep going. "Next, you call me Daddy. The only time I will make an exception is if we're around people we don't know. In front of any of our men, and in front of Cali or Scarlet, you will call me Daddy. They call their men Daddy in front of all of us, so it's quite normal around here. Almost all of our men are either Daddies or Doms."

I drop the shirt over her head and wait until it's in place before I speak again. "Next rule, and it's also an important one. From now on, you don't touch your pussy for anything other than hygiene purposes. No playing with it, using toys on it, or doing anything that might bring your perfect cunt pleasure. Your pussy is mine now, and the only time you're going to come is from my mouth, fingers, or cock. Understood?"

Her mouth goes slack as she starts blinking rapidly. It's fucking adorable. I had a feeling she wouldn't like that rule.

"That is so not fair. I disagree with that rule."

When I turn her to face the mirror again, she crosses her arms and stares at my reflection with her chin lifted in defiance. I chuckle and start pulling pins from her buns, letting her honey-brown locks fall free.

"You can disagree with the rule all you want, but what Daddy says goes. No touching your pretty little pussy."

As gently as I can, I remove the bands from her hair before I grab the brand-new brush I bought for her. It's heavy wood and will be useful for multiple tasks. Like spanking her naughty bottom.

"Don't I get a say in the rules? Like when one is stupid, can't I nix it? Isn't there a safeword or something?"

I chuckle and brush her hair until it's shiny and smooth. "You will absolutely get to have a safeword. Tell me, baby, why do you hate that rule so much? Are you worried Daddy won't pleasure your cunt enough? Because once we get to that point, I'll be making sure you come often, and I assure you it will be better than any kind of orgasm you'll be able to give yourself."

Her lips open and close like a fish searching for water. My eyes trace down her body, and as they land on her pointed nipples, I lick my lips.

"How about this? We'll make it a rule for now and revisit it in a month. If you still don't want that rule, we'll modify it."

"Fine. But you're not always going to get your way, you know. Just because you're the Daddy doesn't mean you always get to be the boss."

Laughter bursts from my lips. I toss the brush on the counter and wrap my arms around her, pulling her back against my chest. When I nuzzle her neck and scrape my beard over it, she whimpers.

"That's exactly what it means, Little girl. I'm the boss. I'm the one who's in charge, and I'm responsible for you. Your only job from now on is to enjoy life. Daddy will take care of the rest."

I SLEPT LIKE SHIT. Apparently, having Chloe wrapped up in my arms all night without being able to put my mouth on her body is an excellent torture tactic. If the FBI had shown up and started questioning me, I would have broken in a heartbeat and sang like a canary.

Even though I was rock hard the entire time, I wasn't going to act on it. I promised her we wouldn't do anything, and while I'm a lot of things, a liar isn't one of them.

She seemed to sleep like a baby, though, so I don't care if I'm a walking zombie for the entire day. If my girl is healthy, happy, and safe, I'm good.

When we pull up in front of Declan's house, she nibbles on her bottom lip. We're all getting together for breakfast so the girls can meet. Declan said he had something work-related to talk about, too.

"It's going to be fine. I'll be with you the entire time. If at any point you want to leave, just whisper in my ear that you want to go home, and we'll be out of there in less than a minute. Okay?"

She fidgets with the hem of her dress. It's the same one she wore last night. I need to buy her some clothes to keep at my house, so when she stays the night, she has stuff to wear besides my shirts. Although, I do like her in those. It's like they're marking her as mine, and I fucking love that.

"They're your friends. We can't just leave if I'm not comfortable."

I grab her hand and bring it to my lips, pressing gentle kisses to her palm. "The fuck we can't. They might be my friends, but you're my girl. Your needs come first."

It's going to take time for her to truly understand that I mean what I say. She's never been put first before. I know she loved her mom, but I don't think even *she* put Chloe first. If Kieran had been able to be a part of her life more, he would have always made her his first priority. It pisses me off that her asshole father kept her from him. Just one more thing to add to the list of sins he'll pay dearly for.

After helping her out of the car, I take her hand and lead her up the stone steps to the house. As soon as we enter the foyer, Cali and Scarlet start screaming with excitement and race down the hall toward us.

"No running!" Declan booms.

Both women come to a skidding stop a few feet away.

"You must be Chloe!" Cali squeals as she springs forward.

Before I can stop her or warn Chloe, Cali has her arms wrapped around my girl and is hugging her for dear life.

"We've heard so much about you from Kieran and Bashie. We've been dying to meet you," Scarlet says, bouncing on her tiptoes.

Chloe giggles and accepts hugs from the women. Not that she had much of a choice.

When she returns to my side, she looks up at me with a smug grin. "Bashie, huh?"

I lean down until my mouth is near her ear. "It's Daddy to you, Little girl, and if you ever call me Bashie, you won't sit for a week."

Her cheeks turn pink as she trembles in my hold. It won't be long before she's over my knee for something. I have no doubt about it. My baby is a good girl, but there's a naughty streak in there. I can feel it, and I can't wait to see it.

"Daddy's housekeeper made us pancakes for breakfast. Do you like pancakes? We also have sausage and fruit and oatmeal and bagels and—"

"Little girl, take a breath," Declan commands as he approaches.

Cali sucks in a breath, and as soon as he gets near, she climbs up on him like a tree. "Sorry. I'm so excited."

Chloe moves a fraction closer to me when Declan's gaze lands on her, and if I could rip off my suit and beat my chest right now, I would. She's seeking me for comfort. It's a win in my book.

"Chloe, you remember Declan?" I ask.

"Yes," she says, offering him a small smile.

"It's good to see you again, Chloe. Sorry for the rambunctious greeting. The girls have been counting down the time until they could meet you."

Kieran and Grady come around the corner, and as soon as Chloe sees her brother, she rushes to him for a hug. When the big bastard wraps his arms around her, I let out a low growl. It's ridiculous. He's her damn brother. I just don't like seeing her in anyone's arms but mine.

"You remember Grady?" Kieran points to Grady.

She nods and gives him a small wave.

"Let's go eat. Grace will have a fit if the food gets cold before we sit down." Declan says.

As soon as we're all seated with plates of food in front of us, Scarlet and Cali begin their interrogation.

"Do you like making bracelets?" Scarlet asks.

Chloe nods. "Yes. I love doing stuff like that."

Cali shoves a bite of pancake in her mouth. "What about diamond art?"

Declan wraps his hand in Cali's ponytail and tugs her head back slightly. "Chew and swallow your food before you speak."

"Sorry, Daddy," she mumbles, still chewing.

The rest of the meal is mostly spent with the women talking and the men observing. My girl fits in perfectly with them, and I have a feeling the three of them will get up to no good whenever they're together.

After we finish eating, Declan asks me and the rest of the guys to meet for a minute in private to discuss business. I look at Chloe. She's already pulling beads from one of the dozen cases Cali has.

"Will you be okay for a few?"

"Yep. Bye, Daddy." As soon as the word comes out of her mouth, her eyes go round.

My lips pull back into a wide smile. I don't want to make a big deal about this and embarrass her more, but holy fuck, she just called me Daddy in front of our friends. In front of her brother.

I lower my mouth to her ear so only she can hear me. "That's my good girl. So proud of you."

Goosebumps rise on her arms. She gives a nod so small that only I notice it, but her eyes sparkle from my praise.

"It's okay. We call our guys Daddy in front of each other too. Don't be embarrassed," Scarlet says.

Chloe's face flushes, but she smiles. I press a kiss to her temple before joining the rest of the guys.

"What's going on?" Grady asks.

"I got a call from Andrei Volkov this morning," Declan says.

I grind my molars so hard it's painful. Andrei Volkov is the head of the Russian Bratva. We don't know him well, and our relationship with the Russians is strained, to say the least. The issues we had with them weren't directly from Andrei, but we're still wary.

"Andrei got a call from one of his guys in Russia. Girls have been going missing. Young girls. Some not even legal."

I raise an eyebrow. "Trafficking?"

Declan nods. "Yes. One of the women got away when she got to the United States and was able to call her family. She was brought over on a container ship that arrived in Seattle. And it wasn't a private port."

The air thickens with tension. We might not trust the Russian Bratva but trafficking in our city is something we work hard to stop.

"How would they have gotten clearance to dock? And who would have that kind of influence here besides us?" I ask.

Killian rubs the back of his neck. "Members of the city council can sign off on clearance. And guess who we know that's a council member?"

Goosebumps rise on my flesh. Jesus.

"Bradley fucking Du Pont," I grit out.

"Is he still alive?" Declan asks.

"Barely. He's probably wishing he weren't. I planned on paying a visit to the warehouse today while Chloe was at work."

Declan grips the table. "Squeeze him for information. If this guy doesn't blink an eye at drugging a woman's drink, he probably wouldn't care if someone shipped a container of girls into Seattle."

My fists clench at my sides. "Gladly."

Kieran lifts his chin. "I'll come too."

I nod. "Does Andrei have any idea how many girls were shipped here? Or what organization might be behind it?"

"The woman who got away guessed there were at least fifty others in the shipping container with her. She said it was pitch black the entire time, so she only remembers some of the women's voices," Declan says quietly. "And so far, Andrei has no idea. He's reached out to all of the syndicates here in the States, and everyone's denied involvement."

"We'll let you know what we find out," I say.

## 15

## CHLOE

"Would you do my makeup sometime? I never know what I'm doing," Scarlet says.

I slide a bead onto the string and smile. "I'd love to. I can teach you some tricks too."

Cali grins from ear to ear. "I'm so glad we got to meet you. Bash was reluctant to introduce us because he thinks we'll be a bad influence."

"Why would he think that?" I hold up my bracelet and sigh. This is my happy place.

"Well, um, we tend to get into trouble together a lot." Cali shrugs.

"They call it trouble, we call it fun," Scarlet adds.

Cali looks at the tray of beads, her gaze totally focused like she's trying to choose just the right one.

"Daddy says we do it on purpose so we can get spanked. Which is kind of true."

Scarlet giggles and bobs her head. "Definitely true."

My eyes go wide. The only person I've talked to about this kind of thing is Paisley. She's going to be so jealous that she's not here to be part of this. I think she'd fit right in.

"You do stuff on purpose to get spanked?" I ask quietly.

Both women stop and look at me like I have a second head.

"Sometimes. Sometimes it happens naturally," Scarlet replies.

Cali goes back to adding to her bracelet. "Have you ever been spanked?"

I shake my head. "Um, no. I've always, you know, thought about it. Bash has threatened it a bunch of times. I'm kind of nervous, but also, I'm really curious."

Scarlet giggles. "Bash threatening you doesn't surprise me. He likes to act all chill, but I had a feeling he'd be a strict Daddy with a twitchy palm."

Heat spreads through my body. "He's definitely not what I first expected."

"What are you nervous about?" Cali asks.

I shrug. "What if I hate it? It hurts, right?"

Both women grin.

"It hurts like hell, but it's also amazing. It brings us closer every time. And the aftercare is the best thing in the world," Cali explains.

Scarlet nods. "I'm always nervous before a spanking, and I don't always want it, but I feel better right afterward. It's like the pain cleanses any bad thoughts or emotions I'm having. And once my punishment is over, Daddy forgets the whole thing. He never holds it over my head when I mess up. It's like a clean slate."

Even though I haven't cut myself in years, I still think about it and how I always felt cleansed of my father's harsh words afterward. Would a spanking give me that kind of feeling? Would it take away the urge to go find a razor when I'm really struggling?

"Do you trust that Bash won't harm you?" Cali asks.

I nod without thinking about it because I do. I know he's a dangerous criminal, but I also know he would die before he let anything happen to me.

Cali lifts her gaze to mine. "Then let him Daddy you. He'll take care of you. Let go. Be naughty. Be a brat. It keeps them on their toes and keeps them humble. They need to be humbled every once in a while."

Our conversation is interrupted when Bash, Kieran, Declan, and Killian walk in.

Bash comes straight over to me and smiles. "Pretty bracelet, baby girl. Did you make me one?"

I tip my head back to look up at him. "No. I didn't think you'd want a piece of plastic jewelry."

He tugs on my hair and leans down to kiss me. "If you make it, I want it."

"I'll keep that in mind."

"Good. We better get going so I can take you home to change before work."

I exchange phone numbers with Cali and Scarlet before Bash finally gets me out of the house. The ball of anxiety that has been in my tummy ever since he told me we were going to Declan's has now turned into a bouncy ball of excitement. We only spent an hour together, and I already feel like I made two good friends.

"Did you have fun, baby?" He reaches in and buckles my seatbelt for me. I don't even try anymore because it gives me a warm gooey feeling when he does it. He's keeping me safe.

"I had so much fun. Thank you for bringing me here."

He smiles and leans in to kiss me. "I can bring you back tonight and you guys can hang out again."

My eyebrows shoot up. "I already have plans tonight."

The air crackles as his jaw flexes and his eyes narrow. "What plans do you have, Chloe?"

Lord. And this must be the possessive side of him that he warned me about.

"Paisley and I are hanging out."

He stares at me for a few seconds before he nods and closes the door. When he gets in on his side, he starts the car. "You and Paisley can come over here, and all four of you can hang out."

Oh. My. God. This man is something else.

"Um, no. Paisley and I are hanging out at our place and having a girls' night."

"Our place, as in my house?"

"Sebastian Gilroy, you're being ridiculous."

He lets out a low growl as we come to a stop at a traffic light. "What did you call me?"

I tip my head back, exasperated with this man. I haven't had enough coffee to deal with his over-the-top demands this morning.

"I called you Daddy. And you're being ridiculous."

"You did not call me Daddy. You called me by my name. Which is against the rules. Then you lied about it. Which is also against the rules."

A shiver works its way down my spine, and when it reaches the base, it spreads over my bottom. Warning bells are going off in my head to tread carefully. It might be already too late, though.

"I didn't mean to," I whisper.

"You've had plenty of warnings, Little one. This

time, your warnings ran out. Is Paisley at your house?"

"No. She's at work."

He gives a slow nod. "When we get to your place, we're going to go up to your room where I'm going to put you over my knee. Then, I'm going to pull up the back of your dress and lower your panties."

I suck my bottom lip in as he continues to drive. My tummy does several flips while my core tightens. My skin is clammy, and I'm finding it difficult to think.

The air is so thick with tension in the car that I start to squirm in my seat. The drive is taking forever. When I glance at Bash, he's calm, cool, and collected, all while I'm over here with my mind racing. I've always thought I wanted to be spanked, but now that I know it's going to happen, I'm scared. What if it really hurts? What if I can't handle it? Will he decide I'm not the girl he wants if I can't take the pain?

As he turns into my neighborhood, he reaches over and grabs my hand. "Breathe, baby. I know you're nervous, but we're in this together. Daddy would never do anything to truly harm you, okay?"

His gentle words soothe me. I'm finally able to take a deep breath, and my tummy uncoils a bit.

We're both silent as he parks and rounds to my side to help me out. Then, he leads me inside and up the stairs to my bedroom. When he shuts the door and locks it, I swallow thickly. This is it. Bash is going to spank me. My Daddy is going to spank me.

"Look at me." His command is gentle, but I still startle.

When I meet his gaze, he smiles softly. "That's my good girl. Do you trust me, Chloe?"

"Yes."

He comes closer and takes my hands in his. "I'm glad. I won't ever harm you, baby. And you will always have a safeword that you can use so if things get to be too much, too painful, or overwhelming, you can say it, and everything stops. Understand?"

"Yes. Are you mad at me?"

His eyes soften, and he takes another step closer before cupping my chin. "Not at all. Baby girl, I need you to know and understand that just because I punish you, doesn't mean I'm mad at you. In our dynamic, you're going to have a ton of rules, some more serious than others, but you will break the rules time and time again. All Little girls do. It's how this works. As long as you know that any time you break the rules, you'll be disciplined. Hell, I'm pretty sure Cali and Scarlet break most of their rules on purpose just so they can get their butts spanked."

My lips twitch as I try to keep from smiling. I don't want to tell him he's spot on.

"You're safe to break the rules in this relationship. You're safe to be Little, and you're safe to be naughty.

Some rules are much more important than others. Anything regarding your health or safety is important, and if you break those rules, your punishment might be harsher. Does that make sense?"

"Yes, Daddy."

He takes my hand and leads me to the edge of my bed so he can sit. With hardly any effort at all, he pulls me, so my tummy is resting on his knees.

"Why are you getting spanked this morning, baby?"

I sigh and twist to look back at him. "Because you were being overbearing, and I was annoyed, so I called you by your name."

He chuckles and swats my bottom over my dress. "Whether I'm being overbearing or not, you're still supposed to address me as Daddy. Correct?"

Even though I want to roll my eyes, I think better of it. "Yes, Daddy."

"And then you lied about it, didn't you?"

"It was just a fib, Daddy."

Another swat. "Fibs are lies, Chloe. We don't lie to each other. Understood?"

A lump forms in my throat. "Yes, Daddy."

He pulls up the back of my dress, exposing the plain white cotton panties I put on before our date last night. Paisley told me they weren't sexy enough, but I've always loved them. They give me an innocent feeling that I crave.

"Kick off your shoes."

I do as he says, and then Bash hooks his fingers into the waistband of my panties and tugs them down. Only, instead of stopping at my thighs, he pulls them all the way off. When I twist to look back at him again, he's wading them up and stuffing them into his suit pocket.

"Daddy!"

He raises an eyebrow. "What? I want your scent with me all day. Especially if I don't get to see you again until tomorrow since you're having a girls' night."

Good gravy. Is this man for real? He stole my panties. And he's keeping them? To smell them? Oh, God. That shouldn't be hot, but my wet vagina thinks differently.

"Do you already have a safeword, Chloe, or would you like to use red as your word?"

What? Oh, safeword. Right. "Um, red is fine."

I'm too busy thinking about my dirty panties in his pocket to focus on anything else.

"Red it is."

Then, his hand comes crashing down onto my bottom, and all thoughts of my underwear disappear, replaced with shocking pain. He smacks the other cheek with the same force, and as soon as the sting registers, I start to squirm.

"Owwie!"

Ignoring my cries, he starts to pepper my entire bottom all the way down to the middle of my thighs. The burning sensation spreads through my entire body, and soon, my chest is tight with all the emotions bubbling up. It's been years since I've felt this kind of sting. This kind of pain. And even though I'm fighting it, I'm also craving it.

"Daddy, I'm sorry!" I cry out.

He pauses and rests his hand on my hot bottom. "What are you sorry for, Chloe?"

I sniffle and hold onto his pant leg. "I'm sorry for not calling you Daddy and then lying about it."

"Is it going to happen again?"

"No!" I shake my head harder than necessary. "It won't, Daddy."

He massages my bottom for a few seconds. "Good."

When he doesn't start spanking me again, I think it's over, and my heart falls a little. Was I expecting more? Hoping for more? I mean, it was painful, but it didn't give me the euphoric feeling that Cali and Scarlet described.

"I want to make sure you remember this lesson for the rest of the day."

Then, as quickly as he started the first time, he starts again, only this time his smacks are faster and harder. I start kicking my feet and whimpering as I grip his calf to keep me steady.

My entire bottom is on fire, but he continues to punish it thoroughly while I try to fight against his hold. My heart is racing. In a weird way, it's like it's soaring high in the sky during a beautiful summer day. It's free.

"Owwie! Owwie!"

My eyes start to burn, and within a few seconds, tears track down my cheeks. Then, a sob breaks free, and years of pain I haven't let go of come pouring out like a fountain.

Bash stops spanking and slowly pulls me up to sit on his lap. I wince when my tender skin brushes against his slacks, but the pain is quickly forgotten as he wraps me up in his arms.

"That's my good girl. My beautiful, sweet, strong girl. You did so good, baby. Daddy's so proud of you. So fucking proud."

His praise makes me cry harder, but the tears are cathartic, and my heart is so full, it could explode any second.

"My good girl. Always Daddy's good girl."

He continues to whisper in my ear for a long time, even once I've stopped crying. I never want to leave the safety of his arms. Maybe I'm losing my mind, but I'm starting to understand why Bash wants to spend every second with me. I kind of want that too. To never leave his side.

When he finally stops, he carries me into the bathroom and sets me in front of the toilet.

"Go potty. I'm going to get you a glass of water, and then I'll get you ready for work."

I look up into his tender gaze and melt. "You don't have to get me ready."

He lowers his mouth to mine and gives me several soft kisses. "I'm your Daddy, and I want to. So let me take care of you, okay?"

As soon as he disappears from the bathroom, I lower myself to the toilet and flinch as the cold seat meets my hot flesh. When I'm done, I stand in front of the mirror and turn my lower body to get a look at my bottom. As soon as I see how fiery red my bottom is, I gasp. He truly covered every inch. It's a good thing I don't have to wear short dresses to work.

His chuckle startles me, and I quickly drop my dress.

"Your red bottom is a beautiful sight. I can't wait to fuck you soon while it's still nice and hot from a spanking."

My clit tingles, and my entire body heats. His cock is rock-hard against his slacks. Holy hell. It looks huge.

"Blink, baby girl," he teases.

I do, several times, and when I raise my gaze to his, he looks smug as hell.

"Here, drink this down." He holds up a bottle of

water to my lips. I try to take it from him, but he shakes his head.

Okay, apparently, he's not letting me do it myself. I take several long drinks before he pulls the bottle away and sets it on the counter. Then he starts opening drawers.

"What are you looking for?"

"Washcloth."

Just as I'm about to tell him where they are, he opens the top drawer of the vanity and freezes. I glance down and grimace.

Slowly, he picks up the package of brand-new razor blades. Shame coats me like a wet blanket. My shoulders slump, and I can't look him in the eye.

"Baby girl, why do you have these?"

The question isn't accusing. He's not being condescending. He asked like he would ask any other question.

"I, um, I've had them for years. I've never used them. I keep them there…"

He drops them on the counter and cups my face in both of his hands. "In case things get so bad you might need them again?"

I drop my eyes and give a slight nod. He's probably so disappointed in me. Or disgusted.

"Look at me, sweet baby," he whispers.

When I do, his eyes are pained. "I hope you never

feel like you need them again. But if you do, will you promise me something?"

I blink.

"Will you promise to come talk to me first? Tell Daddy you're feeling that way so we can deal with it together? Maybe we can explore other ways to give you the relief you seek? Safer ways."

My bottom lip trembles as a tear rolls down my cheek. "I might always be broken, Daddy."

He pulls me closer and kisses the top of my head. "We're all a little broken, baby. But you're no longer alone. And it will kill me if you hurt yourself. I hope being with me, you won't ever have that need again. Just, please, come to me if you ever do, okay? Please, Chloe? Promise me."

The pain lacing his tone breaks my heart. His entire body trembles as he holds me. His fear is so tangible that I can feel it swirling around us. My impenetrable monster isn't so impenetrable.

"I promise, Daddy. You can take those razors. I don't want them here anymore."

When he pulls back to look me in the eye, he strokes my cheek. "Are you sure?"

"Yes."

He tilts his head, glancing to the heavens, then meets my gaze again. "Thank you, baby."

The tightness in my chest eases as he pockets the

blades. I already feel a bit lighter knowing they won't be in that drawer, mocking me.

"Washcloth?"

I point to a different drawer, and he pulls one out and then runs it under the faucet for several minutes. After he wrings it out, he turns to me and gently starts washing my face. Our eyes stay locked together the entire time. I know better than to offer to do it myself. He wants to do this. I think in a way, he needs to do this.

"Do you want me to do your makeup?" he asks with a grin.

We both laugh as I shake my head. "No, Daddy. I can handle that."

He sits on the edge of the tub and watches me the entire time, asking questions about the products I'm using. Every time I glance back at him in the mirror, he's staring at me in awe.

"So, you're going to finish law school. What happens afterward?"

I sweep the eyeshadow brush over my lid and shrug. "I guess I'll find a job as an attorney somewhere."

"But you don't want to be an attorney."

I let out a deep exhale. "No. I don't."

"You want to be a beauty influencer and create a makeup brand of your own."

It's a statement, not a question.

He comes up behind me, his citrus scent filling the space. "After you finish school and pass the bar exam, I'm giving you five hundred thousand dollars to start your makeup line."

My blush brush drops with a clatter into the sink. What?

## 16

## BASH

My girl stares at me like I've lost my mind. Silly girl, she should know I lost it seven years ago when I first laid eyes on her.

"You can't give me that kind of money, Ba—I mean Daddy!"

I place my hands on either side of her hips, trapping her between me and the counter. "I can, and I will. My girl isn't going to live her life doing something she doesn't want to do. She's going to live it happy, doing what she's passionate about, and her Daddy is going to support her along the way."

Her gaze softens as she peers up at me from under her long lashes. "Daddy, it means so much to me that you want me to pursue my passion. Really, it means the whole world to me. You can't give me that kind of money, though. It's not appropriate. We just, you know, started this thing between us."

My lips twitch at her nervous hand motions.

*This thing between us.*

"This thing," I say, "is forever. You're going to be my wife. I'm going to fill you with my babies and watch you become the most beautiful mom in the world. What's mine is all yours, baby. The only thing I want from you is your love and loyalty."

A small squeak escapes her as those beautiful blue eyes go wide. "Who said anything about babies?"

I shrug. "Do you not want babies? If you don't want them, we don't have to have them. I'll just pretend I'm trying to get you pregnant when I'm fucking you. All I need to be happy is you for the rest of my life, everything else is a bonus."

She's completely rigid against me, and for a moment, I worry I've gone too far, too soon. I don't seem to have that warning bell that should go off, telling me to shut the fuck up when I'm around her.

When she huffs out a shaky breath and then starts giggling, my stomach tightens into a ball. Shit. I did. I went too far.

"You are unreal. It's been three days, and you're already talking about marriage and babies. This is… This is weird. Right? People don't do this. Not regular people. They date for a few years and then maybe get married, and then a few years after that, they might have a baby. That's…that's the normal way to do it."

My poor baby. She's panicking.

I wrap my hands around her biceps and gently stroke them with my thumbs. Her eyes soften as she stares up at me. My touch alone seems to center her and bring her back to reality. "Nothing about our lives is normal, sweetheart. We live very differently than the rest of the population. In this life, we don't know how long we'll have. Men in the mafia don't usually die of old age. So maybe I'm moving quickly, but it's because I've been without you for the past seven years, and I don't want to spend another year of my life without you being mine."

Her hands slide into my suit jacket and rest on my pecs. When she raises her gaze to mine, she sighs. "I don't like the thought of you not being here for a long time."

Lowering my face, I nuzzle my nose to hers. "I don't either, baby. But having you by my side, I'm going to do everything in my power to live as long as possible."

A quick, painful pinch catches me off guard, and she smiles. "If you die before me, I'm not going to be with you in heaven. I'll find someone else."

I let out a low growl and pick her up, setting her on the counter roughly, so she gets a reminder of her tender bottom. "First of all, brat, no pinching Daddy.

And second, I'd like to see you try to be with someone else in heaven. You think I'm unhinged now, just you wait."

And then I start tickling her sides until she's screaming and kicking, trying to get free.

"Okay! Okay! I won't be with anyone else!" she squeals.

When I release her, she's grinning and out of breath. "But you have to promise to live as long as possible. Okay?"

"I promise, Little girl."

She raises an eyebrow and lifts her hand in the air. "Pinky promise."

I stare at her delicate pinky and raise mine to it. "Pinky promises are sacred. I'd never break one."

We hook our fingers together, and that seems to soothe her worries because her expression softens, and she lets out a deep sigh.

"Do you want to have babies?" I ask.

Her smile grows wider. "I do. I've always wanted to be a mom one day."

My cock thickens, and I stifle my groan. Fuck. The vision of pregnant Chloe, her belly big and round with our baby, is almost too much to take.

"Good to know, baby. Good to know."

She cocks an eyebrow. "You're not going to try to get me pregnant right away, are you?"

Damn. Smart girl.

"I'll tell you what, baby. I'm probably going to fuck you like I'm trying to get you pregnant, but until you're ready, stay on your birth control. I'll wait as long as you need. Okay?"

"I think I might be as unhinged as you. I should be running for the hills right now. Is this why you're single? All the other women saw your red flags and moved out of the country?"

I bark out a laugh. "You're such a sassy brat. I wouldn't know. I haven't shown my red flags to anyone else for the past seven years."

Her smile falls, her eyes searching my face. "You, uh, you haven't been with anyone in that time?"

"I've had sex. Meaningless sex. No sleepovers or anything. Just quick hookups."

"Oh."

"You're it for me, Chloe. I know it's shocking to you how quickly I want to move, but it's because I feel like I've missed out on so much time with you. And also, I'm a possessive and selfish asshole."

She wraps her arms around my waist and hugs me. My heart pounds against her ear, and I hope she knows it's beating purely for her.

"You still can't give me that much money," she murmurs.

I wrap my fist around her hair and tug her head back. "The fuck I can't. I'm Daddy. I can do whatever I want. And if you really have an issue with it coming from me, then Kieran will give it to you. He's your brother, so you don't have a choice but to accept it from him."

Her mouth falls open as she narrows her eyes. "I don't think it's fair that you two think you can gang up on me."

"Oh, baby, we don't play fair. Especially when it comes to taking care of the people we care about. Now, come on, I need to get you changed so I can get you to work on time."

When I set her on her feet, she puts her hands on her hips. "Daddy, you're not driving me to work."

"Why not?"

She huffs and stalks into her bedroom. "Because I have a car. And I'm coming home when I get off, and you'll be doing whatever it is you do. Don't you have to work?"

"Yes, but I can still drive you." I shrug, baffled as to what the issue is. I mean, why wouldn't she want to be my passenger princess?

"Daddy," she says as she puts her hand on my chest. "You're gonna have to learn that I can do stuff on my own. I love the way you take care of me, but I'm also a big girl."

Determination glints in those beautiful eyes of hers. She's fighting me on some stuff because she doesn't want me to completely take over. Part of me wonders if it has to do with the way her father ran her life. She let him get away with it, and he abused that power. It's going to take time before she understands that my need to control her life has nothing to do with selfish gains. The only thing I want to do is take care of her and make her life easier.

I let out a dramatic sigh and nod. "Fine. But you'll text me when you get there, and when you leave and when you arrive home. Understood?"

Defiance flashes in her eyes as she lifts her chin slightly. I'm prepared for her to say something sassy, but she must see the hard set of my gaze because she finally drops her shoulders and nods. "Okay."

"That's Daddy's good girl."

---

"HEY, MAN," I say to Colt as we step into his house.

Colt shuts the heavy wood door behind us. "You two are in trouble now."

His wife, Ava, bounds toward us. "You didn't bring her?" she asks, pouting.

"Who?" I ask.

"Chloe. Cali and Scarlet were telling us about her."

Kieran gawks at her. "You talk to Cali and Scarlet?"

Ava bobs her head. "Yep. We're all in one giant group chat. Ever since the night our Daddies went to help you and they came over, we've kept in touch."

Warmth spreads through me. I swear, these Little girls are gifts from God. They're the light to all our darkness.

"Chloe's at work. Maybe I'll bring her next time."

Ava shrugs and goes back to the living room where some animated movie is playing.

"So, what brings you guys over?" Colt asks when we're standing around the kitchen island.

I pull out my phone. "Get the surveillance of the coffee shop on my phone, so I can see it whenever I want."

Colt raises an eyebrow and smirks. "Have you ever heard of the word please?"

Shaking my head, I roll my eyes. "Please."

"Having my men keep tabs on the shop isn't enough for you?"

I scowl. "She's my girl. Get it on my damn phone."

"And here I thought Declan was the stalker of the family. Taking it to the next level. Cool. Does she know you've had the cameras at her work tapped into?" Colt asks.

Ava clears her throat, and when we all turn to look at her, she narrows her eyes at Colt.

"Daddy, I don't think you have any room to talk about his stalking habits."

I laugh and arch an eyebrow at Colt. "Sounds like you have some stalking experience of your own."

Colt glares at his wife. "Your bottom is going to pay for that."

She throws her hands on her hips. "I was only speaking the truth, Daddy. Lying is against the rules."

Kieran and I burst out laughing while Colt mumbles something under his breath.

Ava skips back to the couch, and I smile smugly. "So, how about getting my phone set up?"

Colt turns to Kieran. "She's your sister, and you're okay with this?"

Kieran shrugs. "He's doing what he needs to do to take care of his girl. I'd do the same thing if it were my girl."

Finally, Colt takes my phone and starts tapping away at the screen, though the corner of his mouth is pulled back into a half-smile. He handles all of our hacking and security needs and owns several tech firms in the city.

When he's finished, he hands it back. As soon as I get to the camera feed and see my girl working away making a drink, I let out a long breath. My cock aches for her. Just like it's been aching every second of the day since the night I saw her at the bar with that weasel. I hate that she's not here with me physically, but being able to watch her and make sure she's safe is enough for now.

"Is that all you came here for?" Colt asks.

I set my phone down, irritated that I can't keep watching my girl. "Actually, we need something else. Can you hack into the city council's files and see who signed off on the use of a port terminal recently? I have an estimated date it would have happened."

Colt nods and motions for us to follow him. "We'll be in my office, baby girl. Come find me if you need anything."

Ava glances up and grins. "Okay, Daddy. Love you!"

"How's it going, Bradley? I hope the accommodations are up to your standards." I smile at the man handcuffed to the chair. Bright lights shine down on him, the only heat in the massive space.

Blood oozes from his split lip and a deep slice to his cheek. Dark circles brace his eyes. He hasn't slept much—if at all—but I don't give a fuck.

"Please let me go," he begs.

Mr. Broken Record. Again with the pleas. The

promises. We all know they mean nothing. He's a predator... A predator who signed off on the use of a terminal to bring in a shipment of trafficked girls.

"Does this look familiar to you, Bradley?"

I hold up a copy of the form he signed. He squints at it for several seconds. "I can't tell what it's for."

Kieran and I glance at each other and chuckle.

"It's a document that allows access to a shipping terminal here in Seattle. A terminal that was recently used to bring in a bunch of kidnapped women and underage girls from Russia. That's your signature on the page, authorizing the ship to dock."

Bradley's face pales. "No. I didn't know. I didn't know that's what was coming in. I swear."

I set the paper down on the nearby table and crack my knuckles. They're still a little swollen from yesterday's visit. "What did you think you were signing off on, then? A shipment of rainbows?"

He shakes his head and coughs a few times. "I didn't ask questions. I was promised a substantial amount of money for each successful shipment."

Kieran grabs hold of his hair, yanking his head back. "So, the guy who drugged my sister's drink had no idea there were women being trafficked into the US for prostitution? I find that hard to believe."

When Kieran lets go of his hair, Bradley starts to sputter but is cut off when Kieran throws his fist into his face.

"Tell the fucking truth, Bradley!" I shout.

"I didn't know! I swear! At least, not about the underage ones," he cries out between coughs.

This time, I rush forward and punch him in the chest, knocking the air right from his lungs.

I squat in front of him and pull my gun from the holster under my arm. "I'm going to give you one chance to answer my question truthfully. If you're lying, I'll know. Who asked you to sign off on the port usage?"

Sweat rolls down Bradley's face. He squirms as much as the restraints allow, his gaze locked on the barrel of the gun. "You're going to kill me anyway, so why should I tell you?"

The corners of my lips pull back into an evil smile. "You're a smart guy. I'm glad you're already aware of your fate. But here's something you do get to decide. Do you want to die quickly, or do you want to die painfully over the course of several weeks? The option is yours. So, who asked for the terminal usage?"

Bradley is silent for a moment. When he's made up his mind, he lifts his gaze to mine. "Ronald Watts."

My entire body tenses up, and when I look over at Kieran, he's in just as much shock as I am.

"Chloe's father?" I ask.

Bradley nods. Without a word, Kieran and I turn

to leave, nodding to the men we have guarding the warehouse to put Bradley back in his cell.

"Wait!" he shouts. "Just kill me already! Please!"

I toss a gaze over my shoulder as I keep walking. "Oh, we will. After we confirm what you told us."

# 17
# CHLOE

> Chloe: I'm home, Daddy.

> Bash: Good girl. What are you and Paisley doing for your girls' night?

> Chloe: I think we're going to watch movies and eat junk food.

> Bash: You could have done that at my house, you know. My TV is bigger.

> Chloe: Daddy…

> Bash: Yes, baby?

> Chloe: You're impossible.

> Bash: Nah. Just persistent. You'll be living with me soon enough, anyway. Might as well start making yourself at home.

I roll my eyes, but my grin is so wide my cheeks hurt.

> Chloe: We'll see.

> Bash: We'll see is right, Little one. I'm heading into a meeting. Be good and have fun.

It's too soon to think about moving in with Bash. I think. I have a feeling if I talked to my brother about it, he'd encourage it and probably help order a moving truck. Those men are so freaking stubborn.

Despite thinking it might be too soon, the idea of living with Bash, waking up to him every morning, and letting him take care of me in the tender way he does makes my heart beat faster. I almost took him up on his invitation to have our girls' night at his house just so I could be close to him. Sleeping in my bed without him is not appealing in the least. The man was like my own personal heating blanket last night, and without him, I'm going to be cold. I don't know how long it takes to fall in love with someone, but it feels like that's what this is. Maybe it would be different if I had just met him for the first time a few days ago, but I've known him for years.

In all that time, I've learned several things. He's loyal to a fault. He's protective of those he cares about. He's generous. Too much so if you ask me. Five hundred thousand dollars? The guy must have bumped his head if he thinks I'm accepting that from him. Even if I could open the entire makeup line I've thought about and planned since I was a teenager, I don't want him to give me the money. I grew up in a home where my father controlled everything because he was the one who made the money. He used it to his advantage. Hence, me going on a date with Bradley Du Pont. I want to make my own money, so that way I still have control of my life if something were to happen.

I'm going to need to talk to Paisley about the possibility of moving out. I won't leave her high and dry. She's still an entry-level accountant at her firm, so she's not making big bucks yet, plus she's still paying off a mountain of student loans. If I move out, she'll have to get another roommate. The thought of that makes my heart hurt. She's my best friend.

I spend the next while rummaging through the cupboards and freezer, looking for the junkiest of all junk food I can find for the evening ahead. Fruit snacks. Ice cream. Chicken nuggets. Cheetos. Wine. Yes! We are set.

Just as I close the fridge, Paisley comes fluttering into the house, her black cotton dress flowing around her thighs. I have the same one. In yellow, of course.

"Get your dancing shoes on. We're going out tonight."

My eyebrows furrow as I jerk my head back. "What are you talking about? We're doing a girls' night in."

She shakes her head. "Nope. Change of plans. A guy in my office got us on the VIP list at that new club downtown. His brother is a bouncer there or something."

Going out doesn't sound appealing. I was actually looking forward to a night in, wearing comfortable pajamas and watching movies. She looks so excited, though, and it has been a long time since we went out together.

"Are you sure you don't want to stay in? We have a plethora of junk food and wine."

Paisley sticks her hands on her hips and blinks several times. "Go get changed. Let's do girls' night right. Come on. We don't have to stay late."

I let out a deep sigh. "Promise?"

She holds up her pinky. "I promise. We can Uber there and have a couple of drinks, then Uber home and still watch a movie. I've been dying to see the inside of this club. I heard there are cages suspended from the ceilings that women dance in. Plus, there are a lot of sports stars that go there, and you know I'm in my sports romance book era."

Lord, is she ever. All she talks about is hockey romance this and hockey romance that. I keep telling her mafia books are where it's at. Although, there are some sports romance books I've definitely read one-handed.

"Fine. I don't know how you always talk me into this stuff. You should have been the lawyer."

She laughs and shakes her head. "Nah. I prefer to argue for fun. Call Bash and invite him along."

I shake my head as we make our way to the stairs. "He's working. I don't want to bother him."

THE CLUB IS PACKED wall-to-wall with people. Paisley was right, there are huge cages suspended in the air with sexy women dancing in them. By the time we make it up to the bar, I already have a fine sheen of sweat coating my skin. It was a workout trying to muscle past people. Surely, it's a fire hazard to have this many people in here.

With the dim lighting and multi-colored spotlights

moving around every which way, it's hard to see more than a few feet in front of me. The bass of the music is beating so loud, it's vibrating inside my chest.

We get our drinks and slowly make our way through the crowd. With as much as I keep getting bumped, I won't have anything left in my glass soon.

Paisley points and yells over the music, "There's the dance floor! Let's go!"

I nod because there's no use in trying to talk. It's so loud, I can't hear myself think.

When I get jostled between two large men and nearly spill my entire glass, I shake my head and throw the liquid back in one swallow. I'm not going to waste a twenty-dollar Cosmopolitan. Sheesh.

We get to the edge of the dance floor and start to move with the music, staying as close to each other as we can. Paisley laughs and grabs my hips, so we sway in sync with each other.

A new song starts, one of our favorites, and we continue moving to the rhythm. A tall, stocky man comes up behind Paisley and leans down to whisper in her ear. She glances up at him and smiles but shakes her head.

The man frowns and says something else to her. Her smile falls, and she shakes her head harder. I tug her a little closer to me, but the man crowds us both.

"I said no," she yells at him.

He ignores her and starts to grind against her.

The blood in my veins goes ice cold. What is it with these creeps thinking they can do whatever the hell they want? I scowl up at the guy and press my hand to his chest, trying to nudge him away. The guy wraps his meaty fingers around my wrist and squeezes so hard that I yelp and try to yank it away, but his hold is too tight.

Suddenly, out of nowhere, the guy goes flying back into the crowd. Paisley and I gasp and look around to figure out what just happened. Two muscular figures in black suits tower over us, and as my gaze travels upward, my tummy sinks. Bash and Kieran stare at us with dark, murderous expressions.

"You're in so much trouble, Little girl, you're not going to sit for a week," Bash growls in my ear.

A shiver works its way down my spine, but before I can respond, there's another scuffle. The big guy tries to come at my brother, only to be knocked down again. Kieran stands over him and continues to punch him repeatedly. Paisley screams and tries to grab Kieran to pull him back, but he holds his hand out, keeping her from getting too close.

When Kieran stops hitting him, the guy tries to get up, but Bash is on him in a second, throwing more punches.

Several security guys come rushing over, yelling at Bash and Kieran. Bash turns toward them, his eyes dark and deadly, and says something to one of the men, and like a switch, the men back off and move to yank the guy who approached Paisley up from the floor.

When I look at Bash again, his nostrils are flaring, and he's breathing heavily. He grabs my hand and pulls me toward the exit.

"Wait! Paisley!" I call out, but when I turn back to look for her, she's right behind us, being dragged out of the club by Kieran.

Bash's SUV is parked right by the door. We're in some kind of alley behind the club.

"What the hell were you doing there?" Bash demands.

I shrink back slightly. He won't hurt me. I know that without a doubt. But from the way he's looking at me, I feel like a naughty child.

"We came here to go dancing," I say quietly.

He nods and runs his tongue over his teeth. "I see that, baby. I guess the real question is, why didn't you tell me you were coming here?"

My shoulders fall, and I glance over at Paisley. She looks as unsure as I feel. "I thought you were working. I didn't want to bother you."

Bash huffs and shakes his head. "You didn't want to bother me. Even though one of your rules is to tell me your whereabouts. Even though I've told you that you're my first priority over anything. Even though I explained to you that going to certain places without security can be dangerous?"

I glance back at Kieran, but he's scowling at both me and Paisley, his arms crossed over his chest.

"Don't look at me for help, Little girl. He's in charge of you now. You broke his rule, so you'll answer to him," Kieran growls.

"I'm sorry," I whisper when I look at Bash again.

He stares at me for a long moment.

"It's my fault. I forced her to go out," Paisley says.

Bash's gaze slides from me to my best friend then back again. "Chloe is a big girl. She wasn't forced to do anything. It was her choice to disobey."

I lower my eyes from his, tears burning them. "I'm sorry. I didn't want to interrupt you at work."

When he doesn't say anything for a long time, I glance up at him. His green eyes are pained. My heart squeezes, and the first tear falls down my cheek.

"Baby, you *always* come first. I don't care if I'm at work in fucking Antarctica; if it concerns you, I want to be contacted. I don't give a shit if you want to go to a club. But what I do care about is the fact that a place like this isn't safe for you to go alone. I would have come with you if you had just told me. Or if I absolutely couldn't get away, I would have sent security guards to make sure you two were safe. Dammit, Chloe, I can't protect you if you don't follow the rules.

I won't ever stop you from doing fun things, but what I will do is make sure there are safeguards in place to protect you. That asshole was a big guy. What would have happened if we hadn't arrived in time?"

Tears run down my cheeks. Paisley's crying too. Unable to stop myself, I go to Bash and wrap my arms around him and sob. "I'm so sorry, Daddy. I didn't think about all of that."

He returns my embrace, his hands cradling my head against his chest. "That's because it's not your job to think about all that stuff. It's Daddy's job to keep you safe, which is why you have rules to follow."

I nod and sniffle. "It won't happen again."

"You're right about that. After I'm done punishing you tonight, I don't think there will be any question about how serious I am about your safety."

My tummy twists into knots, but my clit swells and my heart is full.

"As for you," Kieran says firmly, pointing at Paisley. "Do not ever try to get in the middle of two men fighting. You're a tiny fucking thing. You could have been badly hurt. Do you understand me?"

I watch from the safety of Bash's arms as my best friend stares up at my brother, her eyes wide. When she doesn't say anything, Kieran takes a step toward her and narrows his gaze.

"I asked you a question, Little girl," he says.

Paisley glares back at him, and it's starting to feel like a standoff between the two. "I was trying to stop you from killing him. And I'm not tiny, so maybe get your eyes checked."

Kieran takes another two steps until he's so close, he's towering over her. "If I wanted to kill him, he'd be dead. Do not *ever* get in the middle of two men fighting. Do. You. Understand?"

She has to tilt her head back to look at his face. "Fine," she grits out.

He lets out a growl of annoyance. "Good. Get in the fucking car before you freeze to death. Jesus. Where are your pants?"

Paisley lets out an irritated huff, then spins around and stomps toward the SUV, where Bash has already opened the door and is helping me into the back seat.

"It's called a dress!" she shouts over her shoulder.

"Yeah, well, it barely covers your ass," Kieran yells back. "And it's only sixty degrees outside, are you trying to die of pneumonia?"

She rolls her eyes, climbs into the SUV, then shouts, "Sixty degrees in Seattle is practically summer weather, you big oaf!"

Before the two men get in the car, Paisley looks over at me. "I don't like your brother."

My lips pull back into a small smile. At least I'm not the only one who's been scolded tonight. Somehow, it's a little easier knowing that she got into trouble with me. Although my bottom is going to pay the price, while she gets to go home and crawl into her comfy bed. Rude.

The air in the SUV is thick with tension. Kieran is running so hot I can feel the heat all the way back here. Paisley has her arms crossed over her chest while she glowers at my brother. If this wasn't such a serious situation, I might giggle.

"How did you know where we were?" I finally ask.

Bash glances at me in the rearview mirror. "GPS on your phone."

I tilt my head and pull my eyebrows together. "How were you able to do that? Did you hack into it or something?"

He raises an eyebrow. "I installed a tracking program on your phone the night I took you home."

"What?" I shout as I sit up straight.

"Little girl, I'd recommend you don't have a tantrum about it right now. If I hadn't installed the program, I wouldn't have known you were here, and then what would have happened? That fucking asshole had his hands on you. If we hadn't shown up, who knows what would have happened."

I shrink back into my seat again, lowering my eyes. I can't believe he was tracking me. Actually, I can believe that. It's Bash. I should have known he would do a thing like that. Whether I like it or not, my Daddy has no boundaries when it comes to keeping me safe.

Warmth spreads through my core. He downloaded that program before he got my brother's blessing. So, even though he didn't think he could have me then, he still wanted to keep tabs on me. I stew on that for a few minutes. I can't decide if I'm ridiculously turned on by what he did or if I should punch him in the balls.

He pulls up to my place, and when he puts the car in park, I reach for the door.

"Don't you dare touch that handle, Chloe. You're coming home with me. We'll be spending the rest of the evening having a nice long chat."

The weight of his words isn't lost on me. By chat, he means he's going to paddle my ass. I clench my bottom without meaning to. When I look at Paisley, she's staring at me.

"Are you going to be okay?" she asks quietly.

I nod. "Yes. Bash won't hurt me."

Kieran yanks open the door on Paisley's side. "Where's your house key?"

She turns and scowls at him before she wiggles out of the car and squeezes past his large frame. "None of your business," she says.

Before my brother can shut the door and catch up to her, Paisley's already slammed the front door.

Well, crap. I guess I'm on my own.

Kieran gets into the SUV and looks back at me, scowling. "I don't like your friend."

Yeah, well, the feeling is mutual from her. Not that I'm going to say that out loud.

## 18

## BASH

By the time I drop Kieran off at his house and I pull into my garage, I'm no longer shaking with rage. I'm not mad at Chloe. Disappointed, yes. She didn't want to bother me? Fuck that. After tonight, my stance on that will be crystal clear.

But that guy. That fucker who touched her? Put his hand around her wrist like she was a toy? Nope. The only reason I didn't finish him off right then and there was because the bouncers at the club will hold him for me. It is *our* club after all. I'll deal with him tomorrow. After I've dealt with my naughty Little girl. She's going to learn a lesson tonight that she'll never forget.

I help her out of the back seat, and neither of us

says anything as we walk through the house. When we pass the kitchen, I pause.

"Are you hungry, baby?"

She won't meet my eyes as she shakes her head. I go to the fridge and grab two bottles of water, then take her by the hand and lead her upstairs. Her fingers tremble in mine as I close the bedroom door behind us.

"Take your shoes off, go potty, and wash your hands. We'll talk when you're done," I say, nudging her toward the bathroom.

When she closes the door, I let out a deep breath and lower myself into one of the armchairs. If Kieran and I hadn't gotten to the club when we had, who knows how badly the girls could have been hurt. My chest hurts thinking about the possibilities. I had thought I wouldn't need to put security on Chloe all the time yet, but I was wrong. Starting tomorrow, she'll have guards with her no matter where she goes when I'm not with her.

The soft snick of the door opening brings me out of my dark thoughts as I look up at my girl. She's wringing her fingers together, and she slowly shuffles toward me. Mascara streaks down her cheeks, and she looks like she's going to burst into a fresh set of tears any second.

I spread my legs wider and hold out my arms. "Come here, Little one."

A sob breaks free as she runs toward me and lunges onto my lap. "I'm so sorry, Daddy."

Holding her tightly, I run my hand up and down her back, shushing her. It takes a few minutes, but her sobs finally subside, and we're left listening to each other's breathing.

"Chloe, I need you to understand that you are my world. The center of my entire universe. And I don't care where I am, what I'm doing, or who I'm with; I want you to interrupt me. It doesn't matter if you have a tiny fucking splinter in your toe, I still want you to interrupt me. My job as your man and your Daddy is to take care of you, and part of me taking care of you is giving you rules to keep you safe. When you break those rules, it puts you at risk, and baby girl, I won't allow you to be at risk."

She sniffles and nods. "I understand, Daddy."

I lean back in the chair so I can look at her face. "I don't think you do, baby. I love you, Chloe. It's okay if you don't love me yet. I've had a lot longer to fall for you. If anything ever happened to you, my heart would stop beating. I wouldn't last a day without you now that I know what it's like for you to be mine. I don't care if you break every other rule I give you, but your safety rules, I need you to follow them to a T. It's the only way I'll be able to breathe when you're not by my side."

Her hand rests over my chest like she needs to

feel my heart beating for her. "I promise to follow your rules, Daddy. It was stupid of me not to let you know. Paisley told me I could call and invite you to come with us, but I told her I didn't want to bother you while you were working. I didn't think about how it could be dangerous."

"Baby, you are never bothering me. Not ever."

She nods and sniffles. "Okay, Daddy."

I let out a sigh. "I want you to go into the bathroom, grab the hairbrush I used last night, and bring it to me."

Her eyes widen, but she doesn't say anything as I help her off my lap. This is going to be a hard lesson for her, but it's one she has to learn.

A few seconds later, she's holding the brush out to me with a shaking hand.

"Since this is your first serious spanking, I'm mostly going to use my hand. If this happens again, though, it will be much harsher than the spanking you're going to get tonight. Understand?"

"Yes, Daddy," she whispers.

I set the brush aside and reach for her. Keeping my gaze on hers, I slide my hands under her dress and pull down her panties. When they drop to the floor, I tap her leg to step out so I can shove them into my pocket. She watches but doesn't say anything about it. Then I take her hand and pull her over my lap, exposing her bottom to me.

"Do you remember your safeword, baby?"

She sniffles and nods. "It's red, Daddy."

"Good girl. Tell me why you're being punished right now."

It takes a few seconds before she speaks, and when she does, her voice cracks. "I disobeyed you. I should have told you I was going to the club, and I didn't."

Resting my hand on her bottom, I sigh. "You scared me, Little one."

Her back goes rigid for a split second. "You don't seem like you're scared of anything."

"I'm scared of something happening to you. Of losing you. That's what scares me."

She hangs her head down and relaxes her body over my lap. When she doesn't say anything, I lift my hand and bring it down on her ass with a loud smack.

Before the pain registers with her, I'm already landing my palm a second time on the other cheek. She cries out and immediately starts wiggling against my hold.

For several minutes, I spank her, peppering her bottom all over until she's kicking and flailing over my lap, promising to be a good girl.

"Owwie!" she howls.

I keep going until her bottom is bright red. She's crying and trying to fight against it, but I don't let up.

When I pause to pick up the hairbrush, she's breathing hard.

"How are you doing, baby girl?"

"My b-bottom hurts," she sobs.

"Do you need to use your safeword, baby?"

She only pauses for a brief second before she shakes her head. "No, Daddy."

I tap her bottom with the back of the hairbrush a few times. "This is going to be hard and fast, but when it's all done, I'll hold you all night long. Okay?"

"'Kay," she whimpers.

As I promised, I start paddling her in a quick rhythm that has her screaming and kicking. I only spank her for a minute or so with the brush since it's her first time, and I want to have a conversation with her tomorrow about it. The last thing I want to do is push her too far. No one is allowed to harm my girl. Not even me.

When I'm done, I gently pull her up and onto my lap. She's shaking with sobs as she buries her face against my chest. I hate making my girl cry. It's the last thing in the world I want to do. I also know she needs this. She needs to know I love her enough to do whatever it takes to keep her safe, even if it means paddling her beautiful bottom. I bury my face in her hair and take in a deep breath, her scent quieting my mind. When I saw she was at the club, I couldn't get there fast enough. Just seeing that asshole's hand on her knocked the wind right from my lungs. Fear hasn't been an emotion I've often felt in my life, but tonight, I was more scared than I can ever recall feeling.

"Daddy's got you. I got you, baby," I croon.

She cries for a solid fifteen minutes until her sobs turn to soft whimpers then to silence.

"My good girl. You're my good girl, Chloe." I continue to stroke her back and cuddle her, and I'll stay right here holding her all night long if that's what she needs.

"Daddy," she whispers.

"Hmm?"

"I love you too. Thank you for showing up tonight. I was scared of that guy."

A lump forms in my throat. Tears fill my eyes, and all I can do is nod my acknowledgment because if I speak, I might be the one sobbing next. She loves me. She loves *me*. I don't deserve it. I know I don't. I also don't give a fuck. She's mine, and if she can love a man like me, I'm not going to question it.

"I was scared, too, baby," I rasp.

Hours pass, and we both doze in and out of sleep. If I don't get us out of this chair and into bed, we're both going to be sore in the morning.

Keeping her wrapped up in my arms, I rise and go into the bathroom then set her on her feet in front of the toilet.

"Go potty, sweet girl."

She peers up at me nervously as I stand, watching her closely. When she doesn't move, I kneel down in front of her and lift her dress over her hips.

"Sit, baby," I murmur.

Slowly, she lowers herself, hissing as her bottom comes into contact with the seat. I stay where I am, keeping my gaze on her face. The dark circles under her eyes are unnerving. She needs to rest. Especially since she has finals coming up in a couple of days. Maybe tomorrow I'll make her stay in bed all day. Maybe I'll stay in bed with her. I can have my men go collect Ronald and hold him in a warehouse until I'm ready to deal with him. He's always put himself first. Well, too bad for him, I'm putting his daughter first. He can rot in a fucking cage for all I care.

Finally, Chloe pees, her cheeks turning bright pink when I smile at her. She's probably never had a man all up in her business like this before. She'll get used to it. She won't be able to make a move without me being in her space.

After she cleans herself up, I lead her to the sink to wash her hands. While she does that, I grab a washcloth and wet it with warm water.

"Turn toward me, baby. Let me see your beautiful face."

She faces me and twists her fingers in my dress shirt. Slowly and gently, I clean off all her makeup with a wipe and then I use the washcloth. We stare into each other's eyes the entire time, silently speaking to each other in a way only we understand.

"Are things always going to be this intense between us?" she whispers.

I smile as I grab the electric toothbrush I bought for her. "I'm sorry to tell you, baby, but it will probably get more intense the longer we're together. In only a few days, you've become the very air I breathe. I'm obsessed, and that obsession will only grow stronger. I'll do whatever it takes to make you the happiest woman in the world, but you'll have no space with me. None. I will be part of every single piece of you, just like you already are every part of me."

The air whooshes from her lungs. "I don't want your money."

Giving a shrug, I hold the toothbrush up to her mouth until she opens for me, and I start brushing her teeth. "You may not want it, but you're still getting it. Everything I have is yours. As soon as finals are over and you're on your break, we'll be going to add your name to all my accounts."

She starts to shake her head, but I capture her chin to hold her still. "No arguing unless you'd like to make a second trip over my knee tonight."

Her eyes go wide, and I chuckle. I figured that

would work. Maybe I need to threaten her with spankings more often.

I finish brushing her teeth and then quickly brush my own before taking her hand to lead her into the bedroom. She's quiet, in her own head, and that's okay. I have my own thoughts swirling too. Mostly wondering how long it will be before I can put a ring on her finger and have her last name changed to mine.

Instead of giving her a shirt to wear to bed, I reach for the hem of her dress and pull it over her head, then remove her bra. It's nearly impossible to keep myself from latching onto one of her rosy nipples, but I keep my lips to myself.

"Get into bed."

She looks down at herself and then back at me. As soon as I raise a stern brow, she crawls into bed, flashing her pink bottom my way. My mouth waters. Fuck. I don't think she realizes how sexy she is without even trying. Pure perfection. And all mine.

## 19

## CHLOE

My skin tingles. I'm naked in Bash's bed, and as much as I hate to admit it, despite having my bottom paddled earlier, I'm incredibly turned on. That spanking was horrible. So painful it took my breath away. It felt like it went on forever, and I thought my poor bottom wasn't going to survive. But the whole time, I felt safe, loved, and secure. I also found the release I used to search for with a razor blade. The pain neutralized all the bad feelings building up inside me.

So now, my mind is clear, and I'm almost high from the aftereffects. I know Bash isn't perfect. But the way he takes care of me, the way he talks to me, and the way he looks at me are perfect. I have no doubt he'll always be intense. He won't give me room to breathe. But I also know he's going to be my biggest cheerleader, and he means it when he says he wants me to be happy. I've never felt as happy as I do around him. My entire soul blossoms when we're together.

He stands at the edge of the bed and slowly starts to undress, folding each piece of clothing as he goes. He likes things neat and tidy. It's one of the many ways he stays in control. I have a feeling my messes will drive him up the wall. I'm going to enjoy watching it. Someone's gotta keep the man humble.

When he unbuckles his belt and lowers his slacks, I hold my breath. His cock is hard. I've never wanted to touch someone so badly in my life. Is he going to leave his underwear on? I'm naked, so he should be too. Slowly, he hooks his thumbs into the waistband of his boxer briefs and lowers them, letting his cock spring free. I swallow, my mouth suddenly dry as I stare at the beautiful piece of art. It's long and thick, with veins I want to trace with my tongue.

"Didn't anyone ever tell you it's rude to stare?"

My gaze snaps to his face. "I wasn't staring."

Crap. I was totally staring. It would be a sin not to.

He smirks at me and tosses the covers back before getting into bed. I roll onto my side to face him, unsure what to do or say. I've never been good at this. It's one of the many reasons why I always wanted a man who took control. Should I talk about the weather? Compliment him on the size of his dick? This is all too much for me to figure out.

"Breathe, Chloe," he says as he brings his hand to my cheek.

I shudder and close my eyes. He runs his thumb over my skin. When he trails his fingers down the column of my neck to the top of my breast, I let out a long exhale. It's amazing how I feel so safe with such a dangerous man.

"Look at me."

I stare into his sparkling eyes. Letting out a low growl, he rolls toward me and pushes me onto my back. His muscles flex as he lifts himself to hover over me, resting his forearms on either side of my head. His erection presses against my core, and I whimper. It glides over my lips, spreading my cream even more.

Slowly, he lowers his lips to mine and kisses me roughly. He pushes his tongue into my mouth, exploring every bit of it as he gently flexes his hips. Every so often, the head of his cock grazes my swollen clit, sending sparks of electricity through me. I whimper and moan, desperate for more. I need him like I need my next breath.

"Daddy."

He lifts his head, staring down at me. His eyes are blazing, and his breaths are coming hard and fast. When he lowers his face again, he starts pressing kisses to my throat. Flexing my fingers on his shoulders, I dig my nails in as I wrap my legs around his waist.

"Daddy," I whine more persistently.

The kisses stop. His jaw flexes as he studies me. A shiver works its way down my body. For a second, I'm worried I've made him mad somehow. Then he cradles my head in his hands, using his thumbs to rub gentle circles at my temples.

"Are you ready for this, Chloe? Ready for me to claim you? Once I fuck you, there's no turning back. There will be no breakups or questioning what we are. You'll be mine. In all ways. My woman. My Little girl. My wife. My everything. Can you handle that? Do you want that?"

A moan escapes as I bob my head. It might be too soon. Hell, it might be insane. I don't care, though. Whatever it is, I want it. I want to be owned by Bash. In every sense of the word.

He stares at me intently, waiting for my words. I lift my hand and place it over his heart.

"Yes, Daddy. I want everything. I want it with you."

When he doesn't say anything, I wiggle my hips, trying to get him to move but he doesn't. "Please? Don't make me beg."

Heat flashes in his gaze and a corner of his mouth

ticks up. His cock jumps against my leg. "You'd look so fucking pretty begging, though."

Before I can respond, he starts to slide down my body, dragging his tongue along my skin.

He ignores my throbbing core and starts pressing his lips to the tops of my thighs. Kissing each scar. I lift my head, and he repeats the action seventeen times, his gaze trained on me the whole time.

"You're beautiful. You deserved better. I'm going to give you everything, Chloe," he says softly.

The lump in my throat prevents me from speaking, so I nod and smile, letting a tear slip from the corner of my eye.

Taking his time, he moves back up my body, passing my core again. When he gets to my belly button, he lifts his head.

"You're going to be Daddy's good girl and come all over my face, aren't you?"

Oh, holy hell. I will do whatever this man wants me to do. Especially if he keeps talking like that.

I bob my head. "Yes."

A wicked smile spreads over his face as he hooks his hands under my thighs, pushing my legs open and back so I'm fully stretched and exposed to him. He closes his eyes and inhales deeply. When he opens them again, his pupils are blown wide. He looks like a hungry beast, ready to attack. My entire core clenches with anticipation and need.

"So pretty. So smooth and pink. Is all this delicious cream for me, baby girl?"

"Uh huh."

He takes a long, lazy lick from my ass to my clit, sending a jolt of surprise through me. When he does it again, I drop my head back and moan. Then he latches onto my clit, sucking it roughly, and I nearly levitate off the bed.

"Oh!"

I whimper and cry as he licks and sucks while holding my legs wide open. My body trembles. Arousal sweeps through me. This man has a magical tongue. Pure fucking magic.

He brings a finger to my opening and swirls it around, collecting my wetness, then slowly eases it inside. It's not enough. I need more. I need him. My cries fill the room as he thrusts in and out while keeping his mouth suctioned to my clit.

"Daddy! Oh! Please!"

"Please, what, baby girl? What do you need? Do you need another finger inside your tight little cunt? Or do you need me to suck harder on your delicate little clit? Hmm? What does my girl need?"

Without waiting for an answer, he does both, and I scream as my climax rips through me like a tidal wave. My entire body convulses, releasing all the pent-up sexual energy I've been feeling for days.

Bash continues to lick and suck softly until I've gone limp against the mattress. Aftershocks of my orgasm ripple through me. As he crawls up my body, I lift my hands to his biceps and sigh as my fingers brush against the thick muscles. He's so strong. In so many ways.

"Are you on birth control?"

I nod. "And I'm clean. I haven't been with anyone in a long time."

He frowns down at me. "How long?"

Shrugging my shoulders, I blink up at him. "Two years or so. I wasn't all that impressed with sex, so I decided to stop doing it."

His warmth soothes me, and between that and my post-orgasm high, I'm practically floating. Is this what drugs feel like?

"Well, I promise you'll be impressed with the sex you have with me."

A soft giggle escapes. "You seem pretty sure of yourself."

He flexes his hips so the head of his cock slides through my folds. "Maybe. Maybe I'm just sure that you and I are meant to be together, so the sex we have is going to be explosive and amazing for both of us."

I wiggle underneath him, trying to get his cock better aligned with my entrance. I need him inside me like I need my next breath.

"Please, Daddy. Please fuck me. Don't hold back. Make me yours."

His emerald eyes darken, and his eyelids drop as he stares at me. "No condom?"

"No. Please, no. Just you."

A low growl escapes. He plunges all the way into me in one swift move. I cry out as the pinch of pain registers. He's so freaking big. Filling me up completely, stretching me to the max. I dig my fingernails into his skin and sweat covers my body.

"That's it, baby. Scratch the fuck out of me. Mark me as yours, Chloe. That's what I am. Yours." His voice is deep and raspy like he's struggling to hold on to his control.

My pussy throbs. He's mine. All mine. It goes both ways. I'm not some piece of property to him. We belong to each other. My heart beats faster as a lump swells in my throat. I have something that belongs to me. Something real and loving.

I dig my nails in deeper until I feel warm wetness on the tips of my fingers. Bash moans and grabs my hips, pulls almost all the way out, then slams back in again. I scream, but the pain I felt before has bloomed into pleasure spreading over my body like wild ivy. Touching every piece of me. All I can do is hold on.

"You're so beautiful. So perfect. Mine. You're mine, Chloe. No one else's. You're my girl. Forever."

My cries fill the room as he fucks me, telling me

all the things I am to him. His girl. His wife. His everything. Over and over.

We're soaring together in our bliss.

"We're forever, Chloe. Husband and wife. Daddy and Little girl. Do you understand?"

A sharp smack to my ass makes me yelp. The zing of pain shoots straight to my pussy and blossoms into pleasure.

"I asked if you understand, baby," he growls.

I bob my head and wrap my fingers around the back of his neck to pull him down for a kiss. "Yes, Daddy. I'm yours. Forever."

His thrusts get harder and faster, and the mix of pleasure and pain is so intense that I can't think.

"You're taking my cock so well, baby. I'm so fucking proud of you. My good girl. Always Daddy's good girl."

He latches his mouth onto one of my nipples and tugs and then gives the other one the same attention. We're both coated in sweat, our bodies gliding against one another.

Suddenly, he sits back on his heels, bringing me up with him so we're facing each other while he fucks me.

"Beautiful," he murmurs.

We watch together as his cock slides in and out of me, wet with a mix of our arousal. He seems too big to fit, but somehow, he does, and it's perfect.

"Daddy's going to put you on all fours and fuck you nice and hard, baby."

Whimpering, I nod. He quickly flips me, and in less than a second, his cock is buried deep. Deeper than it was before. He wraps one hand around my neck and squeezes while he gives my ass a playful slap.

"I never thought you could get any more beautiful, but seeing you taking my cock like such a good fucking girl, you're unbelievable, baby. Just wait until the day I claim every one of your little holes."

His finger presses into my asshole, and I jump in surprise. "Daddy!"

"Shh, baby. I'm not going to fuck you there tonight. Just let me play a bit. Relax. Daddy will take care of you."

He starts to thrust into my pussy in long, deep strokes while continuing to circle my asshole with his thumb. The longer he does it, the better it feels, and the more relaxed I become. When he pushes through the tight ring, I cry out and buck my hips. The sensation is different but so, so good.

"So tight, Chloe. Shit. You're going to kill me with this cunt. Best fucking death ever."

I giggle, but it turns into a moan as he presses his finger deeper into my ass and starts fucking me harder and faster. My entire body is tingling with so many sensations, making this the best sex I could ever imagine.

With his free hand, he reaches around my hip and gives my clit a gentle slap that has me crying out. Then he starts rubbing circles around it, the head of his cock brushing against that perfect spot inside me.

The room starts to blur, and all I can do is feel and hear. Bash. Fucking me. Touching me. Praising me. Telling me I'm his good girl.

"Oh, fuck!" I scream when my entire body tenses and then lets go like an explosion.

"That's my girl. Come all over Daddy's cock. Fuck, you're so tight, Chloe. Goddammit," he growls.

His thrusts become erratic as my pussy throbs around him. His balls slap my clit, and our moans fill the room for several seconds as we ride the beautiful waves of ecstasy while we're still joined together as one.

As soon as his cock stops pulsing inside me, I collapse forward onto the mattress, not caring that my bottom is up in the air, practically swaying in his face. I don't have the brain space to worry about it right now. I'm too busy grinning from ear to ear while my body comes down from the high of multiple orgasms. I was definitely wrong about sex. It is impressive. But only with Bash.

After a few minutes, when we've finally caught our breaths, he gently tugs my ankles so I go flat on the bed and then covers me with a sheet. "Be right back, baby. Stay there."

Yeah, like I'm going to be going anywhere anytime soon. I might need a walker just to get around tomorrow. I'm nearly asleep when the sheet is pulled back, letting cool air brush against my damp skin.

"It's too late for a bath tonight, so I'm going to clean you up with a cloth. I'll give you a bath in the morning."

I hum, not caring about what he's saying because my mind is mush. Then he rolls me over, spreads my legs, and puts a wet washcloth between my thighs. I jolt in surprise. "What are you doing?"

He's kneeling on the bed, still naked, staring at me with intense but loving eyes. "I'm cleaning you up. Lie back and rest. Daddy will take care of you."

When I don't obey right away, he raises an eyebrow. "Do you need a reminder of what happens when you disobey me?"

"Eep! No." I drop down onto the mattress and bring my arms up to my face to hide my embarrassment. He's cleaning up my pussy and ass like I'm a child. Like I can't do it myself. Is there a hole I can crawl into? But also, can I crawl into his lap and sleep in his arms because he makes me feel so special and cared for? I've read a lot of books with Daddy Doms in them, but I never expected they were a thing in real life, or at least if they were, they weren't like this. Bash is better than the ones I've read about. And he's mine.

He pulls the cloth away and covers me with the sheet again. I peek at him from under my arms as he walks back to the bathroom, his perfectly round ass on display. God, how many squats does he do a day? That's hot. I'd like to watch him work out sometime. It would definitely be droolworthy.

A few minutes later, he comes out of the bathroom with something in his arms. I prop myself up on my elbows, trying to see what it is, and when I do, I tilt my head in confusion.

"I wanted you to have a friend to sleep with here until we get you moved in. I know it's not your yellow duck, but it's a baby yellow duck, and I thought they could be friends once they both live here."

My mouth hangs open as he holds out a small, fluffy stuffed duck for me. My hands tremble, and when I bring it to my chest, I catch a whiff of Bash's cologne on the animal. Warmth spreads through me. Something about his scent always calms me and makes me feel safe. Loved.

"You got this for me?"

He shrugs. "I actually bought a whole zoo of stuffed animals for you, but yellow seems to be your favorite color, so I thought I'd give you this one first."

My eyes go round. He's standing so nonchalantly,

like what he just gave me means nothing. I'd never tell him, but this stuffed toy means more to me than the beautiful earrings he gave me. Not that I don't love the earrings. I do. But my stuffies are what bring me comfort. Every time I'm anxious or I can't sleep or I need something to hug, they've always been there for me.

"Daddy," I start, but my voice catches in my throat. "I can't believe this. This is so thoughtful."

"I love you, Little girl. I want you to be happy. I'm hard-headed, and I won't always do things right, but you're my girl, and I want you to have everything you want and need that brings you joy and comfort."

Tears roll down my cheeks, and I pat the bed for him to join me. My throat is too tight for me to get the words out, but I want to tell him that he's the one who brings me joy and comfort now.

He holds up a finger. "I'll be right back."

I wait as he disappears into the bathroom again and reappears a moment later, this time his arms completely full of stuffed animals. A lion, a bear, a giraffe, a monkey, a koala, a leopard, and a tiger. He drops them onto the bed, and I giggle as they fall like it's raining stuffies.

"Daddy! I can't believe you did this."

"Get used to it, my girl. Now, scoot all your friends over to your side. I might be willing to allow them in bed with us, but they stay on your side because nothing is getting between me and my girl."

Giggles erupt as I move each toy to the edge of the bed on my side. He grunts and climbs in next to me, immediately pulling me against his naked body. I melt into him, burying my face in the crook of his arm as he slides it under me. My breathing slows. My entire body relaxes knowing I'm safe, loved, and exactly where I'm meant to be.

"That's my girl. My good girl," he murmurs as we drift off to sleep together.

## 20

## BASH

"I don't want to sit in bed all day."

The corners of my mouth twitch as I button up my black dress shirt. "You don't have a choice. You have finals starting tomorrow, and you were up way too late last night. The only place you're allowed to go today is the potty and then right back to bed. Understood?"

Chloe has her arms crossed over her chest and her bottom lip popped out in a pout. "This doesn't seem fair."

"It might not feel fair, but it's best for your health. I'll see if Cali and Scarlet can come by for a while to hang out. I'm sure they'll bring some activities you can do together."

Her scowl melts slightly. "Where are you going?"

I grab my suit jacket and put it on. "I have to take

care of some work stuff. I'll be home as soon as I can."

Her eyes roam over my body, and that attention alone has my cock hardening. Remembering one more thing, I go to the suit I left folded up on the chair from last night and dig her panties from the pocket. When I turn around, her mouth is hanging open.

"What are you doing with those?"

Keeping my gaze on hers, I bring them up to my nose and inhale deeply. My cock throbs as I take in her addictive scent. "I'm bringing these with me, so I can smell you whenever I need to."

Her pointed nipples press against the T-shirt I put on her before we had breakfast this morning.

"You can't carry around my dirty panties all the time."

I shove them into my pocket and stalk over to where she's sitting with her back resting against the headboard. "Oh, yes, I can. I'm going to buy you truckloads of panties, so I can keep every single dirty pair after you've worn them. I'm going to build a sanctuary for all my girl's dirty panties. I'll visit it every Sunday for blessings."

"You're…"

I grin. "Crazy? Unhinged? Insane? Yeah, baby. I'm all of that and more, and I'm not sorry about it.

Better get used to having a man worship the ground you walk on."

She squirms slightly and makes a small whimpering noise. I wink and lean forward to kiss her.

"I have cameras everywhere in this house. I'll know if you do anything other than go potty. So, unless you want to make another trip over my knee when I get home, I suggest you stay put. Okay?"

"Okaaaay. Sheesh. Maybe you should handcuff me to the bed, so you don't have to worry about me running off."

I cock my head and raise an eyebrow, but she holds up her hands and shakes her head.

"I was kidding, Daddy. It was a joke!"

"The idea has merit, Little one."

She's grinning, and when I lean forward to kiss her again, she wraps her arms around my neck. The thought of leaving her has a ball forming in the pit of my stomach. I'm struggling to take a deep breath. I want to keep her connected to me as much as possible. Unfortunately, the business I need to take care of is dirty, and I won't do anything to bring my girl into the depths of that world.

"I love you. Call or text me if you need anything. Even if it's nothing and you want to talk to me. You're my first priority, baby."

"I know, Daddy. Thank you. Please be careful."

"Always, Little one. I have a reason to come home now."

Kieran, Grady, Killian, and Ronan are already at Declan's when I get there. Scarlet and Cali are perched on their Daddies' laps.

"Chloe is at home with strict orders to stay in bed and rest today since she has finals over the next few days. If you two don't have anything going on, I'm sure she'd love some company," I say to the girls.

Cali's face lights up. "Yes! Can we show her our piranha pond?"

I raise an eyebrow at my sister-in-law. "Can she see it from her bed?"

Her shoulders fall. "No."

"Then the answer is no. You can go over there and watch movies or color or make bracelets. Something that keeps her in bed. Got it?"

Declan taps Cali on the bottom. "If either of you two do anything that causes Chloe to break the rules, you're going to be in trouble too. Understand?"

"Yes," Cali and Scarlet say in unison.

"I need some help with a gift for Chloe. Are you two willing to help me with some crafting later?"

Their eyes light up as they bob their heads. Cali claps her hands together, and Scarlet is practically wiggling right off Killian's lap.

"Okay, but don't say anything to Chloe. It's a surprise."

"Pinky promise," Scarlet offers.

The three of us hook our fingers together, and I know my secret is safe. I'm pretty sure both of these girls would go to their graves with a secret if a pinky promise were involved. The CIA wouldn't be able to break them.

"Your guards will drive you to Bash's house," Killian instructs. "Go get ready."

The girls disappear from Declan's office, and the six of us are left to talk business.

I glance at Kieran. "You filled them in on what we found out?"

Kieran nods. "Yes. We've also alerted Andrei and Alessandro, along with the rest of the syndicates. They all offered their support and resources."

"This is more personal for Andrei since this is happening in his homeland. He asked if he could be part of taking down Ronald and anyone else involved," Declan says.

The room is quiet for a moment. Not long ago, we would have considered Andrei an enemy. Guilty by association and all that. But the way he's been cooperating with us since he took over as the boss of the Bratva, we feel like we can mostly trust him. And if he wants to help in bringing down a bunch of human traffickers and who knows what else, I'm all for it.

"I think it's a good idea. Might help to mend any remaining tension between the Bratva and Irish if we work together on this," I offer.

Kieran, Ronan, and Grady all nod. When we look at Killian, his eyes are dark, and his jaw is tense.

"If the Russians make one wrong move, I'll kill Andrei myself. He may not have been the one who directly hurt my girl, but it doesn't mean I forgive any of them," Killian says firmly.

Declan stares at him for several seconds before he nods. "Agreed. This is their chance to prove they're with us and not against us."

I rise from my chair. "Let's go visit our friend, Ronald, then."

"Looks like someone got out of dodge quick," Declan says.

We're standing in Ronald's closet, where a good portion of the hangers are empty, and drawers are left open with clothes thrown around messily inside.

"Fuck! We need to call Cage and have him do his spy shit," I growl.

Cage Black is some kind of underground, super spy assassin who does freelance jobs. I've never met a man smarter or sneakier than Cage, and he has a whole team of men just like him. They make us look like fucking saints. Always good to have an alliance with a guy like Cage.

Kieran scowls. "Let's go pay Bradley a visit and see whether he knows where Ronald might have gone. Cage can meet us at the warehouse."

I glance at Andrei. "Are you still in contact with the girl who got free? Is she here in the States?"

Andrei nods. "She's afraid to return to Russia. She said there are people everywhere going after young women and girls. I have her in a safe-house for now."

"Would she talk to us?" I ask.

Nikolai, Andrei's underboss, shrugs. "She only speaks Russian, but we can interpret. She's scared, though. She's only sixteen. I'm working on getting her family over here to be with her."

"Let's go deal with Bradley first, and meet with Cage, then we'll talk to the girl," Kieran says.

As we walk through Ronald's house, I take every photograph of my girl I come across. I doubt that the fucker ever looked at them. They were probably set out by her mother when she was alive. Either way,

I'm leaving no trace of my baby in this place. The bastard will never lay eyes on Chloe again. Not even in a picture frame.

On the way to the warehouse, I check the home cameras and smile as I watch my sweet girl talking animatedly to Cali and Scarlet. She fits right in with them. Not that I had any worries about that. Slowly, I reach into my pocket and pull out her panties. Keeping them bunched in my fist, I bring them up to my nose and inhale. Like an addict getting their fix, I relax. I close my mind and take in the mix of her arousal and the spritz of her perfume I sprayed onto them before I left the house.

"Jesus Christ, Bash. Can you be any more fucking obvious about sniffing your woman's panties?" Ronan asks.

He shakes his head in disbelief, but the corners of his lips are tipped up slightly. I know my brother, and when he finds his girl, he'll be even worse than me.

"Don't be jealous you don't have any panties to sniff," I snap.

Kieran turns around in the front passenger seat. "Are you seriously fucking sniffing my sister's underwear? With me right here in the car? You sick fuck."

I shrug and take another whiff before shoving the black silk into my pocket. "What did Paisley smell like last night?"

"Like pineapple and sugar and… You know what, fuck off," Kieran says, flipping me off.

Ronan and I chuckle. I knew Paisley had gotten under Kieran's skin. My best friend sits stiffly in his seat, seething silently. I grin and raise my eyebrows at Ronan, who nods.

Our men greet us as we enter the warehouse. It stinks in here. Like sweat, piss, blood, and impending death. Bradley sits in the same chair as yesterday, his hands and feet bound with chains.

"Did you miss us?" I ask.

When his eyes focus, and he notices how many of us there are, he starts whimpering.

"Our friend Ronald is MIA. Any chance you know where he might have gone?" Kieran asks.

Bradley shakes his head. "No. I have no idea. We didn't know each other like that. It was all a business deal."

Andrei picks up a metal tire wrench and steps forward. "A business deal to bring women from my country here to use them as prostitutes. All so you can fill your greedy fucking pockets! Do you know what I do to people like you? I let them die slowly, painfully, over time, just like those women will when they're being drugged and raped by men like you. Who is behind this business deal?"

I kind of want to slap Andrei on the back right now. Maybe he's not so bad.

Bradley eyes the iron bar and shakes his head. "I don't know."

Andrei swings once, the iron crashing into one of Bradley's knees with a loud crack. Bradley howls in pain as sweat drips down his face.

"You might only have two knees I can break, but you also have two elbows, ten fingers, and many other bones. So, I'm going to ask you again. Who is behind this?"

I grin as Andrei raises the bar.

Bradley screams. "Wait! Okay! Okay! I'll tell you!"

"Smart choice," I say. "Tell us."

His breaths are sharp and shallow. He won't look any of us in the eyes. Cowards never do.

"He goes by Smoke. I don't know his real name. That's what Ronald calls him. He's the leader of some underground gang or something," Bradley rushes out.

"Why would Ronald get involved with a gang?" Kieran asks.

Bradley shakes his head, tears dripping down his face. "I don't know. I swear to God. That's all I know. He offered me a ton of money to sign off on the ship docking and more money for each successful shipment of women."

Andrei takes another step forward. "You knew they were moving women from my country? From my homeland?"

"I'm sorry! I'm so sorry! Please! Please don't!" Bradley begs.

The iron bar slams into his other knee. Andrei growls as he moves back, his face pinched in disgust.

"Anyone else have any questions for this waste of space?" I ask.

Everyone says no, and I move close to Bradley and lean down until we're eye to eye.

"You tried to hurt my girl. I'm sure you understand I can't forgive that."

His face contorts as he sucks in a breath. "I'm sorry. It was a mistake."

I pull my gun from the holster and raise it to his head. "No. It was a choice, Bradley. And for you, it was a deadly one."

A few minutes later, we leave the warehouse and pile into our SUVs. Cage agreed to meet with us at one of his secret locations. After that, I need to stop at Chloe's townhouse before I go home to her because if I have my way, she won't ever return to that place again.

## 21

## CHLOE

If Cali and Scarlet hadn't come to visit me today, I think I would have gone bonkers. They brought all kinds of stuff for us to do, but we spent most of the time talking and laughing while watching animated movies.

Bash texted me a dozen times throughout the day to check in on me and ask how I was doing. A woman by the name of Grace appeared in the bedroom at precisely one o'clock with a tray of sandwiches, fruit, carrot sticks, and chips for all of us. Cali informed me she's technically Declan's house manager, but she tends to take care of everyone on the estate. The sweet older woman had been thrilled to meet me and hugged me before she left us to eat.

"So, I got my first real spanking," I say quietly.

Cali's eyes sparkle as she sits up on her knees. "Oh my God, tell us all about it."

Scarlet bobs her head and grins. "Uh-huh. Don't leave anything out."

My cheeks heat as I replay last night for them, and by the time I'm done, my bottom is tingling.

"That is so hot. Oh my gosh, I knew Bash would be a strict Daddy," Scarlet squeals.

"You poor thing. I hate the hairbrush. I'd prefer Daddy's belt any day over the hairbrush."

I don't say anything because it was awful. But when Bash used the same brush this morning as he gently freed all the tangles from my hair, I got turned on knowing he was using the same thing to take care of me as he used to punish me. I guess in both situations he was caring for me.

"What did Kieran's face look like when Paisley stomped past him? Did he get that pinched scowl going on? Like he couldn't believe anyone would defy him?" Cali asks.

We all giggle hysterically. I probably shouldn't laugh at my brother, but the way Cali described him is spot on.

"He totally did. I thought his head was going to explode."

Scarlet claps her hands. "We need to meet Paisley. She'll fit in perfectly with all of us. Anyone who isn't afraid of Kieran is a friend of ours."

When Cali and Scarlet leave around three, my cheeks hurt from laughing so much. Any concern about them not liking me is gone, and I feel like I have two more best friends.

After a while, I find a movie to watch and curl up with my new duck stuffie. My phone vibrates, bringing an automatic smile to my lips and a tingle rushing to my core. It should be annoying that he's checking on me as often as he is, but I love it. He's taking time out of his busy day for me.

Instead of Bash's name, it's Paisley's.

> Paisley: How's your ass feel today?

> Chloe: Sore. And loved.

> Paisley: I bet. Is Bash less upset now?

> Chloe: Yes. Although, he informed me this morning that he's going to start having bodyguards follow me around soon.

My phone immediately starts ringing, and I swipe to answer it.

"Girl, he said what?" Paisley demands.

I giggle. "It's normal. Cali and Scarlet have guards anywhere they go. It's a precaution. I'm connected to the mafia now, so I could be a target for one of their enemies. He said they will stay out of my way, and after a while, I won't even know they're there."

Paisley's silent for a minute. "Are you sure you want to get mixed up in all of this? It all seems pretty intense. This isn't the norm for people, you know? What if something happens to you?"

I stroke my stuffie's fur and sigh. She isn't wrong. I've had the same thoughts. Bash is more than intense. Maybe it's because I've always known my brother to be a mafia man that it's not as big of a deal for me as it is for her. She's never known anyone in this life. There are dangers to it. Kieran has told me that all my life. That if anything ever happened to him, I needed to remember how much he loves me. I hated when he would say stuff like that. I don't want to think about anything happening to my brother.

"Something could happen to me anywhere. I could get hit by a bus while crossing the street. A maggot could eat my brains while I sleep. I could drown in my bathtub. There's always a risk. I guess I'd prefer to enjoy my life while I'm here and not worry so much about the what-ifs. Besides, Bash is so overprotective. He's not going to let anything happen to me."

Paisley's quiet for a few seconds. "You're in love with him."

I giggle. "I am."

"I fucking knew it," she laughs. "How's his dick?"

"Paisley!"

She huffs. "Fine. Fine. Keep all the deets to yourself. But was it good? Better than your previous lovers?"

"Oh, God. There's no comparison. Bash is… everything and more. I'm talking multiple orgasms in one night. He even cleaned me up with a washcloth afterward. It was amazing."

"Okay. Fine. I approve of your boyfriend. Just, when you bring him around, don't let your brother come, okay? He's a total jerk."

My lips pull back into a wide smile. "Okay. But Kieran is actually a sweetheart. He's just protective."

Paisley snorts. "Let's agree to disagree. Hey, someone's at the door. I'll call you later. Enjoy all your orgasms, and if you meet any of Bash's nice friends, send them my way."

I'm giggling as we end the call. Oh, Paisley. Whoever ends up with that girl is going to have their hands full.

BASH WALKS in through the door not long after I get off the phone with Paisley. With Quackers in his hand. And a huge duffel bag.

"What? How did you get that?"

He smiles and winks. "Daddy has his ways. I wanted you to have your stuffie here so you're more comfortable. We'll get movers to bring the rest this week."

I bolt upright and cock my head. "What are you talking about? Movers? Daddy, I can't move in with you. I have a lease with Paisley. I can't ditch her. She can't afford to live by herself."

Bash sets the bag down and drops Quackers on the bed before he reaches for me. He plucks me up and carries me to the chair that he sat on last night while he spanked my bottom. My skin tingles as panic rushes through me. Is he angry?

When he sits down, he settles me on his lap and holds me against his chest. "Baby, you're an amazing friend. I know Paisley means a lot to you. I would never plan something without making sure she was taken care of too. I've paid the lease in full for the next two years. I've also put a lump sum toward each of the utilities, so she won't have to worry about any bills. Her student loans have also been paid off, and there will be groceries delivered to her weekly. Now, give me your next argument so I can see that it's taken care of."

My mouth drops open as I stare at him in shock. Did all those words actually come from his mouth? I'm no math expert, but I'm pretty sure her student loans were in the hundreds of thousands. What is happening right now? Is this my life? Having a man, a Daddy, who sees a problem and fixes it in the blink of an eye?

Will Paisley be okay by herself? She doesn't make a ton of money but without having any bills to pay, she could start building her savings. We've lived together for so long. I'll miss her.

"She'll get lonely," I whisper as I look up at him with big, round eyes.

He tilts his head slightly, then nods. "I'll get her a dog. Multiple dogs if she wants. You think she's more of a Golden Retriever kind of girl or Pit Bull? I'm guessing Pit Bulls are more her style. Her bark is bigger than her bite. She likes to seem tough, but I can tell it's all a façade."

I press the palm of my hand to his mouth and start giggling. "Daddy! You. Are. Insane."

"Maybe. But you still love me, yeah?"

Shaking my head, I flop against his chest again and sigh. "Daddy, I want to live with you. But I need to talk to Paisley. I don't want her to feel like I'm ditching her or anything. We've lived together since our first day of college."

"You'll miss not seeing her every day," he says thoughtfully.

I nod. "I think so."

"She can move in with us. She'd be safer here on

the estate anyway. She can have the guest suite on the other side of the house. All of the rooms are soundproofed anyway."

My heart pounds, and I'm about two seconds away from jumping this man's bones. He will literally do anything to make me happy. I could ask for a castle in Ireland, and I think he'd have us on a jet tomorrow to go pick one out.

"Can I talk to Paisley about all of this?"

"Of course, baby. Just know that whatever happens, you and I are living together. I'll move into that townhouse if I have to."

A smile spreads so wide my cheeks hurt. He told me he wouldn't give me any space, and he meant it.

"Okay, Daddy."

His cock throbs against my bottom, sending a zing of electricity right to my pussy. I grind against him and moan softly as his cock rolls against my clit.

"Is my girl feeling needy?"

I nod and wiggle against him again. "Yes. I've been thinking about you all day."

He groans and slides his fingers into my hair, tugging slightly. "Thinking naughty thoughts? I should have known you'd be a dirty girl. The feeling's mutual, though. I couldn't stop thinking about the taste of your pussy and how tight it was around my cock."

A soft whimper escapes, and I angle my head so I

can kiss his cheek. First, I kiss, then I nip, getting rewarded with a rougher tug on my scalp.

"Get on your knees, baby," he commands.

With his help, I slide down to the soft floor, kneeling before him. He stares at me with half-lidded eyes, his index finger running gentle circles around my cheek.

"Fuck, I like you like this. On your knees in front of me, looking so damn needy for my cock. Is that what you need, baby? My cock in your pretty mouth?"

I slide my hands up his thighs and bring them together over his bulge. It jumps under my touch. "Uh-huh."

"Take off the shirt," he commands quietly.

Since it's the only thing I'm wearing, as soon as I lift it over my head, I'm left naked before him. And he's still fully clothed in his black suit. It's an interesting feeling. He can see every flaw, every scar, every single thing I hate about myself. His sparkling gaze flickers with heat and hunger. I'm the one who's naked and on my knees, but he's the one who's looking at me like I'm a goddess.

"Who do you belong to, Chloe?"

My fingers tremble as I start to unbuckle his belt. "You, Daddy. Only you."

He slowly nods. "That's right, baby. And I'm going to protect you. Protect you from all your pain, past and present. No one hurts my girl. Do you understand me? Not one fucking person on this earth gets to hurt my girl and live."

It's like he's conveying a secret message, but I'm too focused on getting his cock out to think about it.

"Yes, Daddy. I know you'll keep me safe. Always."

His hand roughly cups my chin. "Always, Chloe."

A shiver works its way down my spine as his stare burns into me.

After a few seconds, he lets go of my chin and leans back in the chair again. "Take out my cock, baby."

Following his instructions makes my hands shake less. I'm doing what he wants me to. Being his good girl. After working the zipper, I tuck my fingers into the waistband of his underwear and pull down, letting his cock spring free. Licking my lips, I glance up at him for approval before wrapping my hand around it. A bead of semen leaks from the tip. Unable to resist, I lean forward to lick it off.

Bash's head falls back against the chair as he groans. "You're such a good girl, Chloe. My good girl. Fuck, I love you."

My cheeks heat as my smile spreads. Every muscle in my body melts over his words. I'll never get tired of his praise. Slowly, I run my tongue along the underside of his cock, and when I get to the crown, I open wider and suck him down as far as I can go. He curses and thrusts his hips up slightly, making me gag. Arousal drips down my legs, and when he thrusts again, I moan.

He reaches out and tugs on one of my nipples, rolling it between his fingers as I move up and down his shaft, sucking and licking every glorious inch of him.

"Fuck, baby. Fuck!" he shouts as he grabs a fistful of my hair and holds my head still. "You keep sucking like a goddamn goddess, and I'm going to explode before I get to fuck your pretty pussy."

I grin and stick my tongue out to flick over the head of his cock. His eyes narrow, and he shakes his head. "Such a tease," he murmurs.

Before I can respond, he reaches down and tugs me up from the floor, setting me on his lap. I whimper as the ridge of his cock presses against my clit. He glides his hand up my tummy and between my breasts, not stopping until he's at the base of my throat. Slowly, he tightens his grip, putting pressure on the sides of my neck.

"You're mine. No one else will ever have you. You belong to me, and I belong to you. It's us against the world, baby."

I nod and whimper as his grip tightens. My clit throbs, loving his rough handling. This man would never harm me, but damn, I love when he's intense like this. It's intimidating, but it doesn't scare me. Nothing about Bash scares me. Not the way he loves me. Not the life he lives. Not the things I know he does. Maybe I'm just as unhinged as he is. Whatever I am, it feels so fucking good. So right.

"Do you trust me, Chloe?"

"Yes," I reply without hesitation.

He stares at me for several seconds, his eyes glittering with hunger. "Good girl. Stand up and come to the edge of the chair, then bend over."

Chills run over my skin as I climb off his lap. He rises and towers over me. When I glance up at him, he raises an eyebrow. Slowly, I lower myself, resting my hands on the cushion.

"Stay." He runs a finger down my spine before leaving my side.

I turn my head to watch him move around the room, stripping off his clothes and then going to the nightstand where he takes something from the drawer. When he returns to me, he leans down so his face is close to mine. The mix of his cologne and the slight scent of whiskey dances around me like a soft cloud. My Daddy. My safe place. My home.

"I'm going to fuck your ass tonight, baby. And you're going to be a good girl and take my cock all the way, aren't you?"

A whimper escapes. Sweat prickles low on my

back. Goosebumps rise as he runs his hand over the curve of my bottom.

"Yes."

He smiles and kisses me. "First, though, I need to eat. I'm fucking starving for my favorite meal."

I squint, trying to understand what he means. Then he moves behind me, drops to his knees, and buries his face in my pussy. His tongue darts out, hitting my clit at the perfect angle, and I jolt, kicking a foot back in surprise.

He chuckles against my clit. "Keep your feet on the floor, princess, or I'll have to tie you up."

"Oh, God."

His laughter vibrates against my pussy. "My girl likes that idea. Noted, baby girl. Noted. Now stop distracting me, I'm trying to focus on my meal."

Using his thumbs, he spreads my lips and starts to lick and suck like his entire life depends on it. I cry out and wiggle against his mouth every time he scrapes his teeth over my sensitive nub.

He lowers one of his hands, and a second later, I hear a cap pop open. I yelp when cold liquid drips onto my asshole. Bash quickly starts massaging it in, gently probing my tight hole with his finger.

"Relax, baby. Breathe for me."

I focus on his instructions instead of the strange intrusion, and with each breath I take, he presses his finger in a bit more. When he starts moving it in and out, the slight burning sensation turns into pleasure. He flicks my clit several times, then sucks, all in perfect rhythm.

"Daddy! Oh! Oh!"

The burning returns as he adds a second finger, stretching my hole to the max. I whimper and moan, unsure if I love it or hate it, but also knowing I don't want it to stop anytime soon.

Pressure builds inside me. I claw at the cushion, chasing the release that's so close yet so far away. Then, he bites down on my clit and sucks hard, and my entire world explodes. I scream and buck, my orgasm crashing through me so hard that my vision blurs and sweat drips down my neck.

Bash moves behind me while I'm still crying out, and a second later, he pulls his fingers from my ass and slowly pushes his cock in through the tight ring.

"Fuck, baby. You're such a good girl. You drive me wild," he grits out as he inches himself deeper.

He wraps his fist in my hair, holding me firmly without causing pain. I take as many deep breaths as I can. His cock is much bigger than his fingers.

"I'm so proud of you, baby. You're taking me so well. I love seeing you stretched around me like this."

His words are like a massage over my skin, helping me to relax completely and let him in all the way. When his hips meet my bottom, he pauses, rubbing his thumb over my ass in slow circles.

"That's my girl. Keep breathing. You're so tight."

"Please, Daddy. Please fuck me. Please, I need more."

The thrusts start out slow and gentle, but soon, he's fucking me hard and fast. I scream and moan, the pressure building within me again. He snakes a hand around my waist. As soon as his fingers start to circle my clit, I shatter.

"Fuck!" he shouts as he bucks erratically until his cock starts to pulse.

As soon as my orgasm subsides, my legs give out, and I go limp over the arm of the chair, letting out a deep sigh.

"Wow," I whisper.

He chuckles and slowly pulls free of my ass. When I don't move, he leans down so his face is near mine, his eyes pinched in concern.

"Are you okay, baby?"

I grin and nod. "Yes. I'm perfect. But I'm not moving from this spot for the rest of the night. My muscles won't work. Just throw a blanket over me."

His laugh is deep and melodic as he shakes his head. "You don't have to move, baby. Daddy will take care of everything."

Just as he always does. This man is nothing like I would have ever expected, yet he's everything I've ever hoped for.

## 22

## BASH

By the time I get my girl in and out of the bath and tucked into bed, she's barely able to keep her eyes open. It's still early, but she needs a good night's sleep so she can be fresh and ready for her first round of finals tomorrow.

I've already arranged for her to be driven to and from school. I would do it myself, but tomorrow, I'll be hunting down Ronald and whoever else is involved in this whole trafficking situation. I will also be putting the finishing touches on her surprise. I hope to hell she loves it. There's no reason she shouldn't. My only concern is that she'll feel like I'm making decisions for her, and that's the last thing I want to do. Ultimately, it will be up to her, and I'll love and support her no matter what.

She clutches Quackers in her arms as she sleeps

beside me while I work. Cage is already hunting for us, and he's sent information regarding Ronald's finances. The asshole is broke. Worse than broke. He's in deep debt.

Until I know the whole picture, I don't want to tell Chloe what we know. There's no doubt in my mind that I'm going to end his life. I'm going to make him pay dearly for hurting my girl before his death. But part of me hopes that whatever he's gotten himself into with this trafficking shit isn't something he's doing because he wants to. It doesn't make it right, but it will hurt Chloe badly if she finds out her father is choosing to traffic young women and girls.

After placing all the online orders I need, I close my laptop and slide down the bed. Chloe hums and curls into me, her face resting on my chest. I stare at her for a long time, wondering how something so precious as her could possibly want someone as fucked-up as me. She's strong. Stronger than she realizes. And I'm never going to pass up an opportunity to tell her that. Her father was her demon, but too bad for him, I'm a fucking monster who will destroy the world for her.

"I'm nervous."

I stand behind her, brushing her hair while she applies contour or whatever it is she calls it. It's brown and does some kind of shading to make her face look skinnier. At least that's what she says. I think her face is pure perfection no matter what, but when I told her that, she grinned and rolled her eyes.

"Don't be nervous. You got this. You've studied and gone through years of schooling. You're going to do great, baby. I believe in you."

She sighs and digs through her makeup bag. When she pulls out a tube of something that I think is lipstick, she grins and holds it up. Then she takes off the cap, and I'm thoroughly confused. It's a pointed blade. Only an inch long, but the glint of metal tells me it's sharp as fuck.

"Baby girl, what is that?"

"Paisley gave it to me," she says with a soft smile. "When we lived on campus, she bought both of us one, and we always carried them in our purses, just in case. We watched videos on where to stab it for the most painful result."

My eyes widen. Fucking Paisley. I like that girl.

"Why's it in your makeup bag then?"

Shrugging, she puts the cap back on. "I don't know. I guess I didn't feel like I needed it after I moved back home."

I stare at the tube for several seconds. "Keep it in

your purse at all times, baby. It's a good thing to have. After finals, I'm going to teach you some other skills to protect yourself."

She looks back at me in the reflection of the mirror, opening her mouth like she's going to argue. I raise an eyebrow and pin her with a stern look.

With a sigh, she slides it into the back pocket of her jeans. "Okay. I'll keep it in my purse."

"You're the most beautiful woman I've ever seen, you know," I whisper.

Her lips pull into a wide smile. "Yeah? Well, you're okay yourself, Daddy."

I chuckle and shake my head. "Brat. Come on. You need to eat before you head to school."

"I can drive myself, you know."

"No. Cullen will drive you and wait in the car. If you need to go anywhere afterward, he can take you. Just make sure you let me know so I'm aware of what you're doing. Understand?"

When I tap on her bottom, she quickly bobs her head. "I know, Daddy. I promise I'll tell you everywhere I go from now on. Do you want me to let you know when I'm going to the bathroom, too?"

"Yes. I would like that."

She stops mid-step and stares at me with her mouth hanging open. "You can't be serious, Daddy."

I turn and cup her chin. "Don't ask sarcastic questions if you don't want sarcastic answers, naughty girl. Although, I do like the idea of knowing all my girl's personal business, so maybe I should make that a rule."

"Daddy," she whines.

I kiss her temple and chuckle. "Okay, we'll put that rule on the back burner for now."

By the time I help her into the SUV, I'm already counting down the minutes until she gets home.

"Good luck today. You're going to do great. I'm so proud of you."

She grins and throws her arms around my neck. "I love you."

"I love you too, Little girl. I'll see you later."

Kieran pulls up in his Range Rover right as Cullen drives away. I get in, and we head to Declan's house. Hopefully, we'll have some more information from Cage this morning.

Alessandro De Luca and Luciano Ricci are in his office when we arrive. Alessandro leads the Cosa Nostra, and Luciano is his second in command. The Italians are our closest allies. The rest of the syndicates have no idea of our working relationship, and we like to keep it that way. It's a secret weapon when we need it.

"Alessandro, Luciano," I say, shaking both men's hands.

"We got some intel from one of our men about this gang that's been operating here in Seattle.

They've been distributing dirty guns to teenage kids. After speaking with Declan, I believe we are both after the same group. The name Smoke was brought to my attention," Alessandro says.

"Smoke is the name of the guy Bradley mentioned...before he was disposed of. He said Smoke and his gang are the ones responsible for the trafficking." I lean against the wall, my arms crossed over my chest.

"So, we have dirty guns on the streets and young women being kidnapped and brought over from Russia. Are the guns coming out of Russia too?" Ronan asks.

Declan shrugs. "No idea."

I cock my head. "When I met with Knox and Angel the other night, they wanted to get their weapons from us because the people they've been using are giving them bad guns. They mentioned they thought there was something else shady going on with their supplier. Let's call Knox and see whether he can shed some light on who they are."

Killian pulls out his phone and starts tapping on the screen.

"Maybe we need to bring Andrei in on this. If anyone can find out what's happening in Russia, it's him. He was livid that girls were being kidnapped from his country," Kieran says.

Declan runs his tongue over his top teeth and glances at Alessandro, who gives a slight nod.

"I want extra guards on the property while he's here. Cali, Scarlet, and Chloe aren't to be in the house while he's inside," Declan says.

Patrick, one of our long-time men who is standing guard near the doorway, nods and gets to work on his phone.

I pull up the GPS app and check my girl's location. "Chloe's at school until late this afternoon. Cali and Scarlet can go to my house so they can finish the project we started."

"Fine, but I want at least a dozen of our guys there with them," Declan says. "I don't think Andrei or Nikolai want to start any problems, but after what we've been through with the Russians recently, I'd like to take extra precautions."

"Definitely, brother. Thanks for including Chloe in that," I say, smiling at him appreciatively.

He nods. "She's family. Always has been. Always will be."

Kieran and I exchange glances, and I know my best friend is as thankful to Declan as I am.

"Any word from Cage?" I ask.

Grady clears his throat. "Only that he hasn't found Ronald yet, and he's sending a couple of his associates to Russia to see what they can find out.

Hopefully Andrei has some men over there who can assist in the effort."

"Andrei and Nikolai will be here in an hour. Let's get the girls ready to go and meet back here after." Killian strolls toward the door and swings it open.

It only takes a few minutes before Cali and Scarlet, their arms full of stuff, are ushered out the front door by Declan and Killian. I follow and get into the SUV that will take them to my house. I want to see their faces when they find out what I've done for Chloe.

Once we're inside, I lead them to the room right next to my office. "Are you ready to see it?"

Scarlet glares at me. "Oh my gosh, stop trying to be dramatic, and let us see. We're dying here."

Killian chuckles, and I roll my eyes, but I push open the French doors. Cali, Scarlet, Declan, and Killian all look around the room.

"Uncle Bash, this is…this is so amazing. Chloe is going to love it. Can I be here when you show her?" Cali asks, swiping at her eyes as tears fall.

I grin and go to her, wrapping an arm around her shoulders. "No. But I'll have her call you and tell you all about it afterward."

The girls huff, but they're beaming.

"Tell Patrick where you want everything, and he'll hang it. I don't want you two smashing your fingers with the hammer," I warn.

Cali rolls her eyes. "You act as if we're total klutzes."

"Baby, you stubbed your toe on the carpet this morning," Declan says.

"Oh my gosh, Daddy. You're being dramatic," she scoffs.

Raising an eyebrow, he grins as he embraces his Little girl. "Am I? I'm pretty sure there's a Care Bears bandage on your big toe that proves I'm not because despite there being no blood, you were sure you were going to die if I didn't put one on you."

"You really didn't have to call me out like that, you know. I'm your wife. You're supposed to be on my side," Cali argues.

Declan leans down and kisses the tip of her nose. "Oh, baby, I'm always on your side. I'd tear this world apart for you. But I'll also call you on your shit when you're being a brat."

She wraps her arms around his waist and huffs. "Yeah, yeah. Don't you guys have some place to be? We have stuff to do here."

After we're practically pushed out of my own house, we return to Declan's right as Andrei and Nikolai pull up.

The air is thick with tension as the Russians and the Italians glare at one another. Alessandro and Andrei shake hands before Declan leads everyone into a large boardroom.

"How's the situation on your end?" Declan asks Andrei.

The Bratva boss shakes his head. "I have men in Russia and here working to find this Smoke individual. So far, it seems no one knows who he is."

"Cage has a few men from his team on a jet right now heading to Russia. Can your guys assist them?" Killian asks.

"Of course. Anything we can do to stop this disgusting piece of shit from hurting women, we'll do it." Andrei looks at me. "Did you find your Little girl's father?"

I shake my head. "No. He left his house in a hurry. We did learn he's broke, though. Could be why he's involved. Either way, as soon as I find him, he's dead."

## 23

## CHLOE

My eyes are so dry from taking tests all day; it feels like my eyelids keep getting stuck when I try to blink. Finals are always intense, but today felt like a lot. Maybe I'm exhausted from getting fucked too deliciously last night. Or maybe I'm just antsy to get home to my Daddy.

After a much-needed trip to the bathroom, I head outside to the courtyard. Even though I'd argued that I could've driven myself today, I'm glad Bash didn't let that happen. I might take a nap on the ride home.

I'm about to cut through the Sciences building to get to the parking lot when a bouquet of flowers appears right in front of me.

"Dad?" I'm not sure why I'm asking. He's definitely my father. But I'm confused.

"Hi, honey," he says. "I knew it was finals week, so I wanted to wish you good luck."

I stare at the pink and white daisies before taking them from him. This is weird. He's never given me flowers.

"I, uh, I also wanted to apologize. You know, for the whole Bradley thing." His voice is wobbly, and my heart constricts.

What do I say to that? It's okay? No. Because it wasn't okay. But he's here, bringing me flowers and apologizing. That means something, right?

"Thank you, Dad."

He rubs the back of his neck. "Do you have time to talk for a few minutes? There's a bench over there we can sit at."

Glancing toward the building, I look back at him and there's hope gleaming in his dark eyes. "Um, sure. Just for a few minutes."

In awkward silence, we cross the courtyard to a cluster of benches. Since it's so late, and the only stuff that's going on this week is finals, the campus is mostly empty, giving us some privacy to talk.

There's something about my father that seems off. Like he's sad or nervous. I'm not used to seeing him express any emotion, so I can't tell for sure what it is. I also kind of hate myself for caring. He's treated me horribly over the years, and yet I'm worried about him. I'm not sure why I'm giving him the time of day.

His apologies don't mean anything. He's told me he was sorry for his behavior before, but it never changed.

Instead of filling the silence with my own nervous chatter, I sit down and wait for him to speak. He came all the way here to see me, and obviously, he has something to say. The sun warms me down to my bones. In a place that gets way too many rainy days, I don't take these nice days for granted. Especially since the weather forecasts a downpour tonight.

"I got into some money trouble."

His voice startles me, then the words sink in. "What do you mean?"

He lifts his shoulders and runs his hand over the back of his neck. "I made some bad investments. Gambled a bit. Used some money I shouldn't have."

My head snaps toward him. "Money you shouldn't have?"

"Some clients' money. I thought I'd be able to pay it back before they noticed but—"

"You stole money?" I bolt up from the bench, my heart racing, and my skin prickling. "How much money? From who? From Bradley? Is that why you forced me to go out with him?"

My dad stands and shakes his head. "No. It's not like that. I didn't take money from Bradley. But, uh, I'm in a lot of debt."

Putting my hands on my hips, I glare at him. "What does a lot mean?"

Why do I care? His debts aren't my responsibility. I'm a grown woman. Kieran or Bash—or both of them together—have already paid my tuition for the rest of law school, so I don't have to worry about that. I don't have any savings to help my father out, so why is he telling me all of this?

"A little over a million dollars." He looks around, not making eye contact with me and it's pissing me off.

Shaking my head, I start pacing. I don't know how to respond to this. Through all the years of him putting me down, treating me like I wasn't good enough, and using me to get ahead in business, I still held a sliver of respect for him. I shouldn't have. But I did because, while deep down I've always known he's an asshole, I thought he was at least a respectable attorney. I chalked up his behavior toward me as not knowing any better because his father treated him horribly too. Why was I so naïve?

I turn around, trying to calm my temper while gathering my scattered thoughts. When I finally stop in front of him and cross my arms over my chest, he shoves his hands in his suit jacket and looks me in the eye.

"Why are you telling me all of this, Dad? I don't have any money. I can't help you."

He takes a step toward me, his eyebrows drawn together and his gaze dark and distant. "That's where you're wrong, honey. You can help me."

Jerking my head back, I narrow my eyes. "What?"

Before I notice he's pulled his hands from his pockets, something sharp pricks my thigh. When I look down, I gasp. He stabbed me with a syringe. What the fuck? My stomach twists, and I think I'm going to vomit.

"Dad, what is that? What did you just do?"

He yanks the syringe away and tosses it. "I did what I had to do."

My head rolls back, and when I look at the sky, it looks like swirls of blue and white dancing around. It's not supposed to move like that.

"Since you fucked up my chance to make the money back, you're going to pay it back personally. Your body for my freedom...*sweetheart*."

His angry, bitter words float through the air as my entire world fades to black.

## 24

## BASH

Something in my gut doesn't feel right. Maybe it's all the coffee I've had today mixing with the whiskey? No. This is something else.

Several hours with Alessandro, Luciano, Andrei, Nikolai, Cage, and our men, and so far, the only thing we've come up with is that the asshole who calls himself Smoke seems to have disappeared. Fitting, given his name. No one knows him, no one knows what he actually looks like, and no one knows how to find him.

Cage has been in contact with his men in Russia, and they stopped the abduction of a young woman. The men who were trying to kidnap her, though, wanted some quick cash. They aren't part of the operation. Whoever is running this thing is smart. No one seems to know anything.

"My brother Luca contacted me this morning. The Colombian Cartel reached out to The Elite Team because there's been a sudden influx of young women going missing from Colombia. Luca and Cassian are on a plane down there to help, but as of right now, it's assumed whoever took the women from Russia is doing the same in Colombia. The patterns are the same." Cage taps his fingers on the tabletop, looking bored. I'm pretty sure it's all an act, but I can never tell with him.

"Jesus, Christ! Who the fuck are these people? We're the goddamn richest syndicates in the US with the most resources. And this is happening right under our noses?" Declan asks.

"For now, we need to secure the ports. My brothers will remain in Russia and Colombia until you give us the order to pull back," Cage says confidently. "It won't take long before we find someone who can give us the answers we need... Once they're properly persuaded."

I don't know who his brothers are. Cage is the only person I've met from The Elite Team, and the fucker is secretive and paranoid as hell. Cage Black might not even be his real name. I guess when you do jobs for the CIA, the mafia, and whatever other organizations they work for, you can't be too careful. But every time we've contracted with him for a job, he and his team do a better job than anyone else on the planet ever could. They're meticulous, sneaky, and terrifyingly smart. Sometimes, I think they may be more dangerous than the mafia.

"We found out that Ronald is not only broke but also stealing from his clients. Based on my calculations, he's in debt for millions. As you all know, politicians don't take kindly to having their money fucked with." Cage laces his fingers together and leans back in his chair like we're all sitting around having a tea party. Completely relaxed. Under the chill façade is a deadly machine that's ready to go to war at the drop of a hat. "I think Smoke might be the name of a politician Ronald stole from. And somehow, he's forced Ronald to get port access in exchange for debt forgiveness."

I glance at Kieran, trying to gauge his thoughts. It's difficult, though, because right now, he looks more pissed than anything.

"I never should have trusted him to take care of Chloe," he grinds out.

Slapping my hand on his shoulder, I give a gentle squeeze. "You didn't know he was that much of a piece of shit."

Kieran stands so fast his chair flies back and hits the wall with a loud crash. "I should have been paying closer attention for fuck's sake! And now this bastard is selling women? He could have tried to sell her."

"She's under our protection now," Declan says firmly.

Andrei nods. "And ours. We don't hurt women, and it doesn't matter which family they're part of, we will protect them."

Meeting the Bratva boss's eyes, I lift my chin in a silent thank you. I won't say I fully trust the guy, but after spending the last few hours talking things out in this room, I'm starting to see the type of man he is. It seems that Andrei and Nikolai want to do good for their families.

My phone rings, and my stomach twists before I pull it free from my suit jacket. When I see Cullen's name on the screen, my blood runs cold.

"Cullen."

"Bash, she's gone! I waited out front. When she didn't come out within ten minutes of her class ending, I went in to search for her. She wasn't anywhere in the building. I tracked her location to the courtyard where her phone was lying on the ground. I also found an empty syringe."

"What?" I roar, jumping from my chair.

"I did a perimeter search of the campus, but I've found nothing else," Cullen says breathlessly.

"Find an admin or a security guard and have them show you the camera feeds. We're on our way."

I'm already moving when the call ends. "Chloe's

missing. Her phone was left on the ground of the campus."

Declan, Alessandro, and Andrei start barking out orders. My vision blurs. My baby. My girl. Is she hurt? Scared? Fuck. I should have had bodyguards on her at all times. Why did I let my guard down? She's the most precious person in the world to me and I didn't keep her safe.

*Get your shit together, Bash. She needs you.*

Shaking all the thoughts from my head, I look around the room as everyone, even men who aren't part of our family, works furiously to help. It's going to be okay. We have all the money and resources in the world. I'll get her back, and hell will rain down on whoever dared to touch what's mine.

Cage sits calmly with his laptop, tapping at the keys, ignoring the rest of us. I've always liked the guy, but his lack of interest is pissing me off. I'll have words with him later about it. Right now, my only focus is finding my girl.

"Let's go to the campus and start there. I want Cali and Scarlet in the safe-room with guards until we know what's going on," Declan says to Grady.

Grady nods and disappears from the office. Andrei and Alessandro are on their phones, Russian and Italian flying too fast for me to understand.

"Got her location," Cage says lazily, his head resting against the back of the chair.

Every single person in the room turns to look at him. I take a step closer, narrowing my eyes. "How do you have her location?"

He shrugs. "Lipstick."

Blinking several times, I try to wrap my mind around whatever the fuck he just said. I've got nothing. I tilt my head. "Come again?"

"She never goes anywhere without at least one of her lipsticks, so I put a tracking device in each of them. Did you know your girl owns over two hundred tubes?"

My knees wobble. For a second, I'm not sure I'm going to be able to keep standing. "How the fuck did you get my girl's lipsticks? Were you near her? Did you touch her?" I'm ready to blow this fucker's brains out.

Cage sits back and sighs. "I've never talked to or touched your girl. I visited your place and her townhouse last night while everyone was sleeping." He pauses for a beat. "I also have trackers on Scarlet and Cali. Scarlet's trackers are all in the bottoms of her shoes. Cali's are sewn into her bras."

"You touched my girl's bras?" Declan demands, his gaze dark and deadly.

Cage shrugs. "You asked me to make sure your women were all as safe as possible. You may not like how I do my work, but I get it done. Your girl is on the highway moving north as we speak."

I stare at the big, muscular, slightly odd man sitting in front of me, and I can't decide if I want to shoot him, hug him, or ask him for tips on how to stalk my girl more thoroughly. I can figure that out later. Once we get my girl back. And after I kill whoever the fuck took her. They're a walking corpse. They just don't know it yet.

## 25

## CHLOE

*Open your eyes, Chloe. Open your eyes.*

I try. I try so hard but they're so heavy. My head pounds like someone's taking a jackhammer to it, and my body is fuzzy. Why am I so tired? What's that sound? An engine? Am I in a car?

Using all my strength, I slowly lift my eyelids as much as I can. Dreary daylight streams in through a window in front of me. Drops of rain run down the glass.

A car. I'm in a car. When did I get into a car? This isn't the Escalade that Cullen drives. The interior is different. It's tan instead of black. It also reeks of cologne. I know that smell. I've never liked it. Where do I know it from, though?

As gently as I can so my brain doesn't pound any

harder against my skull, I turn my head and quietly gasp. My father. Old Spice. His signature scent. He's driving. This is his car. Why am I with my father?

*"Since you fucked up my chance to make the money back, you're going to pay it back personally. Your body for my freedom...sweetheart."*

My thigh twitches. The syringe. He stabbed me with a syringe. That's the last thing I remember. He's dangerous. I felt it when we were talking in the courtyard. Something was off, but I couldn't put my finger on it. He stole money. From whom, I have no idea. What did he mean by my body for his freedom? Is he planning to sell me? Oh, God. He is. He's going to sell me to pay off his debt. What the fuck?

Tears well up in my eyes, and my heart squeezes so hard it's painful. I'm never going to see Daddy again. Or Kieran. Or Paisley. They won't know what happened to me.

No. I can't let that happen. I won't let it happen. I'm not a victim. He's hurt me enough already. My mind spins. I'm lying across the smooth leather seats in the back of his car. Trees pass by quickly, and the road is curvy. We're not in the city. Where is he taking me? If I jump from the car, will I survive with how fast we're going? Probably not. I need to get him to slow down.

Unsure if I'm restrained somehow or whether I can actually move since everything is numb, I try to wiggle my toes. When they move inside my shoe, I let out a breath and roll my ankles. Then I bend my knees slightly and lift my hands. Everything feels heavy, but I'm not paralyzed. It's taking more effort to move than I'd like but the adrenaline is overriding that. This is do or die.

Taking one more look around me in the hope that my purse is back here, I'm quickly disappointed when it's nowhere to be found. My phone. Bash put a tracker on my phone. Maybe he's already tracking me. I can't count on that, though. My father isn't stupid. It's possible he tossed my phone already. I have to save myself.

Several minutes pass while I try to formulate a plan. My mind is foggy still, and I keep fighting the urge to drift off to sleep again. Finally, when I think I know what I'm going to do, I start to stir and let out a low groan.

The noise is loud enough that my father turns to look back at me, his face red and sweaty, his eyes narrowed but his pupils blown wide.

"Dad? What's going on?" I ask, forcing myself to sound weak. It's not too hard to do.

"What the fuck? You shouldn't be awake already." His voice is evil, laced with pure hatred.

Running my hand over my stomach, I cough. "I'm going to throw up."

It's at this very moment I'm so glad my father

loves his Porsche more than me because he swerves and slams on the brakes. I reach out and grab the door handle, ready to bolt when it opens, but nothing happens. He turned on the childproof locks. Shit. Shit. Shit.

"I'm going to throw up," I say between forced coughs.

He jumps out of the car and runs around to the passenger side, then yanks open the back door. Before I can move on my own, he grabs me by the hair and drags me out. I scream and claw at his hands. Fiery pain rips through my skull.

I stumble over my feet but stay upright as he pulls me a few feet away.

"Hurry the fuck up and vomit, bitch. We're already late as it is. The Red Dragons aren't known for their patience, and they've waited long enough for your ass," he growls.

Red Dragons?

With his firm hold on my hair, I can't run. I force myself to cough several times while bending at the hips slightly like I'm about to throw up. Something hard presses against one of my butt cheeks.

My heart lurches. The lipstick knife. I never put it in my purse. It's still in my pocket. The pain searing through my head fades, and my focus sharpens. I have to do this. It doesn't matter that he's my own flesh and blood. He's evil, and if I don't get away from him, I'm going to die.

Continuing my coughing fit, I bring my hands to my hips and ignore the jerk of his hand on my hair while I slide my fingers toward my back pocket.

"Are you going to throw up or not? If you vomit in my car, I'll kill you," he yells, yanking on my hair again.

"You're hurting me," I cry as I slide the tube from my pocket and one-handedly slide the cap off.

"Shut up, bitch!"

I brace myself and swing the knife forward until it sinks into his thigh. He howls and lets go of my hair. I don't waste a second before I start running, but I only make it a few steps before he catches me, yanking my head back by my hair again.

My arms flail, but I start stabbing again. Over and over. Even when he releases me, I keep stabbing.

"You're not going to hurt me anymore! I. Am. Not. A. Victim!" I scream, slashing a new spot with each word.

He falls to the ground, using his hands to try to block me, but I don't stop. I can't stop. He's hurt me one too many times. It's my turn to hurt him. I drop to my knees and keep swinging. When he stops moving, I let out a sob. My shoulders drop, and it's like a weight's been lifted. I killed my father. *I killed my father!* Go me. Maybe I am cut out for the mafia life.

I'm panting as I look around. We're in the middle of nowhere. Not a single car has driven by. At least not that I've seen. I was a little busy killing my jackass father.

Bash. I need Bash. I need my Daddy. The man who will never hurt me. Who will love me unconditionally.

My hands are coated in blood. Splatters of crimson have soaked into my shirt. Looking down at my little lipstick knife, I let out a heavy breath. I always knew lipstick could change a girl's life for the better.

A glimmer of black shines inside my father's open suit jacket when the sun peeks out from the dark clouds. His phone. Hands shaking, I grab it from the inner pocket and try to unlock it. Shit. It's passcode protected. Glancing at his face, I raise an eyebrow and turn the screen toward him. When that doesn't do anything, I look down at his chubby hand resting on the gravel.

Scrunching my nose, I lower the phone to his index finger and press the tip against the home button. The screen immediately lights up. I do a small fist pump. Shit. I don't know Bash's phone number by heart. I start to dial 911, and then I pause. I bet

Kieran's number is in my father's contacts. When I find my brother's name, I press call.

"Where is she?" Kieran shouts the second he answers.

"Kieran!" I cry out.

"Baby. Oh, fuck, baby. Where are you?" Bash asks.

I look around and sigh, a smile tugging at my lips. I sway slightly, a sense of calm washing over me. It doesn't matter that he's not right here. His voice is all I need to know I'm safe. "Hi, Daddy."

"Chloe, baby, where are you?" he shouts.

A giggle escapes. "I don't know, Daddy. In the woods somewhere. I think. Where are you? Can you come get me?"

He huffs out a breath. "Jesus, fuck, baby. I'm coming. I think we're close to you. Your tracker shows you're a mile away. Who took you? Did you get away? Stay hidden, baby. We'll find you."

"Drive faster," Kieran demands in the background.

Unable to hold my own weight, I lean against the Porsche. I stare at my lifeless father, his blood soaking into the ground, and laugh again. Then, I run my hand down the side of the pristine white paint. My lips twitch, and I do it again, finding immense pleasure in using his blood to dirty up his stupid car.

"I'm on the side of the road. I killed him. I killed my bastard of a father. With my lipstick knife."

It's silent for a second before Bash speaks. "That's my fucking girl."

The sound of a roaring engine approaches, and before the SUV comes to a complete stop behind my father's car, Bash jumps out. I take off running to him. As soon as his arms close around me, I collapse, knowing I'm truly safe now.

"Oh, fuck, baby. Fuck. You're bloody. Shit, where are you hurt?" he asks, his voice cracking.

"Get a medic out here," Kieran shouts as he runs toward us.

"It's not my blood. I'm not hurt. I don't think." I try to step back to show them, but Bash won't let me go. Instead, he bends down, places an arm under my knees, and scoops me up.

"I killed him. I'm not a victim," I whisper, trembling before my body goes limp in his arms and my eyes slide shut.

"You're not a victim, baby. You're my fucking world. My Little girl. My everything. My queen."

His words float in my mind as I drift off to sleep knowing he'll take it from here.

## 26

## BASH

She looks so fragile in my arms. I could have lost her. If Cage hadn't put trackers in her lipsticks, we wouldn't have found her so quickly. Not that finding her helped. She'd already handled it.

My lips twitch as I stare down at her. Part of me hates that she was the one to kill Ronald. I was looking forward to torturing the fucker. But from the condition he was in, he got what he deserved. The rest of me is so fucking proud. I want to be her hero for the rest of her life, but today, she was her own hero.

She's going to need therapy after everything soaks in. Even though she knows what a horrible prick her father was, she killed him, and that will stick with her forever. Whatever she needs, I'll be right by her side the entire time. My girl will never have to face anything alone. She'll also never leave my sight without an army of bodyguards ever again.

"It would be easier for me to examine her if you'd lay her on the bed."

I glare at our doctor, Finn, who we keep on the payroll for times like this. "She's staying right here in my arms."

He glances at Declan, who shrugs. "Sorry, Doc. You won't win this one. My brother is a stubborn bastard."

Finn grumbles under his breath as he prepares an IV. "The fluids will help flush any remaining drugs out of her system."

"Why won't she wake up? Can you do something to wake her up?" I ask as I stare at her delicate face.

"It could be a mix of an adrenaline crash and whatever he drugged her with. Her oxygen is good, and her heart rate is stable. She'll wake up when she's ready," he says when he lifts his stethoscope from her chest.

I hate that she's still bloody. I'm not going to let her wake up with that asshole's DNA splattered all over her. "Someone get me some warm wet cloths."

One of our men moves to the wall of cabinets and starts yanking them open in search of what I need. Declan rode back to his house with me to meet the doctor. Everyone else stayed at the scene to clean up.

Now that Chloe's father is dead, we have no leads on finding Smoke and his gang. As much as I want to hunt them down so we can end this human trafficking ring, right now my only concern is my girl. I'm not leaving her side until I know she's okay. Hell, maybe I'll never leave her side anyway. I like that idea.

Cali and Scarlet appear in the doorway, their eyes red with tears.

"Is she okay?" Cali asks. "Oh my God, she's bloody!"

Declan blocks the girls' view of Chloe. "She's fine. It's not her blood. Why don't you two go up to the guest room and put a couple of stuffies and some soft blankets in there for her so Bash can take her up to rest for a bit."

Scarlet and Cali peek around Declan, their eyes roaming over Chloe's body.

"Did she fuck them up good?" Scarlet asks.

My lips twitch, and I nod. "She did."

She grins and nods, then high-fives her sister. "I knew I loved her the second I met her."

Warmth crawls up my neck. I've always had a pretty good life, but with these three girls as part of our family now, I don't think it could get any better. "Me too," I whisper.

She's been sleeping for hours. After giving her two bags of fluids, Finn let me bring her up to one of Declan's guest rooms. I want to take her home where I can get her comfortable and hover over her for the rest of her life, but I'll wait until she's awake.

Cali left a new pair of panties and a pajama shirt on the bed for Chloe. I want to give her a bath, but she needs to rest. Although, my patience is wearing thin. I need to see her beautiful blue eyes and hear her tell me she loves me. I need to know she's okay.

As gently as I can, I undress and redress her, then throw her soiled clothes in the garbage. Even though I cleaned off as much blood as I could downstairs, I go to the bathroom and get some more washcloths wet with warm water.

She doesn't stir when I start wiping her skin again. I'm almost done when Kieran walks in, the corners of his eyes etched with worry.

"How's she doing?" he asks quietly.

"Still sleeping. Everything cleaned up?"

"Yep. No signs of Ronald anywhere. The road he was on leads up to a vacation home he and my mom had. Turns out he was taking her there to meet with one of his clients. He was planning to give her to them in exchange for debt forgiveness."

Rage boils in my stomach, and I wish more than anything I could bring Ronald back to life so I could kill him myself. That fucking bastard.

"Did you kill them?" I ask.

Whoever the hell they are, if Kieran didn't kill them, I'm going to. How dare they even think to take my girl as payment. She's not a possession. She's a fucking treasure. The greatest gift on earth.

Kieran makes his way to the bed. "Not yet. Cage, Andrei, Alessandro, and Ronan are squeezing them for information. Whoever they are, they aren't the boss."

Nodding, I run a cloth down her leg. When I'm satisfied with my job, I sigh and look at Kieran. His face is pale and his eyes dark, zeroed in on Chloe. When I follow his line of sight, my muscles tense. Fuck.

"What the fuck are those?" he demands quietly.

I keep my gaze on the thin scars on her thighs and sigh. Kieran's breaths rush in and out of his chest.

"Bash, what the fuck are those?" he asks, a bit louder this time.

I try to get my best friend to back away from the bed. I've seen Kieran in the worst of times, but I've never seen him look like this. He's scared. He doesn't get scared. He stares down at Chloe, his fist brought up to his mouth.

"Kieran," I whisper.

He shakes his head as a tear slips from his eye. "I never knew. I had no idea. Fuck. What kind of brother am I? I didn't protect her from that asshole. She...she hurt herself. Because of him?"

My only response is a slight nod. There's a lump in my throat I can't seem to swallow. We stand in silence for several seconds before I take a few steps and open my arms to hug him.

"She has you now. She has us. All of us," I say when I pull back.

His expression is as haunted as I felt when I first saw her scars. It's something I'll never recover from, and I have a feeling Kieran won't either.

"Call me when she wakes up?" he asks.

"Yeah. Where are you heading?"

"To let out some rage." He glances back at Chloe before leaving the room. He hasn't killed those guys, but I'm pretty sure that won't be the case when he returns.

ANOTHER TWO HOURS PASS. I've called the doctor up here three times to check on her, and he's assured me she's fine. He also murmured something under his breath about there being something wrong with me. Fucker.

I've been pacing at the end of the bed for the past twenty minutes, trying to keep myself from shaking her awake. The thick carpet is going to be worn thin from how many laps I've done.

"Daddy?" Her voice is raspy and quiet, but it's the most beautiful sound I've ever heard.

I turn to stare at her and nearly drop to my knees when she meets my gaze. Her baby blues are sparkling beneath her drooping eyelids.

"Baby girl."

She nods and tears immediately start rolling down her cheeks, cracking my heart right in half.

"I didn't disobey you. I didn't leave campus on my own. He showed up there and took me."

Rushing to her side, I pull her into my arms. "Shh. I know, baby. I know. It's okay. You're okay. You're safe now. Daddy's got you." My voice cracks, and my eyes burn with tears.

She's safe and in my arms. She'll be okay. I'll make sure of it.

"I was so scared. I never thought I'd see you again. I never thought I'd see Kieran or Paisley either, and you would never know what had happened to me."

Rocking her against my chest, I bury my face in her hair, soaking in the faint soft, sweet scent. For the first time all day, I'm able to take a full breath. "I would have gone to the ends of the earth to find you, baby girl. You're mine, and I'll never give up on you. You're safe now. It's my fault this happened. I should have had bodyguards with you at all times. I fucked up, and I hope you can forgive me."

Her entire body tenses and my stomach lurches. Is she going to hate me because of what happened?

She leans back and cups each side of my face so she can stare at me directly in the eyes. "Don't even think about putting this on yourself. I'll find the hairbrush and spank your ass if I have to until you understand that this wasn't your fault. What happened is on him."

My cock twitches in my slacks as a slow smile spreads on my face. "You think you want to spank me, huh?"

The prettiest rosy hue spreads over her cheeks. "Well, um, no. I don't want to do that. I prefer it the other way around. But I will if you keep blaming yourself. Understood, Mister?"

Raising an eyebrow, I lean closer to her until our foreheads touch. "Understood, Little girl. And if you call me Mister ever again, you'll find yourself over my knee in a heartbeat."

Her breath hitches. "Sorry, Daddy."

I wink and smile. "Better." And then I kiss her, deeply.

We're both wound around each other, kissing, biting, and sucking. My cock is rock-hard, but I don't care about that right now. The only thing I want is to kiss and hold my girl. To listen to her beating heart and run my fingers over her pulse all night to make sure she's okay.

"I love you so much," she whispers.

My throat tightens, and if I could reach into my own chest and rip out my heart to give it to her, I would. She has no idea how much she means to me. "I love you too, Little girl. So fucking much."

"Did the police come?" she asks when we finally pull back enough to see one another clearly again.

"No. The police aren't involved. Do you have any idea where Ronald was taking you or why?"

"He said he was going to make me pay his debt to the Red Dragons. I don't know what he meant by that."

My blood runs cold, and as carefully as I can, I pull my phone from my suit pocket and call Declan.

"Yeah?" he answers.

"Come up here. Chloe might have some information for us."

I end the call and reach for some blankets to cover her legs. I don't want anyone else seeing my girl's creamy soft legs or the scars she feels so much shame over.

Only a few seconds pass before Declan, Killian, Alessandro, Andrei, Cage, Knox, Angel, and a man I've never met before file into the room.

I glance at the man I've never met, then look at Declan.

"This is Jasper. He's Cage's brother," Declan explains.

Nodding, I hold my hand out and shake Jasper's. If he works with Cage, I know we can trust him.

Killian runs his hand over Chloe's head. "How are you feeling, Little one? Glad to see you awake." She lets out a small hiss.

"Shit, did I hurt you? Fuck, Chloe, I'm so sorry." Killian's eyes are wide with fear as I growl at him.

"It's okay. He pulled my hair, so my head is tender. I'm fine. Really. I forgot about that, and it didn't hurt until you touched it."

Anger bubbles low in my stomach. I take several deep and controlled breaths to calm myself. I know Killian didn't intentionally hurt my girl, but Ronald's already dead, and Killian isn't, so it would make me feel better if I shot him. Chloe would be upset with me if I did that, though, so I'll keep practicing this deep-breathing bullshit.

She must sense my inner turmoil because she scoots deeper into my arms until I practically have her cocooned. It's her way of reassuring me, and it's working. Fuck. I'm putty in my girl's hands.

Killian's expression has gone dark like he wishes he could go back and kill Ronald himself. "I'm sorry, sweet girl. I would never hurt you on purpose. Do you want an ice pack for it? Did the doctor check it out?"

"I'm good. Maybe I'll get a cold pack later. Thank you, Killian," she says sweetly, smiling up at him.

"You said Chloe had information?" Cage asks.

I wait for her to answer, but when she twists her fingers in my shirt, I start for her. "Her father said he was taking her to meet with the Red Dragons. He didn't expand on that other than to say he was trading her to pay off his debt to them. Is that name familiar to any of you?"

Cage's and Jasper's eyes darken, their shoulders rigid.

"The Red Dragons are a gang. They sell hard drugs and guns. They'd gone quiet for a while after the leader and several members were killed. I assumed they had disbanded or left to run their business elsewhere. I haven't had them on my radar," Cage answers.

Knox lets out a low growl. "We're the ones who took them out. One of them attacked and kidnapped my girl. When we found her in a rundown warehouse, she was locked in a cage with a dozen other women. We killed every one of them in the building that day and left them hanging by their feet as a message."

I grin at Knox because fuck, these guys are as brutal as we are when the need is there.

"Any idea where to find them?" Andrei asks.

Jasper looks up from his phone. "Our brother, Caine, is sending me the information we have on them. Warehouse locations, hangouts, and the places they like to sell drugs."

"Let's go find them. And find out where all these missing women are," Declan says.

I don't budge. I almost lost my girl earlier, and while I hate to sit this out, I'm not leaving her side.

"Is it cool if I send Cali and Scarlet in here so you can keep an eye on them too?" Killian asks. "Maybe they can all watch a movie together. The bed is big enough for the three of them."

Chloe does a little wiggle in my arms, and I chuckle because I know what she wants me to say. As if I would have ever said no in the first place.

"Of course. Have them get into their pajamas and get ready for bed. I'm going to take Chloe into the bathroom and give her a proper bath. Can someone get me another set of panties and a nightshirt for her?"

My girl's hand tightens around my shirt, and when I glance down at her, her cheeks have turned pink. "Daddyyyy…" she whispers.

I wink at her and smile. She'll get used to all of us taking care of her.

"On it," Declan says as he disappears from the room.

Within seconds, all the men have filed out, leaving just the two of us. I need to get her in the bath, but I'm struggling to let her go at all. I just found the love of my life and then nearly lost her. If she thought I was over the top unhinged before, she has no idea what's coming her way now.

## 27

## CHLOE

I could get used to this being carried everywhere stuff. After all the men left the bedroom, Daddy brought me into the bathroom and set me down on the toilet to pee while he got the bath ready.

As soon as I finish my business, I reach for the toilet paper, but Bash is right by my side in an instant, gently pushing my hands away so he can do it. I should probably be embarrassed about him cleaning me up like this, but I'm not. With him, I feel no shame in anything. He wants to take care of me this way. I want it too, if I'm being totally honest.

There's dried blood under my fingernails, giving me a sick sense of satisfaction. I once loved my father and thought he was a wonderful man, but now all I feel is relief that he's gone. Part of me wishes my mom was still alive so I could talk to her and ask why she always made excuses for him. Why she always stood by his side. Did she see his evil ways or was she blind to it too? Whatever the case, I hope she's proud of me for what I did. She may not have been the perfect mom, but I know without a doubt that she truly did love me and wanted what was best for me. But she allowed my father to rule her life, and I have to be okay with never knowing why.

Daddy lifts me from the toilet and carries me to the tub, slowly lowering me into the hot, foamy water.

"Is it too warm?"

"It's perfect, Daddy. So perfect."

His eyes focus on my face as he relaxes and helps me sit down. My body is heavy, and I still feel the urge to close my eyes. Bash keeps one hand wrapped around my upper arm the entire time as if he's afraid I'm going to slip underwater.

"Daddy?"

"Mm?" He runs a soapy washcloth over my skin, his gaze following his movements.

"I'm not going to be a lawyer. I don't want to do anything that he wanted me to do."

The corners of his lips pull back into a smile. "You're not going to be a lawyer, baby girl. You're going to run your own makeup company, just like you've always wanted."

Shrugging my shoulders, I look up at him, knowing what's coming. "I'm not taking money from you."

His smile widens. "We'll see."

Relief floods me from the inside out. I knew Bash wouldn't force me to be an attorney, but hearing his confirmation makes me so much happier.

"I need to change my last name," I mumble.

"You will, baby. Soon. We can do it tomorrow if you want. Chloe Gilroy has a much better ring to it anyway."

My mouth falls open. That wasn't what I meant. I just want to have a different last name from the man who raised me, but changing it to Bash's last name and being permanently tied to him forever sounds pretty perfect.

"Are you sure you want me to be your wife?"

Dropping his face to mine, he stares at me, his green eyes intense and sparkling. "More than I want to take my next breath."

Well, okay then. Not going to argue with that.

"Hold onto my arm and spread your legs so I can wash you, baby."

His deep voice sends a shockwave to my clit, and as I obey his command and wrap my fingers around his thick muscles, I suck in a breath, anticipating his touch. As soon as the fluffy cloth brushes against my clit, I let out a soft whimper and claw harder at his arm.

"Are you needy, baby girl?"

Peeking up at him from under my lashes, I nod and squirm when he moves his hand again. Slowly, he rubs a circle around my swollen nub.

"Lie back. Daddy will take care of you."

He helps me to lean back before lowering his mouth to mine, capturing my lips. While he kisses me, he lets go of the washcloth and brushes his fingers over my mound.

When he pulls away slightly, he rests his forehead against mine. "I want you to let go and come for me. Let it all go and let me take care of you. I got you, baby. Daddy's always got you."

I nod and moan as he slips a finger inside me while using the heel of his hand against my clit. With one hand wrapped in the front of his shirt and the other gripping the edge of the tub, I start to move my hips in rhythm with him. I don't know why I need this right now, but I'm not going to question it.

Bash adds a second finger and curls them inside, hitting that sensitive spot that makes me see stars.

"Daddy," I plead.

"I know, baby. I know you need to come."

He starts thrusting, and at the same time, he lowers his mouth to my breasts to suck and lick the sensitive peaks. When he latches onto one of my nipples, I jerk and slosh water over the edge of the tub, but he doesn't stop. Instead, he sucks harder and thrusts deeper into my pussy until the ball that's been wound so tight explodes, and I scream.

My orgasm hits me so hard, my entire body shakes as it rocks me, sending waves and waves of pleasure through every nerve. Bash groans as he lifts his head, watching me with half-lidded eyes as I come for him.

"Such a good girl. My good girl. I'm so fucking proud of you, Chloe."

Those words send an aftershock through me. He's proud of me. I'll never get tired of hearing that. Or of the way he looks at me with those sparkling green eyes like I'm the most spectacular thing on earth.

We watch each other in silence for a few seconds before he slips his fingers free and finishes washing me. As soon as he's done, he pulls the drain and uses the handheld sprayer to give me one last rinse before lifting me from the tub. I'm half tempted to tell him I can walk, but I don't want to. I like being in his arms like this.

When we return to the bedroom, there's a fresh set of panties and pajamas on the bed for me. It looks like the bedding has all been replaced as well and is pristinely made without a wrinkle in sight.

Of course, I'm not allowed to dress myself. Daddy does it for me, making me feel Little and loved.

"Crawl under the covers, baby. I don't mind if you and the other girls hang out, but you're staying in bed the entire time. Understood?"

It's adorable that he's using his stern voice right now. I won't tell him that, but if there's one thing I know about my Daddy it's that he's a big marshmallow when it comes to me if my safety isn't a concern. Although I guess it is kind of a health thing, so I better not press my luck.

On all fours, I crawl to the head of the bed and get under the covers. Quackers is perched next to one of the pillows, and when I pull him into my arms, I sigh. Everything is okay. My mind is still foggy and I'm sure in the next few days everything will hit me, but I'm not worried about it. Bash will be there to catch me if I fall.

"Knock knock!" Cali calls out as she opens the door.

Bash raises an eyebrow. "Saying 'knock knock' isn't the same as actually knocking, you know?"

She shrugs and skips into the room with Scarlet at her heels. "Whatever, Bashie." She turns and looks at me, her eyes laced with worry. "How are you feeling? You look good."

I nod and smile. "I'm good. A little sleepy but mostly good. Come sit down."

As soon as I pat the bed, both women leap onto

the mattress, and I swear, I think my Daddy is about to have a heart attack.

"Be careful!" he snaps. "She's recovering."

Cali's eyes get wide. "Are you hurt? Oh my God, did we hurt you?"

Giggling, I shake my head. "I'm not hurt. Daddy is a worry-wart. I'm fine."

Bash grumbles under his breath, but I can see the smile in his eyes. "I love you," I mouth.

His smile breaks free, and he mouths the words back to me as Declan and Killian walk in with trays of food in hand.

"We brought drinks and snacks for the girls," Killian announces.

Scarlet rubs her hands together. "Oooh, Cheetos and wine?"

Killian rolls his eyes. "Nice try, brat. Carrots and juice."

All three of us groan, but as soon as they set the trays down, our noises of protest disappear because while there are carrots and juice, there's also a bunch of other yummy treats too. I find it funny that all these big bad mafia men are so different around us. I love it.

"You're sure you don't mind me staying?" Bash asks.

Declan nods. "Not at all. Someone needs to stay

with them, and you need to be close to your girl. I'll keep you updated."

Bash stares at his brother for several seconds before Declan nods. "Of course. He'll be all yours."

I tilt my head, confused. Bash didn't speak, so why did Declan give him that cryptic answer?

Killian and Declan kiss their women goodbye and disappear, leaving the four of us alone. Bash grabs the remote and turns on the TV.

"What do you Little girls want to watch?"

The three of us look at each other and smile. "*Beauty and the Beast*," we answer at the same time.

"Jesus, fuck," Bash mutters under his breath as he turns on the movie. "You know there are other movies in the world, right?"

We shrug and settle against the pillows. It doesn't take long before my eyes feel heavy again, and I find myself leaning my head against Cali's shoulder before I drift off to sleep.

IT'S NEARLY six in the morning by the time Declan and Killian return to collect their girls. Scarlet doesn't even open her eyes as she's lifted into her Daddy's arms. Bash seems wide awake, and when I crawl out from under the covers, he reaches for me and pulls me onto his lap.

"Did everything go okay?" he asks.

Declan shrugs. "We've captured a dozen Red Dragon members. None who want to tell us where their boss Smoke is. Some of Cage's men intercepted a cargo ship about thirty miles offshore outside of Colombia and found a container ship of Colombian women. They're working with the Cartel right now to get the women back to land."

As I listen, instead of feeling scared, my anger rises. How could people kidnap women like that? Like they mean nothing. I glance at Cali who's sitting on the edge of the bed with the same expression.

"Did you kill them, Daddy? You can feed them to my piranhas if you want to," Cali says as she crosses her arms over her chest.

Declan pins her with a stern look. "We're handling it. What did I say about you and your piranhas?"

Her shoulders drop. "That I could only keep them if I agree that the only food they get is fish food."

I giggle and bury my face against Bash's chest. Watching Declan and Cali together is the cutest thing. She's so spunky, and I love it. She reminds me of Paisley sometimes. Sassy and badass.

"Right now, all the syndicates are on high alert in their home countries. Cage and his team plan to keep searching for Smoke," Declan says before he tilts his head to Bash. "I do have someone special for you to visit at the warehouse whenever you can get there."

Bash nods. "I'll be looking forward to it."

"Come on, Little one. You need a few more hours of sleep, otherwise, you're going to be naughtier than usual all day," Declan says as he picks Cali up.

She buries her face in his neck and sighs. "You like it when I'm naughty."

Declan chuckles. "I love it when you're naughty because then I have a reason to spank your cute butt."

I wave at Cali as she's carried out of the room, and when the door closes, I sit up to look at Bash. "What did he mean when he said he has someone special for you to visit at the warehouse?"

Bash stares at me for several seconds like he's unsure if he wants to answer, but I know he won't lie to me.

"It means they have the man who was planning to meet up with your dad and trade your life for his freedom."

A cold wave of goosebumps runs over my skin. "Are you going to kill him?" I ask quietly.

"Yes," he answers without missing a beat. "First, I'm going to torture him, though, and then I'm going to kill him. No one hurts or tries to hurt what's mine and gets away with it. Not ever."

A whoosh of air rushes out of my lungs as I wrap my arms around his neck and cling to him. "Thank you, Daddy. Can we go home?"

He tenses under me, and when I lift my face to his, I realize he's wondering what I meant by home.

"To our house. The one we're going to share together," I whisper.

His muscles relax, and the corners of his eyes crinkle slightly as he smiles. "Of course we can. Grab Quackers and let's go."

Even though his house is only a short walk from Declan's, Bash loads me into a warm SUV, and we're driven across the estate.

"I've been thinking about Paisley."

Turning his head to look at me, he nods. "And? You want to move her in with us?"

"Would that be okay? I don't want to leave her all alone. She didn't have much of a family growing up, so for the past several years, I've been her family."

Daddy squeezes my hand. "I already have a moving company scheduled to move her into our house this week."

My mouth goes slack, and I try to jump into his lap but am yanked back by the seatbelt he insisted I wear. He chuckles and leans down, kissing the side of my head.

"Safety first, Little one. We'll be home soon."

I roll my eyes, but a slow smile spreads across my

face. This man is going to drive me batty, but I don't want it any other way.

---

WHEN I SAID he was going to drive me batty, that was an understatement. I've been confined to bed for two days, only allowed to get up when I needed to use the restroom, and I'm ready to slit Bash's throat. The doctor even came by and told him I was perfectly fine to go on with my life like normal. I only have some bruising, but otherwise, I'm not injured. Bash said he still wanted me to rest. I want to kick him in the balls. I won't, of course, because when he fucks me and talks about getting me pregnant with his babies, it does something to me I never expected. So, I need to let his balls stay intact. For now.

Cali and Scarlet are here, keeping me from being totally miserable while Bash leaves to go to the warehouse where some of those Red Dragon men are being held. Of course, there are still guards downstairs, and another one, Patrick, is outside the bedroom door, making sure I don't get out of bed. Luckily, Patrick keeps the door closed, so I haven't gotten in trouble the few times I've decided to get up and dance around the room.

They come loaded with supplies. Beading kits, coloring books, pencils, puzzles, a small stash of candy, and some dirty books for me to read to pass the time. I'm coloring a picture of a duck in a pond while they work on their own pictures.

"Are your Daddies over the top like this too?" I ask.

Scarlet blows out a breath. "Oh, you have no idea. Killian would barely let me feed myself when I was hurt and in bed. If I so much as sneeze, he's trying to stick a thermometer up my butt and restricts me to bed for a week."

Cali and I burst out laughing.

"In your butt?" I squeal.

She nods. "Oh yeah. If there's a reason to stick something in my ass, Killian is doing it."

I snort and cover my face as I giggle hysterically. I have a feeling that will be Bash too. He has a bit of an obsession with playing with my butt when we fuck. And when we're not fucking. Hell, the man is just plain obsessed with all of me.

A knock at the door startles us, and I half expect Patrick to pop in and tell us to settle down, but it's not Patrick who walks in. It's my brother.

"Hey." He swallows and looks at the other girls before his eyes land on me. There are dark circles under his eyes like he hasn't been sleeping, and for the first time in my life, I'm worried about him.

"Hi," I say. "Come sit."

He moves to the chair beside the bed. "Cali, Scarlet, can I have some time alone with Chloe?"

Cali tilts her head and purses her lips. "What's the magic word?"

Kieran narrows his eyes at her. "Please."

Rolling her eyes, Cali shakes her head. "That's not even close. The magic word is Cheetos, and it's insulting that you didn't know that."

Raising an eyebrow, he pulls his phone from his pocket and holds it up. "You have three seconds to get moving or I'm calling both your Daddies and telling them about the candy you snuck over here."

Like a fire is roaring under their asses, Cali and Scarlet quickly gather their things and scurry from the room, slamming the door shut behind them.

I grin and shake my head. "And here I thought you'd be the big teddy bear out of the bunch."

When he doesn't crack a smile, mine fades. "What's wrong, Kieran?"

Leaning forward, his elbows resting on his knees, he sighs and looks at the ground. "I walked in the room when Bash was cleaning you up the other day and saw all your scars."

Like a bucket of cold water has been thrown on me, I suck in a breath and blink several times. Shame creeps its way over my skin, and my eyes fill with tears. He must think terribly of me.

"I failed you, Chloe. I'm your big brother, and I was supposed to protect you from assholes like him. It doesn't matter that he was your father, I should have protected you. I'm...I'm so fucking sorry, sweetheart. I hope you can forgive me." His voice cracks and a tear falls to the floor.

Unable to stop myself, I scramble out from under the blankets and crawl across the bed before practically launching myself into his lap. He catches me and squeezes me hard as he buries his face in my hair. A broken sob escapes me as I cling to him.

"You didn't fail me, Kieran. You've never failed me. You've always been the best big brother. No one truly knew how horrible he was, and I certainly didn't tell you anything. I needed another outlet for my pain, and it helped at the time. You did nothing wrong."

He's breathing hard and shaking his head like he doesn't believe a word I'm saying.

"I should have been there more. Forced myself to be part of the family so I could keep a better eye on you."

Pressing my hands to his chest, I push him back until we're facing each other. His eyes are so fucking sad, it makes my own chest ache.

I cup his cheeks in my palms and meet his gaze. "Kieran, it's not your fault. It's only his fault. And Mom's fault. She was a good mom, but she protected him first before anything else. None of this is on you. Okay?"

He stares at me for several seconds, his Adam's apple bobbing as he swallows. "I hope you know how much I love you, Chloe. How special I think you are, and how proud I am of you."

A lump forms in my throat. "I love you, too, Kieran. So much. And I'm sorry I didn't push more to be part of your life. I let him walk all over me, and I feel like we missed out on so much time together."

"I know. We have a lot of catching up to do, don't we?" he asks.

I let go of his face and snuggle against his chest. "We do. And we will. We can't change the past, but we can make the future exactly how we want it."

He wraps his arms around me and kisses the top of my head. "Mind if I stay here and hang out with you for a while?"

My smile goes so wide it makes my cheeks hurt. "I'd love that. Wanna lie down with me and watch a movie?"

When I wiggle out of his hold and climb back into bed, I pat Bash's side for him. He eyes it for a second before he rises and moves around to that side, then kicks off his shoes.

"Bash is going to hate me being in bed with you even though I'm your brother," he says.

I nod. "Yep."

Kieran grins. "So, should I get under the covers too? That would probably give him a heart attack."

We both burst out laughing as my brother gets comfortable next to me.

"I wish you would let Bash give you the money to start your business."

I glare at him. "Did he send you here to try to talk me into it?"

"Define 'send me here.'"

Groaning, I roll my eyes. "I'm not taking his money. My father used money to try to control me, and even though Bash is nothing like him, I don't want to take that chance. I'll do it on my own eventually."

"Let me give you the money, then."

Letting out a huff, I turn and glare at him. "You're no different than taking it from him. I'm not taking your money either. And don't argue with me, or I'm kicking you out of our movie date."

Kieran grumbles under his breath about me being a pain in the ass, but he doesn't argue.

Just as the movie starts, I clear my throat. "Paisley is moving in with us in the next couple of days."

He lets out a low grunt. "Super."

Turning my head, I smile at him. "She's not so bad."

"If you say so."

I rub the blanket between my fingers as I think of what to say next. "She had a rough life growing up. She had to learn how to take care of herself. It's why she can be so prickly sometimes."

His jaw tenses. "Rough? How?"

Laying my hand on his chest, I sigh. "Her story isn't mine to tell. But if you want my opinion, I think all she needs is a good Daddy to love her and she'd flourish."

Almost instantly, his heart starts racing under my touch, but he doesn't say anything. He doesn't have to. His eyes say enough, and I know whether Paisley likes it or not, he just became her protector.

"Where are you taking me?"

"Not far. Keep your eyes closed."

With both his hands wrapped around my upper arms, Bash leads me from our bedroom through the house. At one point, he picked me up and carried me down the stairs, and now he's stopped somewhere and is taking forever to tell me to open my eyes.

"Okay, open."

As soon as I do, I gasp. The French doorway is wide open, and perfect daylight streams in through the enormous windows. Along an entire wall, there's a built-in drawer and shelving system custom-made for makeup artists to neatly store all their supplies. One shelf has dozens of glass jars holding all different kinds of brushes. Another shelf has bottles and bottles of my perfume. The drawers are all see-through on the front, showing off bottles and containers of expensive makeup all lined up perfectly inside.

"Daddy, what did you do?" I ask breathlessly.

In the middle of the room is a large white desk facing the windows, mirrors, and tripod lights surrounding it along with multiple cameras arranged in front. I've never seen such a perfect filming setup in my life.

My heart pounds faster in my chest as I take everything in. Did he do this for me? Because he knows I love makeup and want to film tutorials?

The walls are painted a soft yellow that only adds to the perfect lighting, and when I take a step inside and look around some more, my breathing stops.

Hung throughout the room are dozens of shadowboxes with glittery backgrounds and makeup containers displayed inside them in a way that looks artistic and tasteful. My makeup containers. All the ones I've saved over the years because I couldn't bear to throw away the things that made me most happy.

Tears stream down my face as I go over to look at each one. "You made these?"

"I had some help," he says quietly.

"Do you like them?" Cali asks from behind him.

I spin around to find Cali, Scarlet, and Paisley standing in the doorway with Bash, their eyes wet with tears as well.

"You all did this?" My voice cracks.

"Bash did most of it," Scarlet says with a smile.

Moving my gaze to him, I let out a sob and shake my head. "I...I can't believe this."

He smiles and moves closer to me until he's only a few feet away. "I would do anything for you, Chloe. You're my girl, and my only goal for the rest of my life is to make you happy."

Unable to stop myself, I run and jump into his arms, sobbing as I cling to him. "You make me happy. You're all I need for the rest of my life too."

Slowly, he pulls me off him and sets me on my feet. Then, he lowers himself to one knee. "If you really mean that, then I suppose there's only one thing I need to do right now."

He slips a box from his suit jacket and flips it open, showing me the beautiful ring winking back at me. "My baby girl, my love, my everything, will you be my wife and let me love you and take care of you forever?"

I can't form words, so I bob my head and giggle as he slips the ring on my finger.

"I'm so glad you said yes because I'm not against forced marriage," he murmurs after he stands and pulls me into his arms.

I laugh harder, feeling lighter than I've ever felt before. "You're unhinged."

He laughs and spins me around. "When it comes to you, you have no idea."

Then he kisses me hard and possessively, and it only takes a few seconds before I'm moaning out loud.

The sound of a throat clearing startles me. Shit. We aren't alone. Bash puts me down and swats my bottom.

"Sorry to put a damper on you breaking in your new makeup room, but we wanted to talk to you about something while we're here," Cali says.

I nod and look up at Bash who's trying to look nonchalant, but I can tell he's in on something with the three girls.

"What's going on?" I ask suspiciously.

Cali rocks back and forth on the balls of her feet. "Well, I heard through the grapevine that you want to open your own cosmetic company. I, uh, well, I never had a career for myself, and since I married Daddy, I haven't worked but I'd like to have some kind of job.

So, it got me thinking, and I talked to Scarlet and Paisley; what do you think about the four of us going in and starting a cosmetics line together?" Cali asks nervously.

My eyes widen as I stare at their hopeful expressions. Does she mean that? They want to go into business with me? But...

"That's the sweetest thing ever, but I don't have the startup money right now," I tell them.

Cali smiles. "But I do. It's all sitting in the bank collecting interest. I'd love to be your backer. And Scarlet has experience with marketing and secretarial stuff and Paisley knows accounting. So, we need someone who knows makeup, and that happens to be you, plus you know how to read and negotiate contracts. A multi-woman-owned business. It would be perfect."

My mouth falls open. Cali is offering to back my business?

"Are you serious?" I must be dreaming. This feels like a dream. I might not know Cali and Scarlet all that well yet, but I know enough to know they are my people.

Cali steps forward and holds out a small, rectangular piece of paper. A check. For five hundred thousand dollars. Made out to me. Well, made out to Chloe Gilroy. I'm sure Bash influenced that.

"I've never been more serious. Let's go into business together. We're family. All four of us. And with these assholes hovering all the time, we have to stick together," Cali says with a grin.

"Cali Ann!" Declan shouts from somewhere outside of the room.

A second later, he appears in the doorway, glaring at Cali who's giggling and winking at me. "See what I mean? Hovering."

Tears stream down my face, but I'm grinning from ear to ear. "Yes! Yes, let's do it! But only under one condition. We do it as a team. It's not just my business. It's *our* business."

Cali, Scarlet, and Paisley exchange looks with each other before they turn back to me and nod.

Turning to Bash, I tilt my head back to look up at him. He's grinning, a triumphant look in his eyes that makes me want to kiss him and slap him at the same time.

"This money didn't come from you, did it?" I ask.

He shakes his head. "Nope. It didn't come from me, baby."

I look around the beautiful filming room again and let out a sob before I run to him, throwing myself into his arms. "I love you, Daddy. Thank you for this. It's beyond perfect."

"You're the one who's beyond perfect, Little one. I love you."

## 28

## BASH

Flexing my bloody knuckles, I rest my elbows on my knees and stare at the man sitting before me. His face is in worse shape than my hands, and fuck, it feels good. Satisfying.

"I'm going to ask you again. Where can I find your boss?"

The man hasn't given me any information other than confirming he was the one who was meeting with Ronald to take Chloe in exchange for Ronald's debt. Too bad for this fucker, that sealed his fate. Doesn't matter whether he had plans to do anything to my girl or not.

"I don't know," he says with a groan.

Kieran moves toward him, a knife in hand, and holds it up to his throat. "This isn't a game, asshole.

This is your life. Your family's lives. You really want to fuck with us?"

The guy laughs. "You're going to kill me either way, and I have no family, so fuck you!"

I chuckle and pull my gun from my shoulder holster then point it at his knee and pull the trigger. He howls in pain, screaming out into the empty warehouse.

"Where's Smoke?" I demand.

When he stops crying out in pain, he grits his teeth together. "Somewhere you'll never find him. And he'll come for you for this. He'll come for all of you. Mark my words."

Kieran and I laugh as I get up and move to the table where we have a variety of tools spread out. Choosing the sharpest knife, I spin it in my fingers as I take Kieran's place behind the guy. Leaning down, so my mouth is near his ear, I line the blade up to the perfect spot at his throat.

"Mark *my* words. We'll be ready for him."

WHEN KIERAN and I get back to the estate and pull up to my house, the moving truck is waiting. There's pop music blasting, and when we walk into the living room, Chloe, Paisley, Cali, and Scarlet are having a dance party. Each of them has a glass of wine in hand.

"I wonder how drunk they already are," Kieran says, his gaze landing disapprovingly on Paisley.

I grin and slap him on the shoulder. "Buddy, this is going to be so much fun."

He turns and glares at me. "What the fuck are you talking about?"

"Just can't wait for the show."

Before he can ask more, I close in on Chloe and pull her into my arms, laughing when she lets out a squeal of surprise.

"How's my good girl?" I murmur in her ear.

Her eyes are glassy and twinkling as she looks up at me. "I'm perfect, Daddy. I've never been so happy in my life."

My heart thuds as I stare down at her. "Same, Little girl. What do you think about getting married tonight?"

The glass she's holding slips from her fingers, and if it weren't one of those plastic wine tumblers, there'd be glass shattered all around us.

"Tonight? But I don't have a dress. We don't have a marriage license."

Leaning down, I press a kiss to her lips. "Yes, you do and yes, we do. Daddy's taken care of all of it. There are twenty dresses up in the guest room for you to choose from along with a variety of bridesmaids dresses for your friends. The license is in my pocket. Grace is putting together a feast. And I don't think I can go another day without you tied to me forever."

Her pupils dilate as her breathing shallows. "Really?"

"Really. And if you want a huge wedding later, I'll hire a planner tomorrow, and we'll invite the king and queen of every country to attend."

She giggles and shakes her head. "I don't want a big wedding. I just want you."

My cock hardens and my chest constricts. "You're so fucking perfect. You have me. For the rest of our lives."

"Okay. Let's get married!"

Cali, Scarlet, and Paisley start screaming and jumping up and down, breaking the focus I had on my girl. I forgot they were here.

Kieran grins and pushes me out of the way to hug Chloe. When she wraps her arms around her brother, I let out a low growl but quickly shut up when Chloe glares at me. They might be siblings, but my mind only registers another man touching my girl. Guess I'll need to work on that.

When they part, Chloe shakes her hands in front of her. "Oh my God, I need to sober up and get ready.

You have to go away. You're not supposed to see me before the wedding."

I laugh and grab her, smashing my mouth to hers. She goes limp in my arms, kissing me back, and when I finally let her go, she has a dreamy, far-off look in her eyes.

"I love you, Little girl. I'll see you at the altar."

---

"WE'RE MARRIED!"

Chloe twirls around our bedroom in her flowing white dress. She's the most beautiful sight I've ever seen in my life. I always thought I'd be nervous on my wedding day, but when Kieran led her down the aisle to me, the only thing I felt was unconditional love and adoration. She's my girl. My person. My queen. And now, my wife.

I strip out of my suit jacket and toss it on the nearby chair. My shoes are next, and then I start unbuttoning my shirt. When she notices, she moves to me and closes her fingers over one of the buttons, taking over the job.

When she pushes the material open, her breath hitches. "What is that?"

My lips twitch as I lower my gaze to where she's looking. "It's your name."

Her eyes go wide and round. "I can see that. When did you get it?"

"Today."

"You got my name tattooed on your chest today?"

"Yeah."

She stares at it for several seconds before she tips her head back. "You branded yourself with my name."

I nod. "Yes. I belong to you."

Biting her bottom lip, she runs her finger around the fresh ink, careful not to touch it. "It's beautiful," she whispers.

Letting her fingers trail along my skin, she freezes when she reaches my ribs. "Is that…Is that my name again?"

"Yes."

Pulling her eyebrows together, she looks up at me. "Why did you get my name tattooed on you twice?"

"I didn't. I got your name tattooed on me seventeen times."

She gasps and jerks back slightly. "What?" she shrieks.

I reach out and gently cup her chin. "I wanted your name carved into me the same number of times you were hurt. I needed to feel your pain too. I wanted to absorb it, so you never experience it again.

So you know just how fucking loved you are. I'd cover my entire body in your name if I didn't already have so much ink."

Bringing her hand up to her mouth, she lets out a sob. "Daddy…"

Unable to keep myself from touching her, I pull her into my arms. "I love you, Chloe. You're mine, and I'll spend the rest of my life protecting you, loving you, and shielding you from hurt."

She clings to me for a long time, her face buried against my chest, her tears wetting my skin, my tears dripping into her hair. It's raw and emotional and intimate. It's us. Just us. As it was always meant to be. As it always will be.

Together forever, 'til death do us part.

KIERAN AND PAISLEY'S story is coming in August. Pre-order it now!

I HOPE you loved meeting Cage Black because he's coming out in a new series, Dark Ops Daddies in October. You can pre-order Cage now!

HAVE YOU READ KNOX, Angel, or Colt yet? The entire Daddies of the Shadows series is available on Kindle Unlimited. Check them out!

# ALSO BY KATE OLIVER

**West Coast Daddies Series**

Ally's Christmas Daddy

Haylee's Hero Daddy

Maddie's Daddy Crush

Safe With Daddy

Trusting Her Daddy

Ruby's Forever Daddies

**Daddies of the Shadows Series**

Knox

Ash

Beau

Wolf

Leo

Maddox

Colt

Hawk

Angel

Tate

**Rawhide Ranch**

A Little Fourth of July Fiasco

### Shadowridge Guardians
### (A multi-author series)

Kade

Doc

### Syndicate Kings

Corrupting Cali: Declan's Story

Saving Scarlet: Killian's Story

Controlling Chloe: Bash's Story

Possessing Paisley: Kieran's Story

Keeping Katie: Grady's Story

Taking Tessa: Ronan's Story

### Daddies of Pine Hollow

Jaxon

Dane

Nash

### Dark Ops Daddies

Cage

**KEEP UP WITH KATE!**

Sign up for my newsletter get teasers, cover reveals, updates, and extra content!

The kindest thing you can do for an author is to leave a positive review!

Printed in Great Britain
by Amazon